MW00760441

The Full Nelson

Carole McKee

AuthorHouse™
1663 Liberty Drive
Bloomington, IN 47403
www.authorhouse.com
Phone: 1-800-839-8640

First published by AuthorHouse 6/29/2009

ISBN: 978-1-4389-8984-6 (e)
ISBN: 978-1-4389-8983-9 (sc)

Printed in the United States of America
Bloomington, Indiana

This book is printed on acid-free paper.

Prologue

Counselor Mary Jo pushed the box of tissues toward him as he wiped his eyes on his jumpsuit.

"She's six today. I won't even get to see her. You know....she started kindergarten last September.....and I didn't even get to see her off. They took her away from me...." He sobbed as he grabbed a tissue from the box.

"I feel it is my ethical duty and obligation to remind you that she is not your child, Nelson. She is Lindy and Ricky DeCelli's daughter. She was not taken away from you.....she was returned to her rightful parents. You need to accept that."

"But she cared about me..."

"She was five years old...a five year old that was taught to care and to respect adults. She loves and cares about her parents."

"But....I loved *her*. She was the only person I ever felt love for like that. When she got sick I worried....when she was hungry I gave her food....I bought her clothes. I got her the most beautiful dress for our trip....it was lavender...."

"Nelson....you're still not understanding. Yes, you did all that for her....but you had no business having her there in the first place. You kidnapped her. You can't take another parent's child. Whatever you did for her.....she shouldn't have been in your...proximity....to begin with. Can't you understand that?"

Nelson Sutter appeared to be digesting what she told him as he stared at the floor. He was quiet except for his sniffles. Mary Jo gave him a few moments to think. Suddenly he raised his head and stared at her.

"You don't understand. You have no idea what my life was....how I....hurt so much....all the time.....ever since I was little. You want to know about pain and suffering? I could tell you about it. I could write a book on it."

"Why don't you?"

"Why don't I *what?*"

"Write about it. Write it down. Your story....your life."

"Who would read it?"

"I would....for one. You should....for two. You write it....I'll see about getting it into print....published. I can arrange for a word processor to be brought to your cell. Think about it. You can tell me of your decision when we meet three days from now."

She rang for the guard letting him know that the session was over and said her good-byes to Nelson. She was trying to give him a purpose...something to focus on besides the DeCelli child. She'd hoped he would have pounced on the idea, and maybe he would after he thought about it.

Nelson Sutter was led back to his cell and locked up

again. He had been in the prison facility for almost a year....with nineteen years, three months, and two days to go before he was eligible to apply for parole. After the guard walked away from the front of his cell, he dropped down on his cot and stared at the wall. He thought about what Mary Jo had suggested—about writing a book. She wasn't too bad as far as prison counselors went. He didn't mind seeing her, so when she made the suggestion he didn't just discard it as another stupid counseling idea. He closed his eyes and tried to doze off, but her idea kept surfacing right behind his eyes. Maybe he should. Would Lindy read it? Loraine? He could dedicate it to Samantha. Maybe when she was old enough she would read it, too. Then maybe she would understand that he really loved her like a daughter.

Sighing, he sat up and put his feet on the concrete floor for a moment. He could start it right now—with pen and paper. She said she could get him a word processor. That would be great, but he could start right now and then type up what he wrote down. Hell, why not? Why not write a book? Others who were locked up did it—why not him? Maybe it would end up being a best-seller. *He might finally make it big!* Feeling a little enthusiastic, he walked to the small table and sat down, reaching for his tablet and pen.

Holding the pen poised over the first line on the paper, he mumbled to himself.

"Well, here goes. You want a book, Mary Jo...you'll get a book. You'll get the full story. The full Nelson."

He began to write.

Chapter 1

My first memory of my life was when I was three years old. We lived on a farm in Central Pennsylvania. It was when I was three that I learned to fear three things—roosters, wasps, and my mother. It was late morning, too late for breakfast and too early for lunch when my mother gave me a bowl of chicken feed to take out to feed the chickens in the yard. As I stood there throwing the feed down on the ground for the chickens, a wasp suddenly swooped down and stung me on the forehead. It hurt—it hurt really badly—but I tried not to drop the bowl anyway. As I grabbed my head, the bowl tilted forward giving the rooster an invitation to help himself. I removed my hand from my forehead and began to shoo the rooster away from the bowl. It made him mad—so mad that he began pecking at me on my arms and my legs. He rushed at me and pecked my cheek causing me to drop the bowl and scream. My screaming stopped abruptly when I felt the impact of the strap on my shoulders. My mother lifted me up by my shirt and laid me across the old tree stump and walloped me with the strap.

"That is *not* the way to feed chickens, you moron!" She had yelled at me as she continued to use the strap on me as I screamed.

She sent me to the cellar under our small house where I remained until just before my father came in from the fields. My mother came and got me, dragged me by my arm into the kitchen and sat me down in a chair where she removed the wasp's stinger from my head and washed my face and hands. The sting from the wasp left a big goose egg on my head and the pecks from the rooster left small red scratches on my arms and legs, and a tiny gash on my cheek. The strap had left large red and purple welts on my back and they hurt worse than anything.

"If you weren't so damn stupid these things wouldn't happen," my mother hissed at me. "You don't say *anything* to your father when he asks. *I'll* tell him. Do you understand?"

"Yes, mommy.....I understand," I answered her in a squeaky whisper.

"Good....now go change your clothes. You can play in your room until dinner. Remember to put those into the hamper."

I remember nodding as I made my escape out of the kitchen into the safety of my room. I took off my dirty clothes and put them into the hamper and then put on clean shorts and a tee-shirt. I played with my cars, using the oval braided rug as a roadway. I pushed the cars along the oval rug, two at a time, racing them. I listened to make sure my mother wasn't nearby outside my room before I played out my three-year-old fantasy of driving the car over-top of the figure I called 'mommy'. It was only a piece of straw from the barn that had stuck to my sneaker, but to me it represented my mother. I drove my cars over it again and again. I didn't tire of the thrill I got by doing that. I did it over and over until my father entered my room to gather me up for dinner.

"Hey, pal....I heard you got stung by a wasp. Let me see it."

I pointed to the goose egg on my head and sat still as he examined it.

"Looks like the stinger is out....so it should be okay. Is this where the rooster pecked you?" He had asked pointing to my cheek.

I nodded.

"Now.....your mother says you fell trying to get away from the rooster and that your back is all bruised. Is that right?"

I hesitated, but then nodded. Even at three I knew not to contradict anything she said. Even though I was only three years old, I figured it out that she had told him that story, so I nodded my head in agreement.

"Rough day, huh, pal?" My dad kissed my good cheek and lifted me up into his arms and carried me to the kitchen for dinner.

At that moment, everything seemed okay. I loved my father. He was my hero, my pal, and my protector. As long as he was in the house my mother would not hurt me. She even smiled at me as we entered the kitchen.

"Feeling better, Nelson?"

"Yes, Mommy," I had answered.

"Good. Sit down at your place. Your plate is coming."

My father let me down onto my chair and I stared at the plate my mother put in front of me, my heart sinking.

Liver. I hated it. And mashed potatoes and spinach. I knew I had to eat everything on my plate and I sighed a little as my mother cut up the liver for me.

"Go ahead, Nelson.....eat," she spoke evenly, but I heard the hint of a threat in her voice.

I ate quietly, smothering the liver with the mashed potatoes and then swallowing it whole so I wouldn't taste it. Then I mixed the spinach with the rest of the mashed potatoes.

"Maybe he's too young to feed the livestock," my dad commented. "He's only three."

"Nonsense! He's clumsy, that's all. He has to learn to pull some weight around here. Feeding the chickens is not that hard of a job."

"Well, he may have done a better job if he hadn't gotten stung by the wasp," my dad defended me. "Right, Nelson?"

I nodded at my father and smiled. He was right, of course. I was doing fine until I got stung.

"I'll take him to the barn with me after dinner. That will give you a break," my father told my mother.

My little heart soared! I loved the times when my father took me anywhere with him—just the two of us. I quickly finished everything on my plate and waited patiently for my father to say it was time to go to the barn. I could hardly wait. Being with my father was always such fun, but even more importantly, I would be away from my mother.

When it was time, my father lifted me onto his shoulders and we headed down the path to the barn. I remember my mother's disapproving tone as she told my father that he was spoiling me, making it difficult for her to handle me while he was working in the fields all day.

My father and I walked through the barn checking on the livestock. He used the pitchfork to put hay into the stalls for the horses and then he fed the goats. He checked outside to make sure there was plenty of drinking water for the cattle and then filled the feeding troughs with grain. I followed behind him everywhere he went, picking up dropped pieces of hay and grain and putting those in the proper places. He talked to me while he worked.

"Nelson, you have to respect animals and be good to them. I want you to promise me that you will never, ever hurt an animal. Okay? You promise?"

"Uh-huh….I promise, Daddy. I love the animals, Daddy."

"That's good, Nelson. I do, too."

"I love *you*, Daddy."

"Yeah? Well, guess what? I love you, too," my father smiled at me and ruffled my hair.

My father took care of all the evening chores with me tagging along behind him, and then headed for the house. My mother was sitting on the porch reading the evening paper when we returned. Without looking at me, she ordered me into the house and into the tub. I fairly flew into the house and down the hallway to our small old fashioned bathroom with the claw-footed tub. My father followed behind me and began to run the water for me as I took off my clothes. It was then that he saw my back and backside.

"Nelson, that didn't happen by falling, did it?" He asked me.

I froze. If I told the truth she would punish me, but

I didn't want to lie to my father. I stared up at him not knowing what to do.

"It's okay….you don't have to answer. I know."

He stooped down and stared into my eyes and as I looked back, I saw his eyes glistening with tears. He pulled me to him and hugged me before he put me into the tub.

Chapter 2

We didn't own the farm we lived on. I found that out when I was older. My mother was the resident midwife and emergency nurse and my father was the foreman in the fields. My mother delivered all the babies on the farm, including Richard, the farm owners' son and Alice and Abby, their twin daughters. She even delivered me, with the help of my father, when I entered the world. She also provided first-aid when someone got hurt. Someone besides me, that is. I was always a burden to her. When I was injured, she said it was because I was stupid and clumsy. That was part of the first-aid treatment I got. Even at the age of three, I knew the difference between first-aid and punishment. She would wash out my injury, causing it to burn, and then bandage it roughly, hurting the injury more. The first-aid always ended with a slap on the head and a name like moron or idiot attached to it. That was when I enjoyed playing with my cars and running them over my 'mommy' symbol the most.

I turned five one day in late summer. I remember my father wishing me a happy birthday and reminding me that I would be going to school in a couple of weeks. Kindergarten. I was going to go to Kindergarten and I was excited. My father took me to buy new jeans and shirts, socks and underwear, and new shoes to wear to school. I felt special, especially when he treated me to a cheeseburger and a milkshake at McDonald's. On the way home, my father stopped at a bakery and bought a birthday cake. He had my name put on it! Oh, how I loved my father! I was all smiles when I entered our house, but those smiles ended when I saw my mother.

"That's a waste of money!" She snarled at him.

"Come on, Bertie! All kids should have a birthday cake! He's never had one. It's his last year before he starts school. Anyway, it didn't cost all that much!"

My mother conceded and allowed my father to put candles on the cake and let me blow them out after he sang happy birthday to me. That was the happiest I had ever been. My father cut a big piece for me and allowed me to eat the whole thing. He and my mother ate a piece, too. That made me feel so important. They were eating cake because of me! I remember going to sleep happy that night, and also feeling very grown up. I was five now.

On the first day of Kindergarten, my father told my mother that she should drive me to school. I sat in the front seat of her old blue Chevy as she drove away from the farm toward the school where I would start my academic life. On the way to school on my very first day, she had some hard instructions for me.

"Just keep your mouth shut at school. Maybe they won't notice how stupid you are if you just stay quiet. We can't afford to put you in some special school for retards, so just keep quiet. You understand that?"

"Yes, mommy," I remembered answering.

"Now if they ask you your name you can tell them. Say it. My name is Nelson Sutter. Repeat it."

"My name is Nelson Sutter. Like that?"

"Yes, like that. That's all you should say."

It was not the best advice in the world. I said my name when asked, but nothing else. I feared my mother finding out that I had said anything other than that so I stayed silent most of the time. I didn't speak to other children, nor did I speak to my teacher. I was dubbed 'Dummy' by my peers and considered a non-participating, uncooperative student by my teacher.

In spite of that, I actually did well in Kindergarten and elementary school. I kept quiet but my assignments were graded with marks well above average. Any artwork I did was highly praised by the teacher. This led my peers to chant, "the Dummy can draw, the Dummy can draw" over and over in the school playground during recesses. I ignored them. It wasn't important what they thought or what they said. What was important was the pride I saw in my father's eyes when I took home an A-graded piece of artwork and then an honor roll report card. When I was in the third grade, I made all A's a couple of times. I remember getting off the school bus with Richard, Alice, and Abby and running home waving my report card. My mother grabbed it from my hand and stared at it. She sniffed her dismissal of it and set it down on the counter. She said not one word of praise to me as she handed me the broom to sweep off the porch. I was so disappointed! I thought for sure she would at least say that maybe I wasn't so stupid after all, but she said nothing—nothing at all.

I don't think she would have shown the report card to my father if Mister Canton, the owner of the farm hadn't said something about it to my father. Apparently Abby told her mother that I got all A's and she mentioned it to her husband. He congratulated my father on my accomplishment, so naturally my father asked to see the report card when he got home. I read the pride in his eyes, although he didn't say anything in front of my mother. Later that night when he tucked me in, he handed me a whole dollar! He told me he was proud of me and to keep it up. I remember that I felt like I was going to burst with joy at his words. I fell asleep feeling proud and happy that night. I clutched the dollar bill in my hand and held it all night. In the morning I hid it in my secret hiding place in my room.

The feeling was short-lived. At breakfast the next morning, my mother had a list of chores for me to do. It was Saturday, and I had hoped to go to the main house and play baseball with Richard. He had asked me to come over to play when we got off the school bus the day before. The invitation probably had something to do with my high honor report card. That made me worthy, I suppose. He had never asked me before. I had never played baseball and I really wanted to learn how to play. Richard promised to show me how. Now I knew I wouldn't be allowed to go.

"Since you're so damn smart, I thought you could do a few extra chores around here. Put your brains to good use for a change," my mother said to me as I read over the list. "Now I have to go to town and pick up some things.

Your father is around somewhere.....just do what you have to do and you'll be fine. You're getting old enough to stay by yourself. Have everything on the list done by the time I get back."

She grabbed her purse and car keys and didn't look back. Sighing, I picked up the list again and read it over. Nope, there would be no baseball for me today. I washed my cereal bowl and put it in the dish drainer and resignedly got started on the list. When I was halfway through completing the chores on the list, Richard came by to see if I was going to play. Alice was with him. I didn't like her all that much, but I *did* like Richard and Abby.

"No.....I can't. I have chores to do," I told Richard.

"See? I told you!" Alice whispered. "He can't play because he's the hired help. You can't be friends with him!"

"Shut up, Alice. He's a kid, like us. He just has a mean mother."

Yeah, I did, didn't I? I had never thought about it that way, but now that Richard said it, I knew it was true. I watched them as they walked away from me and I felt the sadness in my chest. I had almost made a friend that day.

I completed the chores, one by one, on the list. I was almost finished. I had one more to do and it was the worst one. I had to clean the chicken coop! The thoughts of the rooster, and the rats ran through my mind. I had heard my father tell my mother he had seen rats in the chicken coop. They were after the eggs and the feed. I squared my shoulders and stood up straight as I walked toward the chicken coop. I was eight now; I could do it. I mentally prepared my eight year old mind for facing rats and the rooster as I entered the coop. I had not prepared myself for the snake, though. It was a rattler, too. I heard the rattles as I pushed the door open and there it was—in the middle of the floor—just starting to coil. I let the door go and I ran—ran across the yard up onto the porch steps. I felt myself shaking and I couldn't hold back the tears. That snake was a big one, too! I had to tell my father about it.

As I started down the steps in the direction of the barn, my mother's Chevy pulled up and stopped just beside the cherry tree.

"Nelson! Help me with these things," she immediately yelled.

"Yes, ma'am," I didn't hesitate, but immediately grabbed a couple of the parcels out of the car and carried them inside, set them on the kitchen table and went out to retrieve more. When all the parcels were inside the house, she asked me if I had completed all the chores on the list.

"I did everything but the chicken coop, Mom. There's a big snake in there. It's a rattler, too."

Before I finished the sentence, I felt the palm of her hand on the side of my head—hard.

"You mean to tell me that there's a rattle snake in the chicken coop and you let it stay there? With the chickens? What if it kills one of them? Idiot!"

"But….it was coiling! It was going to get *me*!"

"Those chickens bring in food and revenue. *You*…you bring problems! Now get out there and clean that coop!"

I don't know what I feared more—the snake or *her*. I willed my feet to trudge back down to the chicken coop, and I gingerly pushed open the door. The snake was nowhere to be seen. I walked inside slowly and quietly, being very cautious, as I moved. No snake. Good. It must have gone. I quickly cleaned the coop as I had been taught, filled the nests with clean straw, and changed the water in the chickens watering trough. I was done! That snake must have left the coop right after I saw it. What a relief that was!

But it hadn't gone far. As I was walking away from the chicken coop I heard my father make a sound and then saw him wielding his axe up and down as he made grunting noises. I stood and watched him as he lifted the headless rattler up in the air.

"Nelson!" He called to me. "I'll bet this is every bit of five feet long!" He carried up to the driveway and stretched it out.

"It's the same one I saw in the chicken coop this morning, I'll bet." I told him.

"You saw one in the chicken coop?"

"Yeah, but it was gone when I went to clean the coop."

"Nelson, you see a rattler, you come get me. You're too young and inexperienced to go up against one. Understand?"

"Yes, Dad."

"Good. I don't want anything to happen to you," he said as he ruffled my hair.

I smiled at him and he grinned back. The moment was ended when she called out through the screen door.

"Nelson! Is the coop cleaned yet?"

"Yes, Mom....it is." I answered.

My father sighed, stood up, and walked into the kitchen. My mother was just putting his lunch on the table. I washed up and made myself a sandwich and sat down with him. I could tell my father was upset about something by the way he quietly stared at his plate. I was hoping he wasn't mad at me for something.

"Something wrong with the food, Neal?" My mother asked him.

"No....there is nothing wrong with the food. Did Nelson tell you there was a rattle snake in the chicken coop, Bertie?"

"Yeah....he mentioned it....why?"

"And you sent him out there to clean the coop after he told you that?"

"Well, I figured the snake would be gone by then."

"What if it hadn't been?"

My mother sat there in silence, her lips were so tightly clamped together they almost disappeared. Her eyes slid toward me and narrowed. I knew I was going to suffer later for this. My father was putting her on the spot—for me and in front of me. That was not going to be good for me. I held my breath.

"Bertie, he is only eight years old. He's too small and too young to take on all the responsibilities of the farm. He needs playtime. Mister Canton told me this morning that Richard was going to teach Nelson how to play baseball today but Nelson had too many chores to do. Why isn't he allowed to play like other kids?"

My mother sat there like a stone statue for what seemed like minutes but was probably only about thirty seconds.

"Are you going to tell me how to raise the boy now? He has to learn responsibility. It won't kill him to do a few chores around here."

"But hours and hours worth of chores? And on a Saturday when other kids enjoy their play time? Let him play once in awhile! That's all I'm saying."

My mother didn't answer my father. They sat in silence just chewing their lunch and staring down at their plates. I sat quietly and ate. I loved my father for sticking up for me but I knew my mother would make me pay for it at some point.

Chapter 3

It didn't happen on Sunday though. We got dressed in our best clothes and went to church like we did every Sunday. The minister spoke to my parents after the sermon and nodded to me with a smile.

"He's growing, isn't he?" The minister commented to my mother.

"Yes, he is. I can't keep up with his clothes any more. He grows out of them so fast." My mother smiled so sweetly at the minister like she was some pious, holy person. She even put her hand on my shoulder like she liked me.

"Well, he's a fine-looking boy," the minister had told her. She smiled and thanked him. The minister bent down a little and stared into my face.

"Nelson, do you play baseball? I'm coaching a little league team next month. Have you thought about joining the little league?"

"I....I have never played....." I answered him quietly.

"He's a little.......clumsy." I heard my mother say.

"Then baseball would be good for him. Help with

coordination. Think you can spare him some time off the farm to play sports, Bertie?"

"Oh, of course, Reverend. He can play if he wants."

I couldn't believe my ears! She was actually saying I could play! I was grateful to the reverend. I knew she would never go back on her word to the reverend. I couldn't wait for the next month to arrive. My dad took me aside and quietly told me we would go find me a baseball mitt at the K-Mart store before little league started and he would show me how to catch and throw.

I waited every day after that, hoping my father would say it was time to go get my baseball mitt. Finally, a week before try-outs, my father took me to K-Mart to buy a baseball mitt! We found one that fit my hand fairly well—my right hand. I was left-handed. I held the mitt all the way back to the house, holding it up to show Richard as we drove by him in his yard. He ran into the house and grabbed his mitt. I watched him running down the road carrying his mitt, chasing our truck. When my father stopped the truck, Richard ran up to his window.

"Mister Sutter, I'll teach Nelson how to throw and catch if ya want!"

"That would be mighty nice of you, Richard. I'm going to show him a couple of things right now, but if you could stay and help him out, I'd be mighty grateful."

"Sure! Let's catch a little.....okay, Nelson?"

Richard was two years older than me, but he never acted like I was a pain in the butt. I believe he felt sorry for me because of my mother. I knew that behind her back, people called her 'Big Bad Bertie' because she had a reputation for being mean. Nobody crossed her but then nobody became friends with her either. Not that she ever wanted friends. She always said she didn't have time for other people who just wanted to get into your business.

Richard and I threw the ball back and forth for a couple of hours that afternoon. My father had to get some of the chores done so he left me and Richard to play in front of our porch. When my father was finished he came to relieve Richard. I was so proud of myself when Richard told him I was learning fast. He said I got better with every throw. My father was impressed with my progress. He threw the ball for me to catch and then I threw it back to him.

"Nelson, I think you're a natural at this. We have to get a bat so you can learn how to hit next. But I think you have potential to be a mighty good ball player."

"Thanks, Dad!" I responded, showing a rare grin. I didn't grin very often and that time the grin was short-lived when my mother appeared at the screen door.

"Are you planning on eating the meal I cooked or are you going to play all day?" She snarled at us.

"Coming!" My father answered for both of us.

My mother was in a bear of a mood at dinner. I believe it was because I was playing catch all afternoon. She really hated to see me do anything but work and she enjoyed it when I was unhappy.

I made the little league team that year. I couldn't have been happier. Richard was one of the older kids on my team and I knew he would look out for me. His parents did, too. They went to every game and watched. I didn't get to play very much that year, but I was proud of my uniform and my baseball mitt. My father attended a few games but my mother never came. That was just as well. I remember when I got my first hit. My father was there watching. I swung the bat and heard the clunking sound of the ball hitting the bat. "Run!" I heard Richard yell. I ran. I ran to first base, smiling. When I stopped at the base I looked over at my father and saw that he was smiling, too. It was one of my proudest, finest moments. My father was proud of me. I was proud of me. And Richard was proud of me, too! I ended up scoring in that inning and it ended up being the winning run. The coach bought us all Dairy-Queens after the game. He talked with my father for a few minutes while we ate the cones.

"He looks like he could be a pretty good ball player in a couple of years, Neal. Keeps it up, there's always scholarships for college. Maybe you'll get a college grad there, huh?"

"We'll see," my father responded.

Chapter 4

I PLAYED LITTLE league baseball until I was almost thirteen. My mother never came to a game and I was happy about that. My father came to them when he could, but sometimes he had to stay away just to keep the peace at home. My mother complained that he was spending all his time at the ball field and never spent any time at home with her. I think he knew that I would pay the consequences for it, so he stayed away from my games to protect me.

I was not too bad of a ball player. I played first base after my first year on the team and I became a good hitter. I hit my first homerun during our last game in my second year in little league. My father was there to see it. The coach told him that as far as he knew, I was the youngest little leaguer to hit a home run. That made my father proud—proud enough to tell my mother. Her response was nothing more than I expected. She let out a sound that sounded something like "Humph" and never even turned around to acknowledge me. She really never acknowledged me. The only words she ever spoke to me were to give me chores or to tell me that I was stupid or clumsy.

I don't remember when it was exactly, but at some point between the ages of three and thirteen, I began to loathe that woman who gave birth to me. I remember entering the eighth grade after a summer of chores and little league baseball. I was thirteen. I had gotten no new school clothes that year. She said we couldn't afford it since my father had to put out money for me to play baseball. I had grown over the summer, and my pants were too short and too tight. My shirts looked like they were going to burst at the seams. Even though my shoes still fit, they were badly scuffed. I tried polishing them, but it didn't help much.

So I started my eighth grade year looking like a refugee. Kids were sniggering behind my back. They began to call me 'flood-ready' because of how short my pants were. Richard became my ally and savior that year.

He was fifteen by then, and bigger than I was. One early evening when my mother was out in the barn delivering a calf, Richard came by with a stack of his clothes that were too small for him. They were perfect fits on me.

"You can have them. Don't worry....I wore them two years ago so nobody will recognize them," he assured me. "I can't help with the shoes because I wear mine out. But... ..I have an idea."

"You do? What is it?" I was all ears.

"You go ask the reverend if there are any odd jobs you can do to earn money for shoes for school."

"My mother would kill me!"

"Here's the beauty of it. You don't *really* have to ask the reverend. Just let your mother think you're going to. There's money, Nelson. My parents pay your parents enough money to afford shoes and clothes for you. They live in your house free and most of the food is home-grown. Your mother is just hateful, that's all. My mother said she wouldn't even be here if she weren't such a good midwife."

His plan worked. The following Saturday night at dinner, I asked if we were going to church the next morning.

"Of course we are. We go every Sunday, don't we? Why?" My father asked me.

"Because I'm going to ask the reverend if he has any odd jobs for me to do so I can buy myself a pair of shoes for school." I spoke confidentially, and I think I sounded determined, as well.

"You'll do no such thing!" My mother bellowed. She glared at me and avoided my father's eyes, hoping he wouldn't question her. It didn't work.

"Bertie....what did you buy Nelson to wear for school this year?"

My mother's mouth opened and then snapped shut, opened again, and then snapped shut again. Her face was becoming the color of a rotten tomato.

"Huh? Bertie.....I'm waiting. What did you buy Nelson for school this year?"

"I.....I...didn't get.....h-him....anything. I....didn't.... t-think h-he n-needed anything." My mother was stammering!

"My God, Bertie! He's grown at least six inches since last year! He's in junior high now. Next year he starts high school. Clothes matter in these years! You don't do anything else for him....at least let him go to school looking halfway decent!"

'Thank you, Dad!' I silently spoke my appreciation.

"Nelson, after we are done eating, I'm taking you out to get you some clothes and shoes. And another thing.... all the chores you do around here....you're going to get an allowance for doing them."

"Really?" I couldn't keep the grin off of my face, even though I knew I should have.

"Yeah.....really," he answered me and then turned to my mother. She was sitting there looking like she was going to breathe fire from her nose. Her face looked like it had swelled up and was about to explode.

"He's my son....and he's just as good as any other kid. You should be ashamed, Bertie....ashamed of yourself for not wanting the best for him."

I didn't dare look up at her. I kept my eyes down and concentrated on the rest of my dinner. I knew that I may have won this battle, but the price of the war was going to be hell. I offered to do the dishes before we left but my mother pushed me out of the way and told me to just go.

We didn't go to K-Mart this time. We went to the mall. I don't know where my father got the money, but he spent quite a bit of it on me that night. I ended up with two pairs of shoes, four pairs of jeans, one pair of dress pants, five new shirts, two polo shirts, two sweaters, socks—black ones and white ones—underwear, two tee-shirts, and a new winter jacket! We stopped and bought soft pretzels and cokes before we left the mall.

"Don't say anything to your mother about any of this," my father warned me. "Just promise me a couple of things."

"Sure, Dad....anything," I responded, knowing that I would oblige him no matter what he wanted.

"First....promise me that you'll wash your own clothes.

I wouldn't want to see them get ruined. Then promise me that you'll continue to follow the path you're on. No drugs, no booze, and no bad grades. Can you promise me that?"

"Well, the first two are easy. Sure. The grade part I'll do the best I can....always....as long as you're my dad."

I remember that night even now. We bonded that night. I knew he loved me and that I could always count on him. He was still my hero, my ally, and my savior. When we got home the house was dark except for a small light in my parents' room. I went directly to my room and carefully hung my things on hangers and put what couldn't be on a hanger in the drawer, all folded neatly. I put my shoes in the bottom of my closet, leaving them in the boxes to keep them from getting scattered. I undressed for bed and then I did something I didn't do very often. I knelt down beside my bed and said a prayer, thanking God for my father, and asking Him to make my mother like me. As an afterthought, I asked God to not let her punish me for my father sticking up for me, then I asked him to bless both of my parents, and Richard.

Chapter 5

RICHARD WAS ALREADY in eleventh grade when I started my freshman year of high school. Although we talked after school and on weekends, he had his own circle of friends. He was always nice to me and he still looked out for me around home, but we rarely associated with each other around school. This was a disappointment to me since Richard was a big shot at school and I looked up to him. He was on the football team and was scoring touchdowns, helping the high school team to win games. He was good-looking, smart, and popular. He hung around with other jocks when he wasn't with his girlfriend, Jackie. She was a pretty blonde girl who was on the cheerleading squad. She was nice to me, too, because of Richard.

I was a school nobody. I had very few friends, I wasn't particularly bright or talented, and I didn't play any sports in my freshman year. I wasn't a nerd, or a jock, or a geek, or a punk, or a hoodlum—I was a *nobody*. I guess I wasn't bad-looking, though, since some girls seemed to look at me more than necessary. I wasn't really interested in girls.

Not that I was gay or anything, I just didn't really see any that I liked that would like me back.

It wasn't until the tenth grade when I saw *her*. *HER*! She was beautiful. She was a *goddess*! Stacey Stockwell. Long blonde silky hair, big blue eyes, gorgeous face, and awesome body! I was in love! She had the sweetest smile of anyone I had ever seen. God, how I wanted to touch her smooth skin! I just knew it would be soft.

I don't know where she came from, but if I had to guess, I would have to say Heaven. In my dreams we were holding hands and walking through fields, and then kissing. Oh, how I wanted to! I had never even seen anyone kiss except for on the television. I knew you put your lips together but I didn't know anything about technique. It was something I couldn't even ask Richard about. He would think I was a jerk. But nevertheless, in my dreams I was kissing Stacey Stockwell. I had a fantasy going where she is standing with Tommy Baker, the most popular boy in school, and she suddenly sees me. She pushes Tommy away and walks towards me and says, *'I've noticed you around school. How about we do something together this weekend?'* I loved that fantasy! I can see Tommy Baker all pissed off in the background as Stacey and I walk away together. It was great.

Stacey was in almost all of my classes that year and she always sat in the seat in front of me. Well, it was because her name began with ST and mine began with SU. Sometimes Pete Stodman was in our class. Then he sat behind Stacey and I sat behind him. I hated him at those times. One time when he was not in our class, Stacey turned around and asked me if I had an extra pencil. I gave her mine—the only one I had. I would have gladly given her everything I owned, which wasn't a whole lot. I wrote with a pen that skipped all class period. It was worth it just to have her smile and thank me. From that day on I always made sure I had two pencils with me in case she should ask again. She never did.

I fantasized and dreamed of Stacey all through my high school sophomore year. What I wouldn't have given for the chance to be her boyfriend! From hearing things around the school, I soon learned that Stacey Stockwell was wealthy. Her parents owned many parcels of land and were heavy investors. Stacey was driven to school in a new Cadillac or a Mercedes every day. Her clothes looked like they were made for her and she wore expensive-looking shoes and jewelry to school.

My fantasy changed. Now I fantasized that she gave up all her wealth just to be with me, and because of her love and faith in me, I became wealthier than her family. In my fantasy I hear her father telling me that I was the only boy who was worthy of his daughter.

That was the fantasy I was having when my mother bellowed for me, snapping me back into reality, the day my life changed. It was eight o'clock on a Saturday morning. I had been up and dressed, but I was cleaning my room and fantasizing as I cleaned. I quickly ran to the kitchen where she stood with her meaty hands on her over-sized sturdy hips.

"I need you to do the chores around here today. Yours and mine. I'll be with that big whiteface all morning and late into the afternoon. She's dropping twin calves, so it'll take awhile."

She left before I could say anything. I would only have said okay anyway. I sighed as I made myself some breakfast. After I ate, I began the daily chores for both of us. I didn't really mind doing any of them, if I could have done them without being called stupid or idiot. I have to admit that she had let up on me a little since that flair-up over my school clothes two years before this. The allowance that my father had promised me came steadily every week. I saved most of it since I rarely ever went anywhere.

I had completed every chore, hers and mine, and my mother still had not returned to the house. I decided to go up to the barn and see if she needed a hand. I knew my father was out in the field supervising the planting of the early crops and as much as I loved my father, I hated planting. I liked animals, not crops.

To this day I am sorry that I was quiet when I walked into the barn. If I had made noise I would not have seen what I saw and heard what I heard. There, in an empty stall was my mother on her hands and knees and old-man Charlie White, one of the farm hands, was behind her with his dick inside her, just pumping away. That part made me want to puke. It was what I heard that forever changed my life. I heard it all.

"Give it to me, Charlie. Give it to me like you did the night we made Nelson. Hard. That's it. That's the way I like it."

"Oh, Bertie.....I'm going to drill you good."

'The night we made Nelson?' What is that supposed to mean? Well, I wasn't a rocket scientist, but I understood. I stood in the shadows listening to them grunting like two pigs. I was frozen. I didn't want to see and hear any more but I couldn't bring myself to leave either. After a loud

dual groan, the noises stopped and they began talking like old friends.

"Bertie, I want to do something for Nelson...seeing he's mine and all."

"Don't worry about it. Neal does everything for him. He loves him like a son....well....he thinks Nelson is his son."

I was becoming sick. I forced my leaden feet to move quietly out of the barn and made my way back down near the chicken coop. My father—my *dad*—the man who I loved and who loved me, had been betrayed by that beast of a woman and that asshole of a guy! He wasn't my real father! Why? Why would she do that? Oh, how I hated her! She was no better than a common whore—only uglier and meaner. I went into the kitchen, got a glass of water, and then left her a note telling her I went out into the field to help dad. I didn't know what else to do. I couldn't look at her, and I wasn't even sure I could look at the man who I always thought was my dad.

He made it easy for me. When he saw me coming he waved and smiled.

"Good to see you out here! How about giving me a hand?"

"Sure....Dad." I made up my mind instantly. No matter who sired me, this man was my dad.

We worked until it was almost sunset and then walked back to the house together. My mother was still in the barn.

"I'll cook us some dinner, Nelson. Want to go up and see how far along that birthing is? Or should I go?"

"I'll go, Dad." I jumped up to go. I wanted to spare my father some pain in case Charlie was still in the barn.

"Okay. See if your mother wants anything."

"Okay."

I flew up to the barn, making noises as I walked in this time. The second calf was just emerging when I got there.

"I would have thought you would have been in here sooner, Nelson. You had to know I needed help."

"I was here....sooner. I left."

She started to say something but she caught on just then. She stared at me hard but said nothing. For once I lifted my eyes and met hers in a steady stare. She knew. She knew what I had seen. I could see how she was calculating the situation and how she was going to keep me under control. The old war was suddenly over, but now we had a colder war going on between us. But I held all the weapons this time. All the years of beatings and mistreatment were gone—gone forever. They would occur no more. I knew it and she knew it.

"Dad wants to know if you want anything. He's cooking dinner."

"Tell him I'll be down as soon as I make sure these two guys are okay. They're both bulls."

"They're beautiful," I acknowledged.

"Yes....they are. The Cantons will be happy." She walked to the telephone installed in the barn and rang up the main house. I heard her telling Mister Canton that he had two new bulls. There was pride in my mother's voice like she had something to do with the gender.

Chapter 6

I ENTERED THE eleventh grade at five feet, ten inches tall. From all the farm work I had muscles, too. Richard had graduated the school year before my eleventh grade year, but before he went away to college he talked me into trying out for the football team. He even drove me to try-outs. I was surprised when the coach called to tell me I made the team. I hadn't even said anything about it at home since I figured I wouldn't make it anyway. Now I was going to have to approach the subject. I hit them with it over dinner that night after the coach called me.

"I want to play football…for the school."

"Yeah?" My father responded with a grin.

"Yeah. I went for try-outs and made the team."

"Nelson, that's great! Any objection, Bertie?"

"Suit yourself," my mother responded. Ever since the calves were born she no longer tried to keep me from doing things. She still treated me like I was a bag of pus, but at least she stopped mistreating me.

"What's it going to cost?" My father asked me.

"Money for insurance and shoes. I have it."

"You do? I'll do my part so just tell me what everything costs."

I couldn't help it. I had to get a shot in there. "Thanks. I'm so glad you're my dad." I saw my mother stiffen and choke a little on the roll she was eating, so it was worth it.

...

Playing football sort of made up for Richard being gone. I missed Richard, but now I was being accepted on my own because I played football. Girls were speaking to me in the halls, guys were giving me high-fives when they passed me, and teachers looked at me instead of through me. I was number eighty-eight, Nelson Sutter, tight end. Tommy Baker was the quarterback, and he had Stacey Stockwell. What I wouldn't have given to be in his shoes.

Stacey was homecoming queen that year. Probably the year after, too, but I wasn't there to see it. Homecoming was my first high school dance. Richard was home for it and he lent me a suit to wear. I remember how dressed up I felt. I studied myself in the mirror and was surprised at how much better-looking I had become. I didn't have my license yet, but I had my permit. Richard offered me a ride to the dance with him and his girlfriend from college. All the way to the school that night I fantasized about dancing with Stacey. If she got crowned queen I would be able to dance with her. It was tradition that the entire football team dance with the homecoming queen. Never mind that I had never danced before; I think I sort of knew how anyway.

Stacey *was* queen and I danced with her—for about

thirty seconds. It was the best thirty seconds of my life. I remember how she smelled and how she felt in my arms. I wasn't very good at the dancing part, so maybe only thirty seconds was a good thing. I remember she smiled at me and said, "You're number eighty-eight, aren't you?" I could have soared to the heavens at that moment! She knew my number! She recognized *me*! Right then the next guy cut in on us. I was content to sit it out the rest of the night after that. Stacey Stockwell knew who I was, and that was all that mattered. I *did* dance a couple of times with girls who asked me. One even gave me her phone number. The dancing part wasn't all that hard. I just watched others for awhile and then I had it. Since Richard had other plans I got a ride home with some of the other players. They let me out at the beginning of our driveway and I walked the rest of the way. I had to pass the main house and I noticed that Richard was not home yet. Abby was sitting on the porch and she called to me.

"Nelson! Were you at homecoming?"

"Yeah. Why weren't you there?" I had asked her.

"Oh....well, because me and Alice aren't old enough yet. My dad says we can go next year."

"Come on up and sit down for awhile," she offered.

"Naw, I better get home. It's late."

"Okay, see ya. Oh, Nelson? Your parents were fighting tonight...so be careful."

"What about? Why were they fighting? And how do you know?"

"Because I was near the house and I heard your mother call your father a couple of names, and then he called her a pig-headed bitch. I heard your name mentioned....so be careful."

"Thanks, Abby. Hopefully they're sleeping now."

I walked the rest of the way to the house just dreading what would be waiting for me. When I entered through the kitchen my mother was nowhere to be found, but my father was sitting at the kitchen table.

"Hi, son....did you enjoy the dance?"

"It was okay. What's wrong?"

"Well, nothing...now. Your mother and I got into it tonight. Listen, tomorrow we're going to go let you take your driving test. Think you're ready for it?"

"Yeah, I'm ready. So what's wrong?"

"Well, I have glaucoma....do you know what that is?"

"N-not really."

"I'm going blind."

I felt the shock run through me. *'Blind! No! There has to be a mistake.'* I remember thinking. My Dad. My hero. He can't be going blind!

"Abby told me you and mom were fighting. Was it about that?"

"Well, sorta. I won't be able to drive any more. I'll still be able to work but just not drive a vehicle. I told her I wanted you to be able to drive to help out and she blew up. I have no idea why."

"Oh....well, Dad....you know you can count on me for anything you need."

"Yeah, son....I know. So....did you dance with anybody tonight?"

My father smiled as he asked me. He stood up and put the kettle on for tea for the two of us. We sat there with a cup of tea and talked. I told him I had danced with three girls and one of them was the prettiest in the school.

"What is her name?" He asked me.

"Stacey. Stacey Stockwell. She's gorgeous, Dad."

"She's her father's pride and joy, Nelson. I've seen her and she is a beauty. She will marry well. Her father will see to it....after college."

"You know the Stockwell's, Dad?"

"Not really. Well, everybody knows them because of their vast wealth. Bill Stockwell is about to sell off some of his land for a hospital. Saw that in the paper. The land is closer to Pittsburgh than to us though. He owns land all over Pennsylvania; I hear....not just around here. The Stockwell's actually lived near Pittsburgh. He built himself a mansion in our county and moved his wife and daughter into it. I hear he wanted the peace and quiet you get out here. They still keep a place in or around the Pittsburgh area somewhere."

"Wow....wouldn't it be great to have that kind of money?"

"Maybe....maybe not. There is a lot of responsibility when you have that kind of wealth. A lot of worry, too.... trying to keep it, paying your taxes on it, and of course trying to increase it. Hell, who am I kidding? It *would* be great."

We laughed together over what my father had said. I felt so close to him that night. I realized that life with my mother wasn't all that great for him either. I wondered whether his life would have been better had he been told the truth about my conception. Not that I would ever tell him.

Chapter 7

I ACTUALLY EARNED a letter in football that year. My father went to the awards banquet with me so I could receive my letter. He made some flimsy excuse as to why my mother couldn't come, but I knew better. What's more, I was glad she didn't come. I went up to receive my letter and I saw the pride shining in my father's now-clouded eyes. He could still see a little, but the vision was badly blurred, he said. I had driven his truck to and from the banquet.

The event was enhanced when I looked across the room and saw Stacey sitting with a couple I believed to be her parents. She looked beautiful—breath-takingly beautiful. Sitting across from her was Tommy Baker and his family. My heart sank. I concentrated on what my father and Jimmy Patterson's father were talking about, so I was surprised when I heard Stacey's voice so close to me. I looked up and *there she was!*

She was standing right next to me with her mother beside her.

"Hi, Jimmy....hi, Nelson," she greeted us. "This is my mom."

"Hello, boys....gentlemen," she added as her eyes swept the table.

"Hello, Missus Stockwell," my father answered.

"Oh, please....it's Belinda. We were just making the rounds of the tables just to say hello to everyone. Is everybody enjoying the meal? Wait until you see the dessert."

She smiled at all of us and she and Stacey moved to the next table. Mister Patterson told us that the Stockwell's had contributed heavily to pay for the banquet, and Stacey didn't even qualify for an award. I guess they didn't have awards for goddesses.

As we got up to leave, Jennifer, the girl who gave me her phone number at the homecoming dance came up to me. She was a majorette and had just earned her first letter for it. I noticed that she was a pretty girl. I had never had eyes for anyone except Stacey so I never noticed Jennifer before.

"Nelson? Why didn't you ever call me?" It was a question, not an accusation.

"Been busy. You know....we farm. I always have lots of chores to do. Trying to fit in school and football made it hard to do much else."

"Oh....well, what are you doing now? Tonight, I mean?"

"I have to drive my dad home."

"Could I get a ride, too? My parents couldn't make it tonight. They are at the hospital with my grandmother. She's dying."

"Oh....sorry to hear it."

"Nelson, we can give her a ride. You can drop me off and then take her out somewhere before you take her home. It's early yet, just past nine. Go have some fun." My father whispered in my ear as he slipped me a twenty dollar bill. I shrugged and said okay.

After I dropped my father off at home, I drove away and pulled onto the two-lane highway. I glanced at Jennifer sitting next to me. She really *was* a pretty girl.

"Where to?" I asked her.

"I don't know. Want to take a drive out to the lake? There are lights around it and they put in a walkway. We could walk around the lake. Want to?"

"Yeah, sure....if you want."

We rode in silence as we approached the local lake, which was really a glorified oversized pond. I had to admit it had been fixed up to look really nice and it was nice walking around it. Jennifer took my hand and held onto it as we walked.

"Your hands are strong....and hard," she noted aloud.

"Yeah, well....lots of hard work does that to a hand," I responded.

"You're shy, aren't you?"

"Quiet, maybe....but I'm not shy. I just don't talk much."

"I like that."

"You do? Oh....is it because it gives you more time to talk?"

She stopped walking, dropped my hand, and stared up at me. I tried to hide the mischievous smile but she saw it anyway and began to laugh. I laughed, too. She grabbed my hand again and pulled me to one of the new high-backed benches that had recently been constructed around the walkway. She sat and pulled me down next to her, and then she put her head on my shoulder. Instinctively, I lifted my arm and put it around her shoulder. We sat like that without talking for several minutes. I glanced at her as she was staring up at the stars.

"What's up there?" I asked her.

"Wishes. Lots and lots of wishes." She answered.

"Are any of those wishes yours?"

"Many of them are mine."

"Yeah? What are they?"

"If I tell they won't come true."

"Maybe the opposite is true. Maybe if you tell them they *will* come true. I mean...have you had any luck by not telling them?"

"No...."

"Well, then maybe you should tell them."

"Okay.....I will then. Here goes. I wish that you would like me."

"Well, now see there? I *do* like you. One wish came true already."

"All right....I wish that you would kiss me."

"Kiss you? You want me to kiss you?" I leaned over and pecked her cheek.

"Not like that."

"Then how?"

"Like this...." She leaned forward and just lightly touched her lips to mine, parting hers ever so slightly.

I had never kissed a girl before but I had instincts. I took her face between my palms and looked into her eyes. "How about like this?"

The kiss made me a little dizzy at first, but she sent up skyrockets when she slipped her tongue into my mouth.

The next thing I knew we were probing each other's mouths with our tongues and my pants were suddenly too small. I came up for air and to catch my breath. I pulled her close and held her for a couple of moments. Her hair smelled nice—like strawberries.

"How's the wish list coming?" I smiled into her long dark tresses.

"You were right. Say them and they may come true. Nelson? Could we...Could we go out again after tonight?"

"Sure....if you want to. Want to go to a movie or something? Maybe stop and get a burger afterward? On Saturday? I'll ask if I can have the truck."

"Yes. Well, that's another wish coming true."

"Do all of your wishes have to do with me?"

"Most of them."

"Maybe I'm the wish-fairy then."

"You are certainly no fairy," she laughed.

I drove her home and I walked her to her door. She wrote down her phone number for me before I walked away. All the way home her warm brown eyes haunted me. Her coloring was quite the contrast from Stacey's big blue eyes and pale blonde hair, but she was pretty just the same. I realized I was looking forward to Saturday night.

The rest of the week flew by with exams to prepare for and assignments to complete. I had asked my father if I could use the truck on the upcoming Saturday and he agreed to it. All I had to do was look at the movie listings to see what was playing. On Saturday morning after my mother drove off to town in her Chevy, I called Jennifer to see what movie she would like to see. She seemed relieved that I called. We decided on a movie and a time and hung up, giving me time to complete my chores and clean out and wash the truck. I had it looking pretty good by the time I was finished.

I showered and dressed in jeans and a short sleeved striped shirt and was almost ready to go when my mother came back. I heard her in the kitchen putting things away and banging things around. I knew she was in a mood. I hoped my father would get back to the house soon. He usually had a calming effect on her. I was in no mood for a confrontation with her. I stood in front of the bathroom mirror combing my dark blonde hair and I scrutinized my face. It wasn't bad. My eyes were light brown, golden actually, and my jaw was squared. I had a nice straight nose and well-defined lips. Is that what Jennifer saw? Did Stacey? I decided to put Stacey out of my mind tonight. Jennifer deserved it. I walked out toward the kitchen and there was the beast in waiting.

"Well, well….going out, pretty boy?"

"Uh-huh." I reached for the truck keys and left it at that.

"Well….it must be nice. You just go and do whatever you want. No rules, no anything."

"I have rules. I'm just going out like other kids my age do. I won't be doing anything wrong. Besides, dad gave me the rules."

"He has no business giving you rules!"

"And why would that be?" I smirked at her and turned toward the door, but not before I saw the shock on her face.

I left quickly so as not to cause a flare-up between us. I got into the truck and revved the engine, looking at the kitchen door as I did it. She was standing there and there was no mistaking the hate on her face. I was determined not to let it ruin my night.

Chapter 8

She wasn't Stacey but Jennifer was fun to be with. We saw a movie that night, and for the life of me I can't remember what we saw. After the movie we went to a local hamburger joint and ordered burgers and fries. Jennifer was sweet if not a little forward, but that was okay since I wasn't used to having a say in anything anyway. After we left the burger place she suggested we take a drive to the lake again. I was happy to oblige.

"Are we looking for more wishes?" I asked her.

"Maybe. You're so good at fulfilling them."

I just smiled at her. Nobody, but nobody had ever made me feel like I was important. Not even my dad, but I knew he loved me. Jennifer made me feel important, and that made her pretty special to me. I parked the truck at the lake and we got out and walked around it, just holding hands. I didn't say much and neither did she this time. We just walked. I felt her shiver.

"Are you cold? I don't have a jacket....."

"No, that's okay. We can just get back into the truck.... okay?"

"Sure. I'll put the heater on if you need it."

"Maybe you should just use the Armstrong heater."

I didn't get it at first, but then I realized what she was hinting and I laughed. I helped her into the truck and ran around to the driver's side and hopped in. She was on me like a magnet on the refrigerator door. Her arms wrapped around me and her lips sought out mine. I was totally excited by that kiss. I shifted in the seat and took her face into my palm and slowly and gently kissed her again. I studied her face when that kiss ended. I wasn't sure what I was supposed to do next. I knew what I wanted to do, but I wasn't sure what was expected of me. She took the lead by removing my hand from her face and putting it on her breast. Oh, the excitement! I started caressing her breast and I felt her nipple get hard. I slipped my hand up under her blouse and then under her bra and touched her bare breast. I was aware of the throbbing ache in my crotch area. I kissed her as I stroked her breast. She moved her lips to my ear and whispered, "Nelson....make love to me."

I didn't have to be asked twice. I unhooked her bra as she slid down her shorts. There it was! In front of me. I had never even seen one except in pictures. Very slowly I ran my hand down to it and stroked it as my lips encircled her nipple. I felt her trying to unzip my pants and I took over. I will never forget that night. I was clumsy and awkward but I managed to get the job done. When she arched her back up to me I knew—I knew what to do. I didn't have a condom, but she did, thank goodness. She gave it to me before I entered her and I almost didn't make it. I don't know if she knew it was my first time or not. Probably, since it wasn't her first time, but she didn't say anything. She just smiled up at me and told me I was wonderful.

We put our clothes back on and sat there for awhile. I was content to just stay like that, but she began to talk.

"Nelson....am I your girlfriend?"

"What? I guess. I mean....you're the only girl I have ever taken out." Girls could ask some strange questions.

"Well, what I mean is....am I the only one you are going to take out?"

"Probably." I winced inwardly at my answer. Somehow I didn't think it was the right one.

"Do you think about me when I'm not around?"

"Yes," I lied. I *knew* the answer to that one. Instincts are good to have.

"Good....because I think about you all the time."

"You do? Why is that?"

"I don't know. I...I just want to be with you. Did I make you happy tonight?"

"Of course. That completed *my* wish list." I chuckled a little and she didn't seem to mind.

"I'm going to make you mine right now, Nelson." She stared into my eyes and eased my zipper down and reached into my shorts. Little Nelson popped right up. Jennifer lowered her head and took Little Nelson into her mouth and accomplished what she set out to do. I was hers.

Afterward, we cuddled in the truck for awhile, neither of us speaking. The night felt special to me. Jennifer felt special to me. I hadn't thought about Stacey all night. How could I think of her again? Not after what just happened. Jennifer deserved to be the one in my thoughts. She was awesome.

I took her home and after kissing her goodnight at the

door, I headed home, too. I promised I would call her the next day, and I did. I called her every day. I saw her in school, and we walked the halls together. Everyone knew we were together now. It felt kind of good, like I belonged to somebody. I finally fit in somewhere, and I liked it.

Jennifer invited me to her house for dinner one Sunday. My mother growled about it but didn't try to stop me. Jennifer's parents seemed to like me. Well, at least they didn't order me out of their house. After the dinner we played Monopoly with her two younger brothers. It was a relaxing evening.

One thing I can say about Jennifer—every time we were together it was worth remembering. She was a great girl. She gave herself to me willingly, she listened to me when I talked, she made me feel important and she made me laugh. I should have been happy to be with her. And I swear I would have been if it hadn't been for Stacey. I couldn't get that girl out of my mind. After a great time out with Jennifer I went home and fantasized about Stacey. That always made me feel guilty since Jennifer gave me her all and I knew she went to bed thinking about me.

Chapter 9

THE SCHOOL YEAR ended. I had one more year to go. Jennifer and I climbed into my dad's truck on the last day, which was only a half-day, and just sat for a moment with our eyes closed.

"What do you want to do?" I remember asking her.

"Let's go to your place."

"No."

"Why? We never go there. I have never met your mother."

"You don't want to meet my mother."

"Yes, I do."

"Be careful what you wish for. If you do ever meet her, be afraid. Be very afraid."

"Oh, come on. She can't be that bad."

"Jenn....no. She *is* that bad."

"What has she done that's so bad?"

"For starters...she hates me. When I was only eight years old she sent me into the chicken coop, knowing that there was a large rattler in there. There are a lot of things....but I can't talk about them."

Jennifer stared at me, unbelieving.

"I mean it, Jenn. I have scars. You do not want to meet my mother."

She let the subject drop, which made me very happy. We ended up going over to Jimmy Patterson's house. His parents weren't home so Jennifer and I were in one bedroom while Jimmy and his girlfriend were in another. It was the first time Jennifer and I had done it in a bed. It was so much more comfortable than the truck and there was room to be less inhibited. It was great. Since my first time with Jennifer, I had developed some style and technique. I had her screaming my name many times and then purring like a kitten. I looked over at the clock in the bedroom and saw that we still had plenty of time. Jimmy said we had to leave by four o'clock, which was okay by me, since I promised my father I would repair the chicken wire around the chicken coop. I reached for Jennifer again and wrapped my arms around her. I was nuzzling her neck and nipping her earlobe when she pushed away from me.

"Nelson....do you think I'm pretty?"

"Yeah, I think you're real pretty," I answered. Not more of those strange questions again!

"Do you think I have a nice body?"

"Oh, hell yeah!"

"Do you think my boobs are too small?"

"What?" I couldn't believe this!

"Seriously....do you think they're too small?"

"Hmmm....let me see," I responded playfully as I took one into my mouth. "Nope....they're the perfect size. To me, they're perfect."

"Perfect for you....but what about anyone else?"

"Now why are you concerned about anyone else? Is there someone else you want to share them with?"

"No....I just....well.....Nelson, do you love me?"

Oh boy! Not the question I wanted to hear! What should I have done? Lie to her? That wouldn't have been fair. I decided to dance around it, but of course that was not acceptable.

"I don't know." Was my answer.

"What do you mean you don't know? You either do or you don't."

"Well....I'm not sure I even know what love is. I've never been exposed to it, except from my dad. I don't feel the same way about you as I do my dad, though. I love being with you, I love talking to you, and I smile when I think of you. If that's love, then yeah, I love you."

She wasn't happy with my answer, I could tell. I could see the disappointment in her eyes and I felt her tense up.

"Hey....can't we just be happy with what we have? I don't want to go out with anybody else. If I think about the future, you're in it. Doesn't that count for something?" *So I lied a little.*

"Yes....yes, it does." She turned to me and snuggled close to me once again. "Nelson....I *do* love you."

"Then show me." I gave her a wicked grin as I rolled her on top of me. We played in the bed another half-hour before we had to get up and leave.

We got up out of the bed, quickly changed the sheets, and made up the bed. I dropped her off with the promise to call her later, and went on home to repair the chicken wire and face the beast, as I now referred to that ogre that gave birth to me. When I was almost finished with the wire, she made an appearance out near the coop.

"What the hell are you doing?" She bellowed.

"Fixing the chicken wire. Had to replace some of it." I added.

"Why are you doing it?"

"I told dad I would."

"Oh....so you do things willingly for him, huh?"

I stopped what I was doing and stared at her. "What is it you would like?"

"I would like to never have to see you again...but aside from that....my car won't start."

"I'll take a look at it. I'm almost done."

She lumbered back into the house. For as big and mean as she was, my mother couldn't drive a standard shift, thankfully, or I would not have had the use of the truck when her car didn't work. She would have taken the truck and let the Chevy sit there.

I finished up with the fence and walked over to the Chevy and raised the hood. I didn't know a lot about cars, but I knew enough to fix hers. I pulled out one of the sparkplugs and saw that it was filed down pretty low. I pulled out another and saw the same thing. The wires were bad, too. I got a brush and cleaned them to see if I could get a spark. It almost turned over for me. Sighing, I went inside to tell her.

"When is the last time you had sparkplugs put in that car?"

She stared at me blankly.

"I assume you haven't?"

"No....I guess I haven't"

"All right....I'm going to go up and get some plugs,

points and wires and put 'em in for you." I told her. "It should be fine after I do that."

She nodded but said nothing.

I tuned up her car and it started right up. She never even thanked me, but of course I really didn't expect her to. She also didn't pay me for the things I bought, which I did expect. I set the receipt on the table and never saw it again. That was the last thing I was ever going to do for her, I promised myself. And I was almost right.

Chapter 10

It was already moving toward the end of June. I had plenty of chores to keep me busy during the day and I had Jennifer to keep me happy at night. With the planting all done and the crops coming up, my father only had to spend time maintaining them during the day. He worked on the sprinkler system a lot since it seemed to always need repaired. He grumbled about how Mister Canton should spend some money modernizing it. I helped him work on it several times. He could still see, but I helped with the intricate parts of the sprinkler system. I enjoyed working alongside of him, as long as he wasn't planting anything. While we were working on the sprinkler system one day, Charlie wandered in our direction. It unnerved me, since I hadn't seen him since that time in the barn. Not up close, anyway.

"Need a hand with that?" He asked.

"No, I think my son and I have it handled," my dad answered him. From the way he said it, I knew. My father knew all along that I wasn't his son. But he loved me anyway! And he didn't really have to! It made me love him more than I already did.

"Want me to try it now, Dad?" I asked. I glared at Charlie and mentally added, 'why don't you go service the cow in the kitchen, you scumbag pig?' I hated that man. I hated him for betraying my father—not because he screwed my mother. As I glared at him I saw something. Of course my father knew! The eyes! I had eyes like Charlie's! Damn, how I wanted to pluck them out of my head! Those golden orbs were a telltale giveaway. My father looked up and saw me glaring at Charlie's back as he walked away.

"Nelson....don't....it's not worth it. You're *my* son.... he don't matter."

My father knew that I knew, too. Somehow that strengthened our bond. I looked down at the man I called dad and I know he saw the love shining in my eyes. He stood up and met my eyes before he spoke.

"I'm the one who wanted you....with all my heart. It don't matter what man or woman made you. I wanted you and I love you. You're all I ever wanted or needed in this world....son."

For the first time in my life I was choked up with emotion. I wanted to tell him I loved him, too but I knew if I started to speak the tears would come pouring out of my eyes and I'd be blubbering like a sissy. I closed the gap between us and just hugged him—hard, like I was afraid to let go, and I think I actually was afraid. He was all I had, too. He was always there for me—protected me from *her* when he could. I kept my face averted from his because I didn't want him to see the tears that were forming in my eyes. I needn't have bothered because when I finally looked at him, I saw that he had been crying.

"You know, dad…you've always been my hero. I *know* she hates me. I knew it from the time I was three. But I always had *you*. I love you, too."

He smiled at me and draped his arm around my shoulders. "Hey, let's have a beer together." He laughed as he opened the old refrigerator that was kept in the pump house. It was my first beer. It tasted bitter and I really didn't like it, but I drank it. I felt a little dizzy but that passed after awhile. We finished up for the day and headed back to the house for dinner. I'm so glad we had that talk, because two days later he was gone.

…

I'll never forget that day. He had been down in the big garage working on one of the Canton's old cars. Mister Canton had asked him to see if he could do something with it. I remember seeing Abby running toward our house—running like she was afraid of something. I was on the porch painting the railing when she came into view.

"Nelson! Nelson! Where's your mother? Your dad! Your dad's hurt. Come quick!" Abby was running out of breath as she spoke. I believe my heart stopped for a second. I felt my insides twisting.

"Mom! Dad's hurt!" I yelled through the screen door before I took off running.

I got to the garage as the ambulance pulled up. He was lying there, ashen, covered in blood. A metal object was sticking out of his chest. It was a flywheel. The flywheel from the car he was working on. I thought I was going to be sick. Instead, I asked Mister Canton what happened. He looked like he was going to collapse.

"He had the car running...and....I don't know how it happened....the wheel was moving and making a noise, and then.....all of a sudden...it flew out of the car....and *hit* him. It looked like it attacked him. God...Nelson I'm sorry."

"It's not your fault, Mister Canton."

I turned to watch the paramedics working on my dad. I could see he was losing blood—losing it fast. I heard one of them say they didn't dare remove the blade. I glanced over at my mother. There was no emotion on her face as she stared at the man she had been married to for more than eighteen years. She was heartless—cold and heartless. My head was swimming. I felt someone's hand on my shoulder and turned to see Richard, his face distorted by concern. Abby stood next to me on the other side. She reached for my hand and held on. It was then that I heard the dreaded words—words that will haunt me forever.

"He's gone. Time of death, fifteen-oh-six."

Just like that. I remember hearing my voice shouting. "NO! NO! DAD!" Richard was pulling me out of the garage and I was fighting him. Mister Canton helped Richard get me out of the garage and I stood there gasping for air. Richard flung his arms around me and held me as I broke down. I learned later that my fucking mother never shed a tear.

Chapter 11

My father was given a nice funeral, paid for by Mister Canton—I think. Many players from my football team showed up to pay their respects as did the cheerleaders and majorettes. When Jennifer came in she hugged me. I saw my mother's eyes narrow so I hugged her back—just to spite my mother. Stacey Stockwell remained absent from the funeral home. I mentioned it to Tommy Baker and he said that Stacey didn't do funerals, and besides, she didn't know me all that well so she wouldn't bother to come. I was disappointed. Jennifer held onto my hand and I found some comfort in that.

Missus Canton held a small reception in their family room, and it extended out onto the patio. She told my mother that it was the least she could do. Jennifer came to it. I was glad until she just *had* to go say something to my mother. She wouldn't take my word for it that my mother was evil. I saw her approaching my mother and I started to intercept but I was too late.

"Missus Sutter, I'm so sorry about Mister Sutter."

Jennifer spoke so sweetly to her! My mother stared at her, almost looking amused, and then narrowed her eyes.

"You're the girl my son is screwing, aren't you?"

Jennifer looked like she'd been slapped. I came up behind her as she backed away from my mother.

"I warned you, didn't I?" I whispered into her ear as I slid my arm around her waist.

Jennifer's cheeks were flushed and she was shaking a little. I pulled her around the side of the house and held her tightly. I just held her.

"Now do you see why I didn't want to introduce you to my mother?"

"Yeah....wow...that isn't what I expected." Jennifer laughed a little. "I'm going to go....okay? My mother has a doctor's appointment and I promised to have the car home."

"Okay....call you later?"

"Yeah."

I walked her to her car and watched her drive away before I went back inside to the family room. What happened next was not my fault—I swear. I was helping myself to a plate of the food Missus Canton prepared when I felt a hand on my shoulder. I turned to see Charlie standing next to me.

"I'm sorry for your loss...son." His voice was a little raspy.

I saw red.

"Keep your hands off me, you piece of shit," I growled at him.

"Hey....that's no way to talk to your elders..." he growled back.

"Yeah? Well, how about I just do this, then?" I showed

all of my teeth as I let him have the whole plate of food—right in his face. I smashed it into his face and held it there. I started to walk out as he began wiping the food from his face. That's when I felt his hand again. He spun me around and drew back his fist. I ducked and hit him square in the gut, knocking the wind out of him. "I told you to keep your hands off of me!" I shouted as I walked out of the door, jumped in the truck and drove off.

I hit the highway and watched the road behind me in the rear view mirror. I saw a car coming at a pretty high rate of speed and started to accelerate until I realized it was Richard. I slowed and pulled off. Richard pulled off behind me and we both emerged from the inside of our vehicles at the same time. Richard was laughing his ass off!

"What the hell made you do that?" He wanted to know.

Well, I told him. We stood there on the side of the road and said nothing for a couple of minutes. Finally he spoke.

"That's some pretty heavy shit. How long have you known this?"

"About two-three years now. Hell, Richard…look at my eyes and then look at Charlie's. My dad knew."

"He did? Wow…he didn't do anything about it?"

"He told me that he wanted me….and that I was all that mattered to him. My dad was a good man, Richard. I'm going to miss him."

Richard just nodded. "Let's go back. You should be there for the people who came to pay their respects. Charlie left."

"You know, Richard….I could be sterile."

"Now why would you say that?"

"Well....when you mate a horse with a jackass you get a mule.....and they're sterile." I responded with a silly grin.

Richard broke up laughing and then I did, too. We got into our vehicles and drove back to the farm. Besides my father, I truly believe that Richard was the only true friend I ever had.

After everyone left I returned to the house and went into my room to change. I took off my jacket and loosened my tie and just stared out the window for a few minutes. I didn't know my mother had come back to the house until I heard her behind me.

"You hate me, don't you?" She asked it without any emotion. I didn't answer.

"You don't have to say anything. I see it every time you look at me. I hate you, too. I never wanted you. I would have had an abortion....but Neal figured it out that I was pregnant. He wouldn't hear of my not having it. It....to me you were an 'it'."

"Is this supposed to be hurting my feelings? Because it doesn't. I'm not three any more. All the hateful words and torture you put me through all my life made me immune to whatever you have to say now. I think we should just stay out of each other's way. You no longer have to cook for me or do anything for me. We can avoid each other entirely."

"What you did to Charlie today....I actually found it amusing. He's your real father, you know."

"Yeah...I know....and so did dad."

"Neal knew?"

"Yeah....how stupid do you think dad was? Look at the eyes. Dad knew. Dad said it didn't matter....Charlie didn't matter. All that mattered was that he wanted me.... *me*...in his eyes I was his son. And in my eyes, he was my father."

My mother turned and walked down the hall toward the kitchen. I got some satisfaction out of letting her know that she hadn't fooled anyone. For the next three weeks we stayed out of each other's way, only speaking when it was necessary. By the time the fourth week after dad's death rolled around, she was gone, too.

Chapter 12

I DIDN'T SEE my mother again that day after our little 'discussion'. I tried to call Jennifer later but didn't get an answer. I figured she went with her mother to her doctor's appointment. When I didn't get an answer by seven that evening, I decided to take a drive and stop by the diner and get something to eat, since I let Charlie wear my food at the Canton's house. When I walked into the diner, Jennifer was there sitting next to some kid I didn't know. He had his arm around her waist. I stood there and stared for a moment before she saw me. When she turned and saw me, I turned and walked out. I never called her again and I never accepted her calls either. I had only known two women up until this point—my mother and Jennifer. Both of them were cheats. I could only assume that all women were.

I worked hard in those four weeks after my father died. I finished painting the porch railing that I had been working on the day of my father's accident, and then I repaired the garage door. I cleaned out the garage next. In the evenings that first week, I replaced the screens in the storm windows and tended the garden every night after that. I washed the truck and my mother's car and cleaned the upholstery and carpeting in both. I never did get a thank you from her on that one. I cut the grass and cleaned the chicken coop every week, pruned the trees, and washed down the porch. I tended to the livestock in the barn every day, and kept fresh water, hay and grain in the troughs for the cattle. I handled the evening milking of the five dairy cattle in the barn. I felt I was doing my part. Mister Canton appointed a new foreman to handle the fields because I was too young. Even *he* admitted that. Apparently nobody noticed the work I was doing or the repairs I completed, but since it all was getting done, they had to realize *somebody* was doing it.

I rarely saw my mother except when we crossed paths in the kitchen or in the barn. One of the horses was giving birth and she was there with it one evening when I was tending to the animals. When I was done, I asked if she needed help or needed anything, just to be civil. She declined, so I went back to the house and turned on the television. Occasionally I would see her in the kitchen while I was making myself breakfast or dinner. I fully expected her to complain about me eating the food until I learned about the social security checks she would be receiving for me because I was the minor child of the deceased. For the next year I would be a source of income to her, and I believe that is why she mellowed up on me. Had it not been for those checks, I believe she would have ordered me out of the house. Not that she was nice to me; she just stopped going out of her way to be cruel.

I had only seen Charlie a couple of times since the funeral. He glared at me and I glared back. Only one time was there an actual face-to-face confrontation. I was in the barn feeding the livestock and he came in looking for some saddle soap. He spoke abruptly and curtly when he asked me for it.

"Where is the saddle soap, Nelson?" He asked, glaring at me at the same time.

I pointed to it and he ran and grabbed it.

"You know....the last time I think I saw you in this barn you were with your dad. You must have been around three."

"Yeah? Well, the last time I saw *you* in this barn you were rutting around and grunting in a stall with my mother...just like a couple of pigs."

Charlie turned sheet white and then red. He walked out and never tried to make conversation with me again.

July was almost over. When I finished up with the chores for the day I showered and dressed to go out. I hadn't been anywhere since I saw Jennifer that night four weeks ago. She had called several times and I didn't return her calls. If I answered the phone when she called, I just gently set the receiver back down in its cradle. It was over, as far as I was concerned. Cheat on me once, okay, but cheat on me twice—well, that just wasn't going to happen. I headed for the diner where everybody usually hung out when there was nowhere else to go. I sat down in a booth and ordered coffee and the cheeseburger platter. As I was sipping my coffee and waiting for the platter, I spied Stacey coming in the door. What luck! Tommy wasn't with her either. I stared as she walked past the booths heading directly toward mine.

"Stacey....hi. Why don't you sit here?"

She stared at me like she was trying to remember me.

"Nelson.....Nelson Sutter. We go to school together."

"Oh, yeah....Nelson. I can't stay. I'm looking for Tommy. Have you seen him?"

"No.....I haven't. Are you okay? You look upset."

"Well.....I hardly know you so I don't feel I can unburden myself on you."

"Sure you can. I'm a good listener."

She stared at me and sighed.

"Well, it's nothing....really. My parents and I are going back to our place near Pittsburgh and I wanted to see Tommy before I left."

"Oh.....for how long? I mean how long will you be there?"

"Until school starts."

"There's Tommy now. He's coming in here."

"Oh good......well....bye....Nelson."

"Okay.....hey, maybe we can do something sometime."

She never answered me as she ran up to Tommy. They left together.

I sat and ate my food when it arrived and was about to leave when Gwen Murphy came in and sat down with me. She was a cute girl with a quick sense of humor. She smiled at me and asked, "Are you and Jennifer broken up?"

"Yep," I responded.

"What happened?"

"Some other guy happened."

"Yeah? Gee....that's too bad. You don't seem all that broken up over it."

"I'm not." Was I supposed to be? I wondered.

"Wanna go do something?" She had a really nice smile.

"Sure. Want anything from here first?" I asked her.

She shook her head so we just headed out the door to the truck. We almost ran smack into Jennifer. I took Gwen by the elbow and began steering her around Jennifer but Jennifer stepped into our path.

"Nelson, I want to talk to you."

"Uh, I'm a little busy, Jenn."

"We need to talk."

"There is really nothing to talk about, Jenn. Now.... let us alone."

She stood there watching as I backed the truck out of the parking space. I don't know how long she stood there, but she was still there crying when I looked into my rear view mirror and drove out of the diner parking lot.

Gwen gave me a night to remember. Her parents were away for the week so we went to her place. Wow! Could that girl make a guy feel good! I would have gone back to her again and again—if I could have. I stayed with her all night and she did things—well, let me just say that I believe that she had a Ph.D. in sexual techniques, if there was such a thing. It was the first time I ever spent the night with a girl. In the morning, we had sex and showered together and then had sex again—once in the shower and then again on the bed. She made me breakfast and it wasn't too bad. She was a great girl.

I left her place around eleven that morning, wondering if my mother would have anything to say about me staying out all night. I pulled into the driveway, shut the truck off, and got out. She wasn't coming out the door screaming at me, so I wasn't too worried. Anyway, I didn't figure she really actually cared if I came home or not. I stepped through the kitchen door and there she was—lying face down on the floor. I could tell she was dead from where I stood so I reached for the telephone and dialed nine-one-one. Then I called Mister Canton. I stood on the porch waiting for them all to get there. I remember speaking to my dead mother, quietly through the screen door. "Well, you got your wish. You never have to see me again."

The coroner said that my mother died of a massive coronary, which surprised me. I thought you had to have a heart for that.

It was a small funeral, smaller than my father's. Again, the team showed up, and then some of the cheerleaders and majorettes. Stacey was noticeably absent again. Jennifer came, as I knew she would. I didn't speak to her, other than to thank her for coming. Gwen showed up and asked me when it happened.

"She was dead on the floor when I got home from your place. They said she had been dead about two hours," I told her.

"Guess what we were doing when she died..." Gwen reminded me. I couldn't help it—I smiled.

Chapter 13

It never dawned on me that there would be a problem with my living arrangements after she was gone. Of course I understood that the house belonged to the Cantons and it was designated for the field foreman, but the new foreman had a home. If I had to leave this one I wouldn't have one. There was also the matter of my living by myself that became an issue. I would be seventeen in August! What was the problem? Apparently there was a problem—I was underage. I had no other family that I knew of. No aunts or uncles that I was aware of, either. It wouldn't have mattered since I really would not have had any intention of going to live with someone I didn't know.

Richard thought he had the solution. He would ask his parents if I could live with them. I didn't like it but at least I knew them. His parents flatly said no. He argued with them but to no avail. Mister Canton vetoed it because of my fight with Charlie. Richard told him why I fought with Charlie but it didn't matter. He said he needed Charlie on the farm. Missus Canton vetoed it because she didn't want an unrelated teenaged boy living under the same roof as her beautiful teenaged twin daughters. Beautiful? Had she taken a look at those two lately? Richard had all the looks in that family and there had been nothing left over for the twins. Richard had gray flashing eyes and a nice head of thick black hair, while the twins had watery blue eyes, frizzy mouse brown hair and skin that resembled biscuit dough—not to mention that they must have weighed three hundred and fifty pounds together. Now three hundred and fifty pounds isn't bad if you're talking about new-born twin bulls. Plus, they had mouths that looked so cute on chipmunks but not so cute on humans. Missus Canton needn't have worried. Sandwiched between those two naked in bed would have had *me* screaming for my mommy. Anyway, this wasn't solving the problem of my living arrangements. In a matter of a month I would be out of a home and nowhere to go.

Children and Family Services showed up. I guess I have Missus Canton to thank for that. After several meetings with them, I was ordered to pack my things and come with them. Richard helped me get my things together and he looked like he was going to cry. I have to admit I was kind of sad and more than a little scared. I think it should be noted that up to this point I had been a pretty good kid. I never smoked, drank, or did drugs; I worked hard around the farm, and I managed to keep my grades up in the honor roll level. Yet I was being treated like a criminal. Go figure.

Richard had a couple of questions for these agents from Children and Family Services, but I only had one.

"I know about the social security check for me every month. What happens to it?" I asked.

"It is used for your upkeep," the older gentleman told me.

"Upkeep? What am I? A Chevy? And speaking of that, what about the cars? My dad gave me the truck. Shouldn't I be allowed to have it?"

"No....it will be sold off and the money will be put into an account for you, just like any other asset your parents may have had. But it doesn't look like they had too much, does it?"

"No....I guess not," I admitted. *That* was kind of embarrassing.

"Where will Nelson be going? Will I be able to visit him?" Richard asked.

"There is an opening at a nice boys' shelter just southeast of Pittsburgh. We worked at getting him in there and it looks like they have accepted him. If you can get there, you can visit him. Just call and make arrangements first. They're strict about letting strangers come in."

"Can I write to him? And can he write to me?"

"Sure...that's permitted. You must be a good friend."

"Well....he's kind of like a brother."

When Richard said that I almost teared up. I didn't know Richard saw me as that. Richard told them to wait a moment and he ran down the driveway. He was back shortly with stamps, envelopes and a large writing tablet. He put them in one of the boxes that held my things.

"You better write to me, Buddy."

"I promise, Richard....I will."

I knew I could handle anything having been the son of the devil woman, but when I thought about not ever getting to have sex with Gwen again, it sort of bothered me. And then I thought about Stacey Stockwell. I may never see *her* again! The source of all my fantasies—the one who I would do anything for—was slipping through my fingers because these people made a decision that I shouldn't live alone! I took out the student directory and jammed it into the side of one of the boxes. Her address was in it. Gwen's was there, too. I would drop her a line as well. It was the least I could do to thank her for the wonderful night she gave me. I had been silent while I packed, but I made one last-ditch effort to keep my freedom.

"Hey, why can't I just have the social security checks and support myself until I get a job? I don't need to be sheltered somewhere." "It's the law that a minor child under the age of eighteen cannot live on his own."

That was the end of the discussion. One thing I thought about that I hadn't thought about earlier. I was going to be closer to Pittsburgh. Stacey's family had a place close to Pittsburgh. Maybe I could find out where it was and go see her once in awhile. Tommy Baker wouldn't be there. I could have Stacey all to myself.

I was ready to go. I sighed as I looked at Richard. He no longer had a handle on himself—*he was crying!* Richard. To this day I never had another friend like Richard. Mister Canton came in to say goodbye. He took me aside and told me there was a small account started for me for college if I wanted it.

"There's five thousand dollars in there for you. I'll add what I can. If you choose a community college it may cover a year...maybe more. I'm sorry, Nelson. I wish I could have offered you a better arrangement."

"Yeah....it's okay, Mister Canton. I understand." *Like Hell I did!*

Richard and Mister Canton helped me carry my boxes of things down to the car. Abby was sitting on the old tree stump waiting for me. She ran up to me and hugged me before I got into the car. Alice wasn't there. Fine. I didn't like her anyway. Missus Canton stayed away, too. Because of guilt, maybe? I climbed into the back seat after one more hug from Richard and a surprising one from Mister Canton.

"Take care," he said. "Let us know how you're doing."

The younger guy started the car and put it in gear. As he drove slowly down the driveway, I looked back and saw Richard saying something to his father, and from the looks of it, he wasn't being too nice. It was the last time I ever saw either one of them. Richard and I kept in touch through the mail for awhile, but then after a time, I quit writing. The life I had there in Central Pennsylvania was gone—over. There was no sense trying to keep it alive. I had written Gwen a letter, too. She answered it but I never wrote back. I wrote to Stacey and didn't hear from her. I sat down and wrote her another long letter, just pouring my heart out to her. In the letter I told her that I would make it big and then come back for her. I never mailed the letter, but I kept it for years.

After riding for about a half hour, the driver exited the two-lane in order to get onto the Pennsylvania Turnpike. Our first stop was in Somerset for fuel and a bathroom and McDonald's.

"You won't be seeing much fast food after this so go ahead and get what you want. The shelter serves well-balanced nutritious meals."

I ordered a Big Mac and a Quarter Pounder, large fries,

and a chocolate shake. To me it was like getting a last meal before an execution.

Chapter 14

We arrived at my destination just before dark. I looked up at the austere gray bricked building and a sense of doom came over me. This cold institution was to be my home for a whole year. I squared my shoulders and stood up straight. So be it. I could handle it. I looked at the older gentleman whose name was Mister Harrison, I learned en route, and nodded. We started up the wide steps and entered though the massive steel door. We were greeted by a booming voice belonging to a man of about forty.

"Well....you must be Nelson......welcome! I'm Father Timothy Olson. I'm the director here. Come on in and sit. You have things to bring in? Mister Harrison, take a couple of the boys down with you and bring his things up. Put them in the holding room." He said all this before I could say anything. The two men I came with disappeared, leaving me alone with—was he a priest?

"Okay.....Nelson. Let's get acquainted, shall we? Let's see...you will be seventeen in...three weeks. Good....we'll plan on birthday cake for dinner that night. Now...we do encourage foster parents...but I'll be honest with you....

they like them a lot younger than you. Some people take teens but never over sixteen.....at least not to my knowledge. But we needn't worry about that...you just got here. So.... tell me about school....your grades. Do you play sports?"

"My grades are good—all A's and B's. I played football at my high school."

"Good! Very good! Now....can you be open about some other things?"

"I guess....like what?" I shrugged.

"Any drugs or alcohol?"

"No."

"Cigarettes?"

"No."

"Sex?"

"Uh....yes."

"We don't permit that here."

"Isn't it all guys?"

"Yes."

"Then....no problem."

He smiled at me. "Well, I guess we know your sexual orientation."

"Straight as an arrow," I answered as I stared into his eyes and grinned.

"Good. Now you'll be rooming with three other boys. We try to match everybody up by age but sometimes that's not possible. Two of the boys in your room are seventeen and one is sixteen. It should work out."

The sound of footsteps indicated that my things had been brought up. Father Olson leaned out through the doorway. "Just put them in that room there. We'll go through them." He told Mister Harrison.

"We watched him pack so I'm sure everything is okay," Mister Harrison assured the good priest.

"Oh, I'm sure it is, too. We still have to go through it."

I sat quietly listening to the exchange while I watched the three boys who helped carry everything try to get a good look at me. One of them caught me staring and he halfway waved at me. I nodded to him. So far I had not spoken, except to answer the questions the priest asked me. I was too busy observing and listening. The men indicated that I was to follow them into what was called the holding room. The boxes holding my belongings were lined up on the table. Father Olson told me to sit in the chair at one end of the table, and I obeyed. The priest began going through the boxes, carefully lifting everything out and neatly piling it up in front of the box, one at a time. An older lady came in carrying a plate holding a sandwich and a glass of milk. She set it in front of me and I remembered to thank her for it. She gave me a tight-lipped smile and quietly left the room. Mister Harrison was putting everything back into the boxes as Father Olson finished each one. As he emptied the last box, he nodded his approval.

"Everything is in order. There is nothing here you can't keep. I can tell we will have no trouble with you. Are you ready to see your room and meet your roommates?"

"I guess." I stood up and reached for the empty plate and glass.

"Leave that. Missus Eaton will come and collect it."

Each of us grabbed a box and followed the priest up a staircase to the second floor and down a hall. We made a left down another corridor and entered the third room on the right. The large room held four small cots, four four-drawer dressers and four small desks, each holding a small lamp. The middle of the floor was filled by a sofa and a coffee table. The room wasn't bad. There was a large closet that I could see was divided into four equal sections.

"You can start putting your things away. I'll go down and see if I can find the other boys. You can meet them."

"I'll stay and keep him company," the younger man who did the driving volunteered. His name was Bill Kent, he told me while we were standing in line at McDonald's earlier on the turnpike.

When the others left the room, Mister Kent handed me a card. "If you have any problems, I want you to call me. You seem like a really nice kid. I don't want to see you have to go through any...unnecessary problems."

"Thanks," I said as I stuffed the card into my pocket.

He helped me empty out boxes as I put my things away. As we were working on this a black kid entered the room. He stopped and stared at me and then dropped down onto the sofa and stared at me some more.

"You Nelson?"

"Yeah," I said warily. Now I don't want to sound like a racist, but this was the first time I had ever encountered a black person. He was very dark, as tall as I was, had about the same build, and had what I called braids in his hair. Later I learned that they were called Dreadlocks. I wasn't sure how I was supposed to act or react to him. Finally, he stood up and walked over to me, extending his hand.

"Ronald....Ronald Green....glad to meet you," he said, exposing a big toothy grin. I accepted his hand and shook it.

"Nelson Sutter.....glad to meet you. This your room, too?"

"Yeah....we're roomies.....and we'll get along fine. I can tell. You play football?"

"Yeah....I was on the team at school."

"Good....maybe you can get on the team here."

"I'll try." I responded.

Ronald and I did get along for the year I was there. He was an easy-going kid who had lost his parents in a car accident when he was fifteen. He didn't fight and he played fair. I only wish I could say the same for my other two roommates.

Chapter 15

JUST AS MISTER Harrison and Mister Kent were getting ready to leave, my other two roommates showed up—with major attitudes. Ronald introduced them to me as Shake and Bake, but I learned within the next minutes that they were actually Curtis and Jimmy. Curtis, a light-skinned African American, was the older and the bigger of the two. He looked like he could hold his own in a confrontation and I judged that he was confident of that. Jimmy, a white dude, was smaller and had the bigger attitude. Little guy syndrome—I spotted it immediately. They both sized me up as I watched them warily. Mister Kent cleared his throat and shifted from one foot to the other. He extended his hand to me and I shook it. Mister Harrison did the same.

"Remember, Nelson....call if there are any problems."

"Okay.....thanks for the food earlier," I responded as they walked out the door. I had a sudden urge to yell, 'don't leave me here!' but I quickly got a grip.

When I turned toward the three roommates, they

were staring at me like my dick was hanging out. I stood my ground and stared back.

"Something wrong?" I asked, my eyes taking in all three of them.

"So what are you in for?" Curtis asked.

"Dead parents," I responded.

"You kill 'em?" He retorted.

"No....well, maybe my mother. I didn't come home all night and when I did, I found her lying on the floor, dead."

"Yeah? Where were you all night? Getting a little?"

"Maybe.....but now you *sound* like my mother."

Ronald started laughing. "You're all right, Nelson." He laughed, and so did Curtis. Jimmy remained silent and brooding.

Lights out was at eleven, since it was still the summer vacation. When school started it would change to ten o'clock. Until then, the three roommates filled me in on the way things were. We were all assigned chores in order to keep the house clean, and everybody had to take a turn in the kitchen. The food wasn't bad, but just not enough of it, they informed me. If we went anywhere, we had to let Father Olson know, and we had to be back by nine—unless it was something special. Visitors came on visitors' day and we all had to go down to the rec room, dressed in nice clothes on that day, since some visitors were looking for potential foster children. Cigarettes, booze, drugs, and sex were not permitted on the premises. However, Curtis informed me that they were obtained and used when nobody was looking. Getting a hold of cigarettes and selling them was a nice little money-making scheme, I learned. I silently counted in my head the money I carefully kept hidden from everybody when I checked in here. I would not share the fact that I had almost thirty dollars on me—not even with Ronald, who I believed I could trust.

"What do you do to get laid?" I asked.

"Well, that's a little difficult.....but there are opportunities. You just have to be careful.....not of getting caught, but of getting the clap. Some real skanks around here," Curtis informed me. "Best bet is to find a nice girl in school and sweet talk her into it. As long as you're home by nine, you're good to go."

I was satisfied with that answer. Hadn't I done about the same thing out in the country? I wanted to know about the good priest. Was he a good priest? Or was he someone I had to be wary of?

"Father Olson is okay. He doesn't try to hit ya up the ass, if that's what you're worried about," Jimmy offered. "He's fair, and he does treat us pretty okay. Just don't break one of his rules...you follow the rules and you'll be okay."

Ronald seemed to be studying me as I listened and absorbed all this information. He didn't say much, but just nodded his head in agreement a couple of times. Curtis and Jimmy left the room together because they had a cigarette deal going on in a couple of rooms down the hall. Ronald stayed back and observed me some more. Finally he spoke what was on his mind.

"Dude....don't put a lot of trust into those two. You're a nice guy. Don't let them know it. You have to hold your own in here. Stay nice on the surface, but be ready for anything. I like you....and I want you to know....I got your back."

And he did, too—for the entire next year.

Because of the abuse I took as the child of the beast, I was a light sleeper. And because of all the farm chores and football, I was fast and strong. Both elements came in handy that first night at the shelter. The outcome of the event that occurred that first night earned me the respect of all three roommates. I had just fallen asleep when I felt his presence near my cot. I had no idea what he had in mind, but I wasn't going to give him the opportunity to act on it. Quick as a cat, I sprung on him and pinned him to the floor by his throat, one knee pressed into his solar plexus, and my fist drawn back to smash his face in. Ronald jumped out of bed and turned on a lamp, illuminating the scene. Jimmy sat up and stared at the sight of Curtis under me in a bad position. I was looking into the eyes of pure fear as I stared down at Curtis. I don't think he expected such a reaction from me.

"Did you want something, Curtis?" I asked, intentionally keeping my voice low.

He shook his head. I kept my position over him, unwavering.

"Then why were you there? Were you sleep-walking?"

He saw that question as a way out, so he nodded.

"If that's a problem, maybe we should tie you to the bed....do you think?"

He shook his head again, his eyes widened with more fear.

"Do you think that when you sleep-walk from now on it will be a direction away from my corner of the room?"

Curtis vigorously nodded.

"If I let you up are you going to crawl back to your

corner and stay there? Or will you need to be convinced that you should stay there?"

"No....I won't bother you again. I swear," he said through gritted teeth.

Slowly, I released him and he crawled back to his cot.

"How about you, Jimmy? Do you sleep-walk, too?"

"No, I don't," he answered quickly.

Ronald began to laugh. "You're one bad-assed dude. I wouldn't want to mess with you. Where'd you learn to handle yourself?"

"My mother taught me."

Ronald laughed at my joke. He couldn't possibly know how close to the truth it was. I never had another incident like that one for the entire year I lived at the shelter. Curtis and Jimmy didn't like me, but they respected me and gave me a wide berth because of that night. Ronald, on the other hand, chose to hang around with me.

Chapter 16

BIRTHDAY CAKE, IN honor of my birthday, was served at dinner on the day I turned seventeen. That was only the third birthday cake I had ever had. I had been in the shelter for close to three weeks now and was looking forward to leaving. It really wasn't all that bad, I guess. At least I wasn't getting abused. But over the years I had learned to be self-reliant and was relatively a loner. Here, in the shelter I had people too close to me all the time. If I stepped outside onto the concrete somebody was right beside me. If I went to the TV room to sit for awhile, there was somebody already there, or somebody soon would be. I couldn't even go to the bathroom in private. There was always somebody there. I tried to think of a way to use this to my advantage, but so far I couldn't think of a thing, except to know that these kids wanted me for a friend.

It was a Saturday. The Saturday, a week before school started, actually. Ronald asked me if I wanted to go to the mall with him. Our clothing allowance from our social security checks was handed to us to go shopping for school clothes. Big deal. We each received $104 to spend on clothes and shoes. Thanks to Richard and my father, I had plenty of clothes. I just needed shoes. The rest of the money I spent on cartons of cigarettes, booze, and condoms. My idea was brilliant. I stood outside of a State Store, just watching people go in and out. Now a State Store in Pennsylvania is the only place you can buy liquor. Beer you can buy at a distributor or at a bar, but a bottle of booze can only be purchased at a State Store. I watched for about an hour before I found my mark. He looked like he was down on his luck and a little thirsty. I watched him emerge from the store, carrying a brown bag, and I waited for him to cross the street before I approached him.

"Hi.....what do you have in there?"
"Just a bottle of whiskey," he responded nervously.

"Let me see it. How much did you pay for it?" I asked him.

"I paid nine dollars for it," he answered defiantly.

"I'll give you twenty for it," I bargained.

"Are you crazy?"

"No...just underage. Sell it to me for twenty bucks?"

"Sure," he said as he grinned at me, thinking that he was ripping me off.

My next stop was at a science store to purchase vials like they use in laboratories. A dozen of them came with a stand to hold them. Perfect. I would be open for business by the evening. I had to let Ronald in on my plan since I would need some advertising for my merchandise.

"So, Ronald....here's the deal. Cigarettes are a quarter apiece. Now the way I figure it, by the carton a pack of cigarettes is worth a buck-eighty-five. Every pack carries a three dollar and fifteen cent profit. Now the whiskey....

each vial holds about two ounces....two bucks apiece. This bottle is worth about sixty-five dollars or better."

"And the condoms?" He asked.

"Come on....who in this place has a need for them?"

"They're for you?"

"Yeah.....and I plan on using them, too."

Ronald laughed and grinned at me. "So you have an easy time with the ladies, do you?"

"Usually. I never have to ask. *They* ask *me*," I boasted. It was true enough, if you think about it. I never asked Jennifer or Gwen for sex. I didn't even expect it. It was always their idea.

So my illicit contraband operation began. Ronald had a subtle way of getting the word out and before I knew it, I was looking at profits. I paid Ronald twenty-five percent of the profits. He was satisfied with that since I had put up all the front money and took all the risks. All he had to do was advertise. Before the first week was out I was down to one carton of cigarettes and only enough whiskey for two vials. Sadly, I still had all the condoms, too. Oh well, school was starting on Monday. My luck would be changing. In the meantime, I had to get out there and get some more merchandise. The cigarettes were easy to get since stores were not required to check ID yet and most clerks thought I looked older anyway. Now the alcohol was tougher. I decided I would purchase enough to last awhile since it was riskier and harder to obtain. I just had to find my mark. On the Saturday right before school started, I stood across the street from the State Store and waited. Ronald was standing by at another State Store. Before dinner time, Ronald and I had three different varieties of booze to offer our customers. We stopped to get more vials from the science store before we headed back to the shelter.

Ronald and I ran this lucrative business for the entire year we remained at the shelter. Business boomed and there was never a lull in the demand for our products. I made Ronald an equal partner, since he was purchasing items for the business, too. I was smart enough to realize that I needed to walk out of there with money in the bank, so I started a small savings account for myself at a local bank. Not only would there be a little interest, but the cash was safe from sticky fingers.

For that entire year, I went to school, did my homework, sold my products, and thought of Stacey. I soon learned that being from the shelter made you unpopular with the students, especially the female ones. There were not many opportunities to hook up with girls—nice ones, that is. Curtis was right about there being a lot of skanks around. They were a dime a dozen, but nice girls didn't go with boys from the shelter.

Until I met Kathy. She transferred to my English class in late October and she sat in the seat directly across the aisle from me. She had a cute face, pretty green eyes, shiny dark brown hair, and a gorgeous set of knockers. She smiled at me and I smiled back on that first encounter. Now English class was just before lunch, so it wasn't surprising to see her in the cafeteria right after class. What was surprising was that she came directly to me and asked if she could sit at my table. I had no objection. I saw her again after school and again the next day in class. We had lunch together and ended up at her house in her bed after school. She was no skank either. So much for nice girls not going with boys from the shelter! I passed the time with Kathy that year. I was relieved when she told me she was going away to college, since I didn't want a permanent thing once I was out of the shelter.

Chapter 17

You really know you're all alone and have nobody when you graduate from high school and there is nobody there for you to see you graduate. I had no family, and no friends. Outside of the shelter, I really didn't know anybody except Kathy. Her parents did not approve of me so we had to sneak around that year. I was one of those boys from the shelter and her parents told her I was beneath her. I could have told them that I was beneath her sometimes, but most of the time I was on top, but I didn't think they would appreciate the beauty in that. Anyway, we managed to keep everything a secret from them. On graduation day, she stood with her parents after the ceremony and I just went back to the shelter. I never saw her again.

I had a little more than two months to decide what I was going to do. I still had that college fund from Mister Canton, so I thought I would maybe try night school at the community college in Pittsburgh while I worked during the day. But where would I work during the day? I really had no marketable skills. There were not many fences to mend, crops to tend to, or cows to milk in the city of Pittsburgh—that I knew of, anyway.

Father Olson called me into his office the day after graduation. At first I thought maybe he found out about my business operation and I was a little nervous. As I sat there outside his office door waiting for him to get off the phone, I was silently forming my defense. Finally the door opened and he called me inside.

"Nelson…first let me congratulate you on your graduation. You ended your high school years in high standing. When I checked on your grades about a month ago, it looked like you were graduating with honors. How did your finals go?"

"Not too bad, Father."

"Good. Now…what I want to talk to you about…"

'Oh, boy....here it comes.' I secretly winced inside.

"Have you thought about what you're going to do? You can stay here until you officially turn eighteen, but after that…."

So this was just the old 'out you go' talk. Okay, I could handle this.

"I don't know, Sir….I may try to get into the community college at night….and work somewhere in the days."

"Do you have any experience at anything?"

"Farming," I answered and shrugged.

"Not much of that around here. I suppose you could go back to the area where you grew up. What are your thoughts?"

"Know anybody who is hiring?" I asked in response.

He smiled a little before he answered. "I'll look into it and let you know."

He stood up signaling that our talk was over. I went

to my room and checked my inventory. I had enough inventory to make another hundred and a half, after I paid Ronald.

Ronald and Curtis didn't graduate that year. Curtis was behind a year and Ronald's birthday fell after the cutoff date. I was the only graduate in the shelter. A special dinner in my honor was given that night after our talk. Father Olson had bought graduation decorations and the cook baked a graduation cake. At dinner he announced my graduation and my honor standing in the class. Everyone applauded as they were expected to do. Ronald gave me a high five.

"See? If you had played football you might have gotten a scholarship," Ronald reminded me.

"I didn't play because I got here too late for tryouts. The team was already picked," I responded.

"Yeah, you probably would have been a damn good player, too," Ronald complained. "Jerks! They could have let you try out."

"Over and done, my friend....over and done. Now I have to think about a job."

When I returned to my room that night, there was a package on my bed. It was from Mister Canton and Richard. The passbook for the college fund was included in the box along with my yearbook from the previous year and some other memorabilia from my old high school. There was a graduation card with a hundred dollar bill in it, which really surprised me. It was Richard's idea, I'm sure. I wrote them a thank you note and sent it off the next morning. Funny how I never really thought about my life on the farm, and I rarely thought about the people I knew there. Except Stacey.

...

Sometimes help comes to you from somewhere you least expect it. I was lying on my bed looking through the jobs section of the newspaper a week after graduation when Timothy Jones wandered into my room. I glanced up at him when I noticed he was in the room, but paid no attention to him. I was a little annoyed when he tried to strike up a conversation, but I tried not to show it. The kid was usually very quiet and shy but he had something to tell me that day.

"Nelson?" He ventured. I lifted my eyes from the newspaper to look in his direction but I didn't answer him.

"Nelson...do you know anything about cars?"

"Some....not much. Why?"

"Well, I have an ex-stepfather that owns a used car lot and he's looking for a salesman. He tries to run the lot himself but there are too many people milling around it looking at cars. He says he needs help."

"Yeah?" I questioned as I up-righted myself on my cot. "And you think I would be able to sell cars?"

"Well....yeah....I do. You got that....thing about you. People stop and listen. I think you'd sell lots of cars."

"Where is this car lot?" I smiled at him a little. Timothy was a good kid.

"Here.....here is my ex-stepfather's card. Go see him."

...

I did go see him and he hired me. You would have thought I was born into it, too. I sold four cars that first week and continued to sell after that. I quietly stashed my money into my bank account so that I would have enough to get myself a place to live after I left the shelter. Timothy's ex-stepfather turned out to be his step-father, twice removed, and he was called Big Jim. The car lot was 'Big Jim's Auto Sales' which was not surprising. Big Jim started referring to me as Nelson the Giant because I surpassed him in sales every week. He was happy with me.

Toward the middle of August I enrolled in night classes at the community college about the same time I found myself a small apartment near the car lot. I didn't have a car of my own yet, but I was working on it. On the nights I had classes I either took a bus or Big Jim gave me a ride. Because of the expense of registration and insurance, owning a car would have to wait. I was living frugally, paying my rent and electric bill, earning a decent amount of money every week, while I attended night courses at the community college. I still had no friends, not even a girl friend at this point. That changed on Halloween. I bought some candy bars in case anybody came to my door that night. It was the idea of the elderly lady across the hall. She was such a sweet old lady. She told me that every once in awhile some would show up and she always liked to have something to give them. I shrugged my shoulders and bought a bag of Snickers bars. If nobody came, I could eat them.

I hadn't expected anyone to knock on my door so I was pretty surprised when the knock came. I was sitting at my little kitchen table working on an assignment for school when I heard it. I got up and opened the door to a tiny witch standing there holding open a bag. There was a voice prompting her from around the corner in the hallway.

"Go ahead, Haley....say it. Trick or treat!"

"Trick or treat!" the tiny voice mimicked, as she held the bag open.

"Wait a minute," I responded as I walked to the kitchen cupboard to retrieve the Snicker's bars. "How many do you want?" I asked as I opened the bag.

"All of 'em!" She answered.

"Haley! That's rude!" The disembodied voice emerged in the form of a very pretty girl.

"I apologize for her rudeness," the voice owner added quickly.

"It's okay. Cute kid. Is she yours?"

"Hardly. My sister is in the hospital. She had another one yesterday....a boy this time. I agreed to help her out by taking Haley trick or treating."

"Aunt Renee....we can go now." Haley's voice rose above her aunt's.

"Haley, I'm talking to the nice man. Now just settle down or we won't go to any more houses."

So her name was Renee. She was cute, with shoulder-length auburn hair, green eyes and a dimple in each cheek and one in her chin. After she made her threat to her niece, she turned back to me. "I guess I better get going. Oh, I see books on the table. Are you in college?"

"Yeah," I answered her. What else was there to say about it?

"Do you go to Community? I go there, but I've never seen you there."

"It's a pretty big campus. I have all night classes."

"Oh....that would explain it. I'm studying to be an x-ray technician. How about you?"

"Business courses. I sell cars during the day," I told her.

She looked over at the little witch and started to laugh. Little Haley had fallen asleep on my lumpy old sofa. It made me laugh, too.

"Well...I guess the night ends for Haley. I guess I'd better take her home to bed."

I just nodded, but I was thinking the exact same thing about Renee. I closed the door behind them as they walked out of the apartment. I didn't expect to see either one of them again, so it was quite a surprise to see Renee camped out on the front stoop of my apartment building when I came home from work the next day.

Chapter 18

I SAW HER as I was walking from where Big Jim dropped me off. I had almost a whole block to walk while I planned my greeting to her. In the end, I didn't have to plan it since she immediately greeted me when she saw me.

"Hi....Nelson....remember me? Renee?"

"Oh yeah....the aunt of the witch."

"Yeah...you remember," she laughed and then smiled, looking very pleased.

"So what brings you to my door step?" I hoped I sounded nonchalant.

"I don't know....I thought maybe you would like to do something tonight. You know...hang out."

"I have to work tomorrow. Saturday's a big day for selling cars."

"Oh...." She looked dejected and I felt kind of bad.

"Well....look....I don't have much money.....but how about we walk over to Wendy's and I buy you some artery-clogging dinner? If you want, we could hang out at my place afterward. Maybe sit on my stoop or something."

The look of dejection turned into a bright smile as she nodded. "Great!"

"Just let me change clothes first," I told her.

After I changed we walked to Wendy's and had burgers and fries. The weather was turning colder, but it wasn't too bad out yet. The night was clear so after we finished eating we walked for a little while. She slipped her hand into mine and started the probing questions that seem to be so important to girls.

"So Nelson...where did you grow up?" This was the first question.

"In Central Pennsylvania," I obliged. "On a farm."

"Do your parents still live there?"

"Dead."

"What?" She asked, looking shocked.

"They're dead."

"Oh...wow....I'm sorry."

"Sorry for what? It's not your fault."

"I mean.....I don't know....never mind." She really didn't know. She didn't know what to say either. "Do you have a girlfriend?" She dove back in quickly.

"Now if I had a girlfriend would I be here with you right now?"

"I would hope not....I guess. So you don't have a girlfriend?"

"No," I answered. I could be totally honest about that.

We walked a couple more blocks and then headed toward my apartment. It may not have been very cold yet, but you began to feel it if you spent some time outside. We stopped into the local pharmacy and picked up a two liter bottle of Pepsi before getting to my place. As soon as we got inside my apartment I filled two glasses with ice and Pepsi and carried them to the small coffee table that sat in front of the dilapidated sofa. The apartment came with a nineteen-inch color television and a remote to go with it. I paid extra for the cable installation. She was already holding the remote when I sat down next to her.

"I have one movie channel. It's all I could afford," I told her.

"It's fine. Maybe the movie coming on next will be a good one."

The movie turned out to be 'Blazing Saddles' which was pretty funny. I had never seen it before. I noticed Renee kept giving me sidelong glances during the movie. I pretended to be indifferent. If she wanted me she was going to have to make the first move. When the movie ended she asked to use the bathroom. While she was gone from the room I began reading out of one of my textbooks. I didn't want her to think that I was sitting there waiting for her. She came back and sat down next to me again. Her subtlety was almost laughable.

"Want me to rub your back?"

"Why? Do I look like my back hurts?"

"No….I guess I just thought….most guys liked their back rubbed. I didn't mean…."

I laughed lightly and then smiled at her. "I would love a back rub. Are you sure you don't mind?" I asked her, playing the game as I went.

"No….I offered."

"Right. So do you want me to lie here on the sofa?"

"Well….it might be more comfortable for you if you stretched out on your bed."

"Well....yeah, I guess it would," I conceded, continuing the cat and mouse game.

She followed me into my bedroom as I plopped down on my bed, face down. As I recall, it really wasn't a very good back rub, but it got her where she wanted to be. I let her rub my back for awhile and then I rolled over and smiled up at her. She took that as an invitation and immediately locked lips with me. The sex was okay—not the greatest—but okay. I had to do most of the work. Afterwards, as we lay there in the dark room, she began stroking my chest. I braced myself and waited for—something—I wasn't sure what. That something was a question.

"Nelson....did I....was I....okay...for you? Did I...... satisfy you?"

"What? What kind of a question is that?" It was one I couldn't believe she was asking. That's what kind of a question it was.

"Well...were you....happy...with me?"

"Renee....of course I was. Look at it. It's lying there like it's dead. That's a sign that I was satisfied. Now why would you think I wasn't happy with you?"

"Well...because....it took you so long to...you know." I could hear the quiver in her voice.

"Well, I waited for you. I wanted you to come first. That's what a guy should do."

"Oh.....wow...that's the first time I ever did. It was my first orgasm."

"Yeah? Now you're making me feel special," I teased.

"It's because you are," she responded.

I rolled over on my side and held her, stroking her back. Her skin felt soft under my hands that were still hardened and calloused from farm work. Surprisingly, she had a pretty nice body. I felt myself being aroused again so I started kissing her. This time I worked on giving her an orgasm before I even entered her. She gasped and breathlessly spoke my name as her orgasm began.

...

Renee and I hung out together for the rest of that year. I can't say we dated because I rarely had money to take her anywhere. Once in awhile I managed to take her to a movie or an inexpensive place to eat, but mostly we stayed at my place and watched television and had sex. She understood about my money situation. For Christmas that year I bought her a small gold locket and a green sweater with the bonus money Big Jim bestowed upon me. After all, I had nobody else to buy anything for. A couple of days before Christmas she came to my apartment dragging a small tree, tree lights, and ornaments for it. We spent a couple of hours decorating it before we fell into bed for a couple of hours of sex. When we were hungry for food I suggested she get dressed so I could take her to dinner. Via the port authority, we went to a nice restaurant for dinner since I had some of the bonus money left. I walked her home and we made plans for Christmas Eve together. Since we were on a winter holiday break from school we had some free time. She had taken a job in Kaufman's Department Store for the holidays and her schedule was varied, but she knew she had Christmas Eve off. I was invited to her house for a late Christmas Eve dinner, so she came to my apartment early. She was surprised when I handed her the wrapped Christmas gifts, but not nearly as surprised as I was when she handed me one. I had never had a gift before—from anyone. It was a watch. I had never had a watch before this. She sat and watched me expectantly as I opened it.

"Do you like it?"

"Like it? Oh hell yeah, I like it. Thanks, Renee. Thank you." I hugged her to me. I had never known this kind of sweetness before. She was truly a giving person. "But you didn't say whether you liked what I gave you. I mean....if you don't we can exchange it. I know I'm not that good at buying gifts...."

"Nelson....they're wonderful. I love the locket and the sweater is beautiful. I love them both. Thank you." She smiled a genuine smile and hugged me.

Christmas Eve dinner at her house was okay—actually, it was better than okay. The food was good and her family was warm and friendly. Her father gave me a ride home and her mother insisted that I take a doggie bag. On the way to my apartment, her father asked me where I was spending Christmas for dinner. Embarrassed, I told him I didn't have any plans.

"No family?"

"No, Sir....my parents are dead and I was an only child."

"Well, Renee and I will be here to pick you up at one tomorrow. You can have dinner with us. Renee's grandparents will be there but they don't bite, so you should enjoy the day."

"Thank you, Daddy!" Renee piped up.

"Are you sure it's not an imposition, Sir?" I asked him.

"Absolutely not. We'd love having you." He answered.

So I spent Christmas day at Renee's house, too. What

a family! Renee had a younger sister and a brother, besides the older sister who was Haley's mother. Everybody seemed to like each other. I could feel the closeness and the love as I sat in their family room watching a Christmas movie. I had never had a nice Christmas. We never had a tree or presents, and dinner was nothing more than a regular meal—not like the spread Renee's mother put out. They were by no means wealthy, but I found it obvious that they felt blessed to be together. They were rich in love and warmth for one another. I vowed that someday I would have that, too. It was that Christmas holiday that made me realize that I was lonely.

...

I ended my college year with a 3.2 GPA and never went back. Renee had gotten a scholarship to Edinboro University and was going to be leaving the area. Originally, she planned on being an x-ray technician but later decided to become a teacher. She applied for a scholarship and got it. We saw each other during the summer but we let each other go when it was time for her to leave for Edinboro. It was a tearful parting—well, on her part. Don't get me wrong—it wasn't easy to let her go. She had been a wonderful girlfriend, lover, and friend. I just didn't outwardly cry. I had only cried one time in my adult life, and that was when my father died. Although I didn't cry, letting Renee go felt almost the same. It was more than just losing her. She had shared her family with me. I spent holidays with them, went on picnics with them, went to parties and even one wedding reception with them. Renee had provided something to me that I had never had before, and for that, I wished her the best—always—and still do.

Chapter 19

Some people have very eventful and exciting lives. I was never one of them. After Renee left for Edinboro, I went back to my old routine life, except that I couldn't afford classes any more. I would have been able to if it hadn't been for the fire at Big Jim's Auto Sales. I had planned on enrolling for classes again in the fall and I had just enough left in the bank to pay for tuition for another year when Big Jim's burned down. It was no fault of mine that caused the fire. I didn't smoke. Apparently Big Jim forgot to put his cigar out and it rolled onto the floor onto some scrunched up papers that didn't quite make the trash can during one of his 'basketball practice' sessions. The papers caught a flame and the flame rose to a couple of petroleum-soaked rags that were draped over the trash can. That flame rose to the curtains on the window and the fire escalated from there. Some of our inventory that was closest to the building was badly damaged from fire, smoke, and fire department firefighting. Big Jim had to remain closed for more than two months until the place was rebuilt. I thought about getting another job but Jim asked me to try to hang on. Hey, the guy was good to me, so I hung in there. I lived on my college money while I waited for the place to be rebuilt. Had I known about college grant money and student loans, I may have continued going while I sat on my ass, out of work.

With Renee gone, and not having classes or a job to go to, I had plenty time on my hands—time to reacquaint my fantasies with Stacey. I had rarely thought about Stacey when Renee was around, but now she was back in my head, my heart, and my dreams. I wondered where she was and what she was doing. Did she go to college? Or did she marry Tommy Baker? No, she couldn't have. Tommy Baker came from a nice family with a little money. Stacey's father would not have let her marry down like that. I thought about writing a couple of letters to Gwen, Richard, and Tommy Baker. The more I thought about it the better the idea sounded. Why not Tommy Baker? I could ask him how it was going, was he in college, and was he and Stacey still together. Yes! That was even a better idea! So I sat down and wrote to Tommy and hurriedly ran to the mailbox on the corner and dropped it in. All I had to do was wait for a response. I never wrote the letters to Richard or Gwen. The answer I was waiting for would come in the form of a letter from Tommy. I waited three weeks for an answer. I had just about given up waiting for him to write back when I pulled an envelope showing his return address out of my mailbox. As soon as I got inside my apartment I tore the envelope open and sat down to read, not even taking my jacket off first.

I scanned the letter and saw Stacey's name so I went back to the beginning and began reading it. He said that he was surprised to hear from me and that he was going to college in Philadelphia. He wasn't with Stacey any more since she was going to some college near or in Pittsburgh. The letter stated that they had broken up over a year ago and as far as he knew she was in college and had not married anyone. Then he asked me how I was and what was I doing. He wanted to know what happened to me. I had my answer to my question so I never bothered to write him back with any answers to his questions. Stacey was somewhere in Pittsburgh! Where, I wondered. My fantasies about Stacey continued only now another scene was added: *It's raining—pouring actually—and I hail a cab to get home. As I'm stepping into the cab Stacey comes out of nowhere, soaked to the skin, and asks if we can share the cab. Of course I agree and then give the driver my address. She turns and looks at me and says, "Nelson! Where have you been? I think about you a lot." The cab pulls up to my place, which is not my place now, but the one in the fantasy, and she says, "Mind if I come in to get dry?" Of course, I agree. Inside my upscale apartment I offer her a drink and a chance to change out of her wet clothes. She disappears and comes back into my living room wearing my robe. In a fluid motion she sits down on my expensive white sofa and smiles at me. I hand her a small snifter of Brandy and sit down beside her. We make small talk and then she lifts her arm up and runs her fingers through my hair and then puts her hand behind my head and pulls me towards her. We kiss. The kiss is passionate and we melt into each other for more. The sex is incredible and when it's over we lay in each other's arms and she tells me she always loved me but Tommy was in the way.* Anyway, the fantasy ends differently every time. There were other fantasies. In one, I pull her from a burning building and go back for her father. Since I save his life he gives me permission to marry his daughter. In others, I pull her out of the river, rescue her from a wrecked car, or take her in from the cold and warm her. In all of them I am her hero.

For the two months I spent waiting for Big Jim's to reopen I tried to find Stacey. I looked in the phone book and found nothing. I took buses to the area campuses and just walked around. I asked a couple of people if they knew her and nobody did. Tommy may have been wrong. I mean, if she was in school here how could anybody not know her? She was so beautiful!

Two months after the fire, I was lying on my bed with my eyes closed, drifting in and out of a Stacey fantasy when my telephone rang. It was Big Jim.

"Hey....ready to go back to work?"

"Yeah....when?"

"Grand opening Monday. Be here at eight. Oh, and Nelson....I have a bit of a bonus for you....for being loyal."

I hung up and briefly thought about that. Oh well, I would find out what the bonus was on Monday. It felt good to be getting back to work.

...

"It ain't much...but she runs good."

Jim and I stood side by side staring at the little green compact Ford. He handed me the keys.

"Take it for a spin. You'll see that she runs like a new car. It's wheels for you. I know it's not much to look at but you can get back and forth in it. We'll keep dealer plates on it so it will be covered by the dealer insurance. It's registered to the dealership. It's not much of a bonus....

I know....I'll try to do more for you. I appreciate your loyalty...and....hell....you're one hell of a salesman."

As I stood there staring at the car I realized that Jim thought I was unhappy or disappointed with the car. He couldn't be further off from the truth. I was stunned that he would do this for me. It was more than a generous overture—it was trust. He trusted me by giving me a vehicle registered to the business. That was solid gold.

"Jim....it's great. I appreciate it. Now if I can only figure out how to make enough money to get back into classes. Let's start the selling marathon!"

I gave him a high five and slid behind the wheel of the little green Ford. I took it around the block and had to admit that Jim was right. She drove like a new car.

I sold three cars that first day back, and two every day after for the entire week. In six days I had thirteen sales. I hoped the streak would continue. If it did, I would have my tuition money together before the next semester began.

The streak didn't continue. I was selling enough to keep myself afloat but not enough to gather tuition. My college education would have to be on hold for awhile.

The Christmas season was upon us. Sales were normally down this time of year and picked back up in late January. I came home just bushed one night, a few days before Christmas. All I wanted to do was get undressed and drop down on the sofa with a cup of coffee and watch television. I had only been inside my apartment for two minutes when someone knocked on my door. Renee was standing there smiling at me when I opened the door. I was so overwhelmed at seeing her.

"Renee! It's great to see you. Come in."

"Is this a bad time?"

"For you to come here? Never. So tell me how everything is going for you."

"Really great. I'm on the Dean's List. How about you?"

I told her about the fire and how I had to drop out of college until I had money to go. She was very sympathetic and encouraged me to apply for a scholarship. Before I realized it my arms were around her, just holding her. I didn't want to sleep with her at that moment. I just wanted to hold her—feel her against me. I needed her. We held each other for awhile and then she let me go. Our eyes locked and she must have seen the loneliness and the sadness in them because she took my hand and led me to the bedroom.

"Renee, we don't have to..."

"Shhh...Nelson....kiss me."

As we kissed she began undressing me. The kiss started out soft and gentle but as my clothes where shed, it became urgent. I unbuttoned her blouse and unhooked her bra. I could have cried as I touched her. Then I couldn't believe I said it.

"Renee....I think I love you. I have missed you....so much."

"Me, too...Nelson, I've thought about you every day."

When our clothes were in a heap beside the bed she pushed me down and climbed on top of me. When she put me inside of her I almost screamed from the sheer joy of being in her. It was quick for both of us. We lay there together in comfortable silence as I stroked her arm. I wanted to hold her all night. I never realized how in need of human contact I was.

"Can I take you out…tomorrow night?"

"Sure….where do you want to take me?"

"Wherever you want to go. I have a car now."

"Yeah? How about we go grab something to eat and then just go see Christmas lights? You know, just ride around."

"If that's your choice….then that's what we do," I responded, and then brushed my lips against hers.

I took her face between my palms and studied her. Damn, it felt good to have her there! Stacey was fantasy, but Renee was real. She was very real and right there, in my bed. I found myself asking the question that seemed so important to girls.

"So….you haven't found anyone else?"

"Nobody like you. I won't lie to you, Nelson. I've been out with other guys. But you're the one I think about. When I kiss another guy, it's your face I see behind my closed eyes. When I come home from a date, I think about you as I get undressed and ready for bed. I've missed you….and there will never be anybody like you."

I admired and appreciated her honesty. We spent as much time together as was permitted during her Christmas break. I went to her house for the holiday dinners again and was surprisingly happy to see all of them. Little Haley had grown in the past few months, I noticed. Her baby brother was over a year old now, and Renee's sister was chasing him all over. He had an affinity for the tree and that was where she didn't want him to be. I tried my hand at gift buying for Renee again. Gees, that was hard! I didn't even shop for myself let alone someone else. But I really wanted to get her something nice. I discussed it with Big Jim and he took me to see his friend who sold good gold jewelry at wholesale prices. I found a beautiful chain that wouldn't set me back too far and I bought it. I also bought her a dress. I had never bought anything like that for any girl so I was apprehensive about whether she would like it. I knew her size from the couple of things she had left at my place so I knew it would fit. As an afterthought I bought her a sexy nightgown which was to be opened and worn at my place only. She loved everything I gave her, and I was equally pleased with her gifts to me. I had never had anybody buy me clothes as a gift and it felt good receiving them. It felt—personal.

The holiday ended too soon. Renee left for Edinboro and I was hit with the realization that I would be all alone again. This time she had given me a phone number to call her. Maybe I would be able to take a ride up and visit, we both speculated. After she left I went back to my routine of nothingness, hoping that she would come back for spring break.

She did. She came back again, and again. For two years I looked forward to seeing her on her school breaks. I visited her once during those two years. She was all I lived for, and then she quit coming.

Chapter 20

I WONDERED WHAT happened to Renee and why she quit coming around. Then after awhile I stopped wondering and just assumed she found someone else.

I was twenty-three years old now. I was alone, and I was lonely. Even the little old lady across the hall was gone. Her kids put her into a nursing home one day while I was at work. I saw them removing the last of her things as I was coming in through the front entrance so I asked about her.

"She's not able to take care of herself," the tall, gray-haired guy said. "Mother held out as long as she could..... then...well, when my sister came to visit her she found her lying in bed in her own body waste. We should have checked on her more frequently....but she was a proud woman who loved being on her own."

"I wish I would have come over more often," I offered.

"She wasn't your responsibility.....she was ours. I thank you for the time you did give her. She talked about you a lot."

This made me smile. No, I hadn't spent a lot of time with her, but the times I went over there to visit her are fond memories.

...

There were a few changes the year I was twenty-three. I lost Renee, and Missus Wilson (that was the little old lady's name), and I lost my job.

Big Jim called me into the office right at quitting time one Friday.

"Sit down, Nelson....I have some bad news for you."

'Uh-oh,' I said to myself. I immediately tried to remember if I may have done something wrong. I couldn't think of a thing.

"I'll get right to it rather than sugar-coat it. I'm selling out."

"Why? Business has been so good."

"Cancer....I'm terminal."

He couldn't have shocked me more had he told me he was pregnant. I felt my insides go numb for a couple of seconds. I studied him to see if I maybe hadn't heard him right, but by the look in his eyes, I knew I had. I had been noticing how tired he looked the last couple of months, but I thought his age may have been catching up with him. He was past forty, but under fifty. I didn't know exactly how old he was.

"Cancer....where?" It was an ignorant question but the best I could come up with at that time.

"Liver first....now it's in the bones. Yesterday they found a spot on my lung. I have about six months at best right now."

"Jim...I don't know what to say." And I didn't, either. I was stunned.

"It's okay, Nelson...you don't have to say anything. Nothing is going to help or change it now. But just listen to me. You have been a loyal employee. You have made me a lot of money. I don't want to go and not compensate you."

"Hey....Jim....that's not what this is about. You..... you've been fair to me and I've enjoyed working for you. I made myself some money, too."

Jim smiled at me and then chuckled. "Anyway, you get the pick of the lot. You'll have to get your own insurance and register the car in your name...but the best one on the lot is yours. Also...."

He stopped talking right there and I saw the pain come into his eyes. He reached for a bottle of pills and I instinctively got up and poured some water from the water cooler into a cup. I handed him the cup and waited while the pain pill began to take effect.

"See....that's one of the things I like about you, Nelson. Your instincts....you knew what to do. Anyway, let's get back to the business. Pick out the car you want and let me know. Now....whatever you sell until the lot is cleared off....your percentage is doubled on it. Also, here is a bit of a bonus for you."

He took an envelope out of his pocket and slid it across the desk to me. I stared at it but left it sit there.

"Hard to pick it up, huh?" He sighed. "It's not much, but I remember how you spent your tuition money to keep yourself going while I rebuilt after the fire. Maybe that will get you a couple more classes under your belt." He did his best to smile at me, but I could see he was still in pain. "Also, I have a letter of recommendation for you, and a couple of names. You're good, Nelson. You're a born salesman. Maybe you should try new cars next."

"Jim....at the moment I can't think of working for anybody but you." And I meant that, too.

...

We had a major car sale going on for the next two weeks. I was making money hand over fist and the lot was emptying out. I chose the silver Grand Prix to be mine. It was only two years old and looked brand new. Jim registered it for me after I purchased an insurance policy. Finally, I had good-looking wheels.

I choked up a little on the last day of business. There were three cars left on the lot and the office was being cleared out. It was the end of an era for me. I spotted a young couple looking at one of the cars left on the lot. She was very young and very pregnant and he was just as young. I decided to approach them.

"Hi....interested in one of these?" Jim had already told me to just get rid of them, and not to worry about price.

"We don't have very much to spend, but we need a car....to get to the hospital when the time comes."

"This one here is the best of the three." I herded them toward a red Chevy sedan. "I can work out a price for you."

"Well, okay....at least we can see what we could get it for," the boy answered with hesitation as he looked at his young girlfriend. I said girlfriend because there was no ring on her finger. Later I found out I was right.

"Honey, we can't afford it. Look how nice this car

looks. We only have seven hundred dollars." I head her whisper to him.

So they had seven hundred dollars. They were in for a surprise. They were not going to pay a dime over three-hundred and fifty, plus registration and insurance. I made the deal and took four-hundred and ninety-eight dollars of their money. This included car, taxes, registration, and a six month no-fault insurance policy. Thank goodness our insurance agent was still on the premises. They were ecstatic and I felt pretty good myself. The other two cars were donated to a government-sponsored mechanics school.

...

I walked into my apartment with a heavy heart after that last day at Big Jim's Auto Sales. I was twenty-three, uneducated, out of work, and I was lonely. Soon I would lose Big Jim to the disease that was slowly rotting his body away.

I could have sat down and cried. I sure wanted to. Looking at life as a poker game, I had been dealt a lousy hand. Was this karma? Why did I lose everybody I cared about? Lethargy set in, and I spent the entire weekend sitting on the sofa or lying in my bed. I don't remember eating, but I do remember sleeping a hell of a lot.

On Monday morning, I knew I had to snap out of it. Maybe I *had* been dealt a bad hand. Either I could fold, or ask for another card. I chose another card. Way before daylight, I ran down to the box on the corner and bought a newspaper. It was a Sunday paper, since the box hadn't been serviced yet. After I put on coffee, I showered and put on a robe and sat down at the kitchen table with the newspaper spread out. There were plenty of sales jobs in the want-ads. I grabbed a highlighter out of the drawer and began highlighting the ones I might be interested in. In between cups of coffee my eyes strayed to the manila envelope I had brought home from Big Jim's. He said there was a letter of recommendation and a couple of names and phone numbers. That couldn't hurt. I dragged the envelope across the table and opened it. Yes, there was a letter in there, and some names of dealerships, with the names of contacts at each place. The manila envelope held the title, free and clear, to my car, my insurance policy, and the white envelope holding the check. I hadn't opened that envelope yet, so I guess now was as good a time as any. Five-thousand dollars. Five-thousand dollars! That's what I started out with! Yes, indeed, Big Jim was all right. It was also what I needed to boost me out of my slump.

I began making the phone calls from the phone numbers Jim provided and landed two interviews. One was at another used car lot dealer and the other was a new car dealership-Chevrolet. I made it to both interviews that day and returned home to wait for a phone call. In the meantime, I ordered myself a pizza with everything on it, and called Big Jim's house. He answered and he sounded good. I asked his advice about the two dealerships and he advised me to go with the new cars if I had the choice. I felt both interviews went well, so I was surprised when I didn't get a phone call by five o'clock Tuesday afternoon. In fact, I didn't get a phone call until Friday morning—from both dealerships. I took the new cars and was told to come in Monday, in casual dress, for orientation. I was back on the road to success. I could feel it.

Chapter 21

Selling new cars may have been a little more difficult than selling used ones, but the commission was so much better. I could make as much as five thousand dollars on one car if I played it right. Very rarely, was my commission that high, but if I sold three cars a week, I definitely put myself in a higher tax bracket. Selling one car a week enhanced my lifestyle as it was, and my average per week was two.

I had been selling new Chevrolets for almost a year by now, and I had taken no time off work except for one day to attend Big Jim's funeral. That's all I'm going to say about Big Jim or his funeral. It was one of the saddest days of my life and I refuse to feel that pain or that sadness again.

I had quite a bit of money in the bank. I had given up the idea of college since I was doing so well at selling cars, but I decided it was time for a nicer apartment and new furniture. I found the perfect apartment. It was advertised as one bedroom and a den or two bedrooms. The building was fairly modern and in a nice area. The apartment itself had great amenities—appliances included, sliding glass door leading onto a balcony, large closets, dishwasher, parking, and an exercise room. I signed the lease and moved in the following month, after I went shopping for furniture. I paid cash for three rooms of furniture, plus a desk and chair for the den, and a twenty-six inch television. Everything was delivered the day I left the little apartment for the new one. I felt proud—proud and happy. These things were mine. I paid for them. I looked around the new apartment and just felt good. The light beige carpet and the white walls looked and felt so clean and uncluttered. The sofa and chair I chose were dark green and the lamps were gold and beige with some dark green in them. My new cocktail tables were knotty pine with glass tops and they sat low. My bedroom furniture was black lacquered and expensive-looking, and I chose a glass topped dinette table with four gold chairs. I still needed to get some things to go on the walls, and a comforter for the bed. I thought about Renee and how nice it would be to go shopping with her and let her help me pick it out. Then I thought about Stacey and pictured her lounging on my sofa.

It's funny, but I realized something that day I moved in. When I thought of Renee, the two of us were doing things together, and when I thought about Stacey I was just admiring her as she sat in my line of vision. I just couldn't see us going to movies, or shopping, or anything. Maybe it was because we never had. Renee and I had been pals as well as lovers, and at that very moment as I was in my new apartment putting things away, I missed her terribly.

...

I continued to prosper by selling new cars. I had moved

from the Chevrolet dealership up to selling Cadillacs after two years. Selling one of those babies every two weeks kept me in my current lifestyle. Selling more than that—well, it was definitely money in the bank. One of my finest moments was when some stuffy old guy came in and grabbed me by the arm and pulled me aside.

"I need a good, honest salesman. Is that you?" He whispered to me.

"I'd like to think so, Sir. Can I assist you in any way?" I asked him.

The guy sized me up and then asked me to sit down with him at one of our tables we had strategically placed around the showroom.

"I need more than one of these," he said, as he pointed to the top of the line Cadillac parked in front of the table.

I could feel goose bumps on the back of my neck.

"How many were you thinking you needed?" I asked hesitantly, thinking that this guy was going to just disappear before my eyes, like a magician or maybe like an April fool's joke.

"Six," he stated, flatly.

"Six," I repeated, thinking I hadn't heard him right.

"Yes....I need six. What colors do you have in stock?" He was talking like we were discussing shoes.

"Let me check, Sir. Can I get you some coffee or something? Soft drink, maybe?" Anything to keep him there. He shook his head.

I ran over to check the inventory and wrote down the colors and the number of them in stock. When I came back my heart sank He wasn't sitting there. I was about to go back on the lot when I heard his voice behind me.

"So what colors do you have?"

I showed him the glossy swatches of the car colors and he sat back down, laying the colors out on the table.

"Do you have at least one of each of these six colors?"

"Yes, we do."

"Good.....I'll take one of each, all top of the line, fully loaded. Can you meet that demand....Nelson?" He asked as he leaned forward to read my name tag.

I checked the inventory sheet once more, and assured him that I could.

"Okay....let's talk price."

I came away that night with six sales under my belt. I took a beating on my commission, but I made nine thousand dollars in two hours' time. He signed the contracts and gave me a deposit in the form of cash, and returned the next day with all of his sons, his daughter, his wife, and a cashier's check for the balance owed. It was a done deal. All the cars were detailed and ready to drive away when he got there. I was top salesman for the day, the week, the month, and then the whole year. I was promoted to sales manager, which meant that not only did I get commission on my own sales, but I got a small commission on everybody else's sales. The money was rolling in and I had no one to share it with. Until I met Ann, that is. I was washing my car one pleasant Sunday morning in June and she was in the stall next to mine, washing her Nissan. Since I was now a sales manager I was given a lease on a Cadillac of my own and that is the one I was washing when I met her. As I was rinsing the soap off of mine she came into my stall to see if I had change for a dollar. I always had lots of change so I obliged her. Ann had a look about her. She wasn't gorgeous or even pretty, but she had a look that shouted 'tigress on the prowl' and

I was intrigued. I pulled my white Cadillac out of the stall over to the vacuums and began vacuuming the carpeting. I could see her watching me but I didn't let on that I was paying attention. I was finished with the car but I made it look like I was checking things in the trunk. I spent just enough time for her to pull her car over to the vacuums. I knew she would need quarters, so I waited.

"Could I trouble you for another four quarters?" She asked me, and again, I obliged. "Nice car," she added.

"Thanks," I responded, playing it cool, as I shut my trunk and made a move to go.

"Uh....is the car yours....or your wife's?" She asked hurriedly.

I stopped and took a couple of steps towards her. "It's mine...and I don't have a wife." I responded.

"Girlfriend?"

"No."

"Gay?"

"Definitely not."

"Wanna do something?"

"Sure." I smiled at her.

She followed me back to my place and she parked her car and hopped into mine.

"So what do you want to do?" She asked me once she was seated in the passenger seat with the seatbelt on.

"Whatever you want," I told her.

"Ever go to an amusement park?"

"No. I've seen them in movies and on television though."

She laughed like she thought I was kidding. "Want to do that?"

"Sure," I responded.

I was ready for anything rather than go back to my place and be alone for the rest of the day. I followed her directions and we entered a huge parking lot. I could see lots of flashing lights and movement to my left. One intriguing sight was a huge pirate ship swinging back and forth. This was going to be a new experience. I wondered why Renee never suggested it. We spent the entire Sunday at the park, riding the rides, eating, and playing the games. Ann was delighted when I won a large teddy bear for her. I'm not sure which of us had more fun, but I made myself a promise that I would go back there again. As we were leaving the parking lot, she turned to me.

"Nelson.....thank you for the wonderful day," she purred.

"Hey, I had fun, too....so thank *you*."

"I don't want the day to end." I caught on to the suggestion.

"And what would you like to do next?"

"Well....we *could* go to my place....but I have a roommate. How about you?"

"No roommate, no wife, no girlfriend, no lover...want to go there?"

"Sounds good....that's where my car is anyway."

"Fine with me," I told her.

We drove to my apartment and we went inside. I could tell she was impressed with it by the way she looked around and touched things.

"Want something to drink? I don't have much in the way of booze, but I have some wine."

"That will be fine," she said almost absently. "Oh, you have a balcony....can we sit out there for awhile?"

"Yeah, sure," I obliged.

I led the way through the sliding door onto the balcony. I was glad I had just purchased some furniture for out there. We sat down on the two-seater piece of patio furniture and at first we didn't talk, but I wanted to know more about her.

"You know, Ann…we spent the entire day together and I know nothing about you. What do you do for a living? You never said whether you had a boyfriend. Come on, girls *like* to talk."

"Okay," she laughed. "I'm twenty-four, I don't have a boyfriend, and I'm a receptionist. I was lonely when I woke up this morning and when I saw you at the car wash I knew I wouldn't be lonely tonight."

"Oh, yeah? Really? And why is that?" I chuckled.

"Because I decided I wanted you."

She did that purr again and then stood up and walked inside. I followed her in. I was about to ask her if she wanted more wine when she abruptly turned into me, wrapped her arms around my neck, and pressed her lips against mine. We shared a kiss and then she immediately rubbed her face over my cheek and took my earlobe between her teeth. Gently she nibbled my earlobe and whispered into my ear.

"Don't make me beg for it."

As surprised as I was, I was also aroused. I never had a girl come on quite that strong before. I had yet to ask for it from any girl, but never had a girl been so direct and to the point.

"I wouldn't dream of it," I whispered back as I began to undress her in my living room. We made it to the bedroom and I had the best sex I have ever had to this day. I pegged her right—a tigress—a very skilled tigress. I would no sooner let loose a shot when she had me up and aroused again, and again, and again. I got no sleep that night. Her appetite was insatiable. She left at five in the morning and I caught a couple of hours of sleep since I didn't have to be there until nine.

Ann and I dated and had marathon sex for about six months, and then all hell broke loose. I learned never to trust a woman with that kind of sex appetite.

Chapter 22

It all happened one evening when I got home from work. I had only been home long enough to take off my jacket and tie when there was a knock at the door. I pulled open the door halfway and it was forced open the rest of the way. A guy about ten years older than me burst in through the doorway and stood there glaring at me. My first reaction was surprise, and then my second reaction was anger.

"Who the hell are you? You can't just come bursting through my door. Get the hell out before I knock you out."

"I think I have the right to do anything I want here, Pal, since you're sleeping with my wife."

"What are you talking about? I'm not sleeping with anybody's wife."

"You deny sleeping with Ann? My wife?"

"*Your wife?* Ann is your *wife?* Hey, I had no idea. I didn't know she was married. I'm sorry....I don't know what else to say."

"Yeah....unfortunately, I believe you."

"How can she be married when she seems to be

available all the time? Sorry...I mean married women usually have to be home at night."

"I travel.....a lot. It's my job. You're not the first, but I know when it started between you two. I was supposed to take her to Kennywood Park, but I got called out of town. You took her that day."

"Hey, look...if I had known she was married nothing would have ever gotten started. She asked me if I was married and she said she....didn't have a boyfriend. I guess she never really said she wasn't married....I just assumed...."

"Yeah, I know. I'm going to ask you not to see her any more."

"No problem. I don't want to be involved with a married woman...man, dude...I feel sorry for you. Don't worry...Ann and I are done...as of this moment."

"Thank you," he said with honest gratitude. He sounded almost pathetic.

"Can I ask you something? Why would you want to stay with her if you know what she does?"

"You've been to bed with her. Where else could I get that kind of great sex?"

After he left I sat down with a glass of wine. Wow, I felt sorry for him! I don't know what I felt sorrier about—the knowledge that she cheated on him or that he would stay with her just because of the great sex. It sounded pretty sad to me.

She called later that night and I told her it was over, and that I promised her husband that I wouldn't see her any more. She sounded angry and I couldn't figure out if she was angry at her husband for making me promise that or with me for actually making the promise. I never saw her again. After Ann, I promised myself that I would be a little more cautious from then on.

...

And I was cautious. I never went to bars, and I never just picked up women. Mostly, they found me. I was sort of a private person, and I kept to myself. I guess you could say I was a loner. I got along well with my bosses and co-workers but I never socialized with them. I guess I really wasn't a social person.

One afternoon I had a conversation with my boss and I learned a few things about myself. The first thing was that my co-workers admired my sales ability, but he said it wasn't my ability that attracted customers. He said I had the look and demeanor of an honest person. He said that there was no way a customer could look at me and think that I wasn't telling the truth. In sales, that was a huge plus, he added.

"I have to tell you what my wife said about you," he confided that afternoon.

I had only met his wife a couple of times and other than formalities, we did very little conversing. I was curious about what she said.

"My wife said you are that strong, silent type and that you have such a nonchalant, non-judgmental personality that makes women want to climb all over you. Do you do okay with women?"

"I guess," I shrugged. "I don't date much but when I do it's because *they* picked *me*. As long as they aren't fat and ugly I'm usually pretty agreeable to it."

"Ever have somebody really special? Somebody you really cared about?" He probed.

"Yeah, I guess....sorta," I answered as I saw Renee in my mind's eye, and then Stacey.

"What happened?" He continued.

"I don't know." I shrugged again. "Why are you asking? This is kind of personal stuff, don't you think?"

"I'm sorry....you're right. I'm asking because my wife wants to fix you up with her niece."

"No....no way," I protested as I stood up. "No....I work here...you're my boss...I don't want any conflict over that. Thanks...but no thanks."

"I'm sorry....you're right again. Nelson, I really do apologize. I shouldn't have even thought about it."

I went home that night and started job hunting. I knew that it wouldn't end there. The wife would figure out ways to put her niece in my face, and hell, I might even like her. But there was no way I was going to get involved with the boss's relative. What would happen if it didn't work out? Or what if it ended badly? Certainly he couldn't fire her from being his relative, but he sure as hell could fire me.

...

It didn't take me long to get another job offer. I was well-known in the business by this time and any dealer knew I would increase his revenue. My boss at the Cadillac dealership was pretty upset when I told him I was leaving. He didn't ask it, but I'm sure he knew the reason why I was leaving. This time I tried Lincoln. The commission was not much different and the sales market was the same.

I worked at this dealership up until I was thirty years old. The year I turned thirty I had plenty of money in the bank, a whole wardrobe of suits, sports jackets, ties, and dress shirts, a brand new Lincoln, and a great apartment. Two things happened in my thirtieth year. I changed sales careers and I met my wife.

Chapter 23

I HAD BEEN selling cars, old and new, for twelve years. Although I loved it, I began to wonder if I would be any good at selling anything else. Big Jim had said that I was a born salesman. Did he mean car salesman? Or did he mean salesman of anything? I wanted to explore my options and just look into other types of sales. I had enough money in the bank along with a growing portfolio of investments, so I decided to leave the car business and try something else.

I searched through the want-ads again and saw that sales jobs were plenty—especially commission jobs. I thought I'd try insurance, so I took the exams and paid for my licensure and began my career as an insurance salesman. I made money at it, but I seemed to be working all the time. I had no time for a social life—not that I had one anyway. After the experience with Ann, I sort of went back into hibernation where I had always felt safe. I decided that I wanted no more husbands knocking on my door.

One thing about selling insurance—once you got

the initial policy written, you always had the potential of increasing that policy either by making the policy amount higher or just selling the client additional insurance. Many of my clients called me back to increase the amounts on their policies or to add another policy on. Policyholders didn't usually disappear. One of my biggest sales was an increase-slash-add-on. It was on a Saturday morning. On the previous Monday evening, I had sold a joint life insurance policy to a married couple in their early forties. I was surprised when they called me early the following Saturday morning and asked if it was possible for me to come to their house that morning because they wanted additional policies written. I was more than happy to oblige. They lived way out in the boonies, so it was a bit of a drive out there. They made it worth it for me to go, though, since they bought a policy for each of their four children and a couple of indemnity policies on themselves. They also increased their life insurance on their original policy. Yes, I wondered about it, since it seemed so sudden, but they explained that they were taking a year off to go to Alaska and follow their dream of living in the wild. The children would be home-schooled in Alaska and they had planned on living simply and maybe writing a book. They said they had saved up for over fifteen years to do it. They felt they should carry the extra insurance since it was wilderness and they would be new at living in it. I wasn't sure it was a smart thing to do, but I was in no position to question them. My commission was steep on the deal.

After I left their house I drove back to civilization and stopped at a small restaurant for lunch. It had started to rain as I was driving back and by the time I got inside the restaurant it had turned into a torrential downpour. I took my damp suit jacket off and draped it over one of the empty chairs at the table I chose, and waited for a waitress to bring me coffee and a menu.

The rain seemed to be good for business and I was glad I had gotten there when I had. As I was reading my menu, every table had been filled by diners wanting to get out of the rain. Since the place became so crowded so quickly, I had plenty of time to dawdle over the menu. Just as I decided on what I wanted, I heard a feminine voice beside me.

"Excuse me....I hate to bother you....but would you mind sharing your table with me? There seems to be no place to sit."

She was lovely. She was classy. Without knowing anything about her, I knew she was well-bred and intelligent. Her grey eyes were sharp and they sparkled as she stared at me waiting for my answer. I noticed her glowing tan and knew instantly that it had not been acquired in Pennsylvania. She had style—style from her chicly-styled dark blonde hair down to her expensive bone colored high-heeled pumps. (Yes, I knew what pumps were—Renee taught me.) One other thing I knew instantly was that she was only interested in sharing the table and was not just hitting on me.

"Of course," I said. "Please...sit down. You should probably use the other empty chair to hang your jacket. It looks pretty wet."

"Thank you....thank you so much for being so kind," she spoke with such sincerity in her voice.

I handed her the menu. "Here...save the waitress a trip. She's pretty swamped."

"I see that. Rain pushed people indoors, I guess.

You look like you are in the middle of a workday," she commented.

"Well….I had an appointment this morning, but I'm off for the rest of the weekend. How about you? You don't dress like that to go to the mall or the park…at least I hope not."

She smiled easily. I liked that. "I had a big corporate meeting this morning."

"On a Saturday?"

"Yes…well, every time we have a big meeting like this during the week the rumors begin to fly though the company. The employees get on edge and wait for a bomb to drop…even if there isn't one ignited."

"What about this time? A Saturday meeting would have to be…one hell of a bomb coming down."

"Not really…it's actually all good."

"Yeah, but if the employees get wind of a Saturday meeting…behind their backs…they will really be anxious."

"Well put. But…we are making the announcements on Monday….first thing. We have acquired another company and there will be quite a few promotions…and a couple of firings of course….but mostly….it's all good."

"Well, I'm glad of that. By the way, my name is Nelson Sutter."

"Oh….I'm sorry. Where are my manners? I'm Loraine Carter."

"Well, Miss Carter…I'm pleased to meet you. What company is lucky enough to have you on board?"

"Walsh Industries, Incorporated. I'm the supervising operations manager. I oversee all of the supervisors in operations."

"Big job. Walsh…I've heard of that company…what do they do?"

"Well….mostly they are known for advertising…. newspaper and magazines….television and radio…but there is a small operation that handles outdoor advertising as well as mobile."

"Mobile?"

"Yes…. Busses and cabs for example. You see the ads on them?"

"Oh….okay…..so what company did yours acquire?"

"Price-West Productions….another ad agency. They were sinking fast….mainly because of the competition… us."

We had a pleasant lunch with good conversation. My first impression of Loraine proved to be accurate. She was extremely intelligent, educated, well-bred, and to be exact, way out of my league. I gave her a brief history of my sales career and she acted like she was impressed.

"I have never been able to sell anything," she told me. "Even as a little girl, the only Girl Scout cookies I ever sold were the ones my mother and my aunts bought from me. I admire that skill in other people." She told me with a genuine smile.

"I've been told that I'm a born salesman. One of the guys I worked for said it was how I looked that drew people to me. I look like an honest man. That's what he told me, anyway," I explained, smiling sheepishly.

"I think he was right. I mean, I would probably buy ocean front property in Arizona from you if you offered it," she said with half of a laugh. "You *do* look honest."

"Thank you," I responded as I glanced out of the

restaurant window. "Oh, look…it stopped raining. The Sun's coming out."

"Even without looking, I believe you. See how honest you look?"

We both laughed. The rain had stopped and our lunches were eaten. The plates were being cleared from our table, so there was no reason to continue sitting there. Yet we stayed seated and ordered another cup of coffee. By the time there were no more excuses to sit there and talk, I was convinced of two things. First, Loraine was everything I didn't deserve, and second, I desperately wanted to see her again. I don't know if it was her or the loneliness that made me so desperate, but whatever it was, I knew I had to ask her to go out. My mind was reaching as she began to put her suit jacket on, and gather her purse together. I was struck with an idea, hoping it was something she would be interested in.

"Listen….tomorrow is Sunday and it's supposed to rain again. I was wondering…I planned on going to the museum just to walk around. I have never been to the big museum over in Oakland. I was wondering if you'd like to tag along."

She cocked her head to the side like she was considering the invitation, and then she smiled. "Okay….yes….I think I would truly enjoy that. I'll tell you what. After the museum, I'll drag you to Phipps Conservatory…with your permission, of course."

"I'll go with very little resistance, I promise. But then I get to buy you dinner as a reward for being dragged to the conservatory…sound fair?"

"Fair enough," she laughed.

That was how it began. We started seeing each other

regularly every Saturday night and sometimes on Sunday. It was strictly platonic at first. I just enjoyed being with her. She was more than just pleasant and fun to be with—she was interesting, too. I was actually learning things from her—things I didn't even think I wanted to learn became fascinating. *She* was fascinating. Our dates always ended with a chaste kiss and the promise of a phone call the next day. Yet I always walked away smiling.

We had been going out together for almost six weeks before we reached another level in our relationship. Loraine had a wedding to go to and she asked me to go with her. I was more than happy to go with her. We danced several times at the wedding and we both went up to try to catch the garter and the bouquet. I had never participated in anything like that but it was fun, especially when I was victorious in grabbing the garter. As luck would have it, Loraine caught the bouquet and I had to put the garter on her thigh, which was tradition, they told me. I remember sliding the garter up to her thigh and feeling a tugging sensation as I did. I glanced up at her face and saw that she was feeling it, too! As we danced after that, I felt a new beginning starting to bloom in our relationship. We couldn't take our eyes off of each other. When the music stopped, we said our good-nights and drove home in uncomfortable silence. I walked her to her door and she turned to me and asked if I wanted to come in for a nightcap. I nodded.

I opened the bottle of wine she offered as she reached up and retrieved the wine goblets from her cupboard. I watched her from behind as she reached and I couldn't help but notice the agility of her sleek body. She moved a lot like a cat. I had never really noticed that before. Just by watching her, I was being turned on. She brought the goblets to the counter, I poured the wine, and we went and sat on her sofa. We didn't talk. I was beginning to think maybe I had it all wrong. Maybe what I thought she was feeling wasn't sexual, but maybe repulsion. Maybe I repulsed her and she was getting ready to tell me we couldn't see each other any more. I felt myself already starting to feel bad—so bad that I almost didn't hear her say my name.

"Nelson?" She said my name like a question.

I turned to face her.

"You don't find me very attractive, do you?" She asked me.

I was floored. "What? That's crazy! Of course I do!"

"Then you don't find me sexually attractive."

"Where is that coming from? I find you attractive in every way."

"Then why haven't you made a pass at me?"

I was too surprised to answer at first. Hell, I never had to. The girls always made the first move, but I didn't think I could tell her that. But I had to say something.

"I guess I didn't want to seem too pushy. I didn't want to scare you away."

"Scare me, Nelson," she whispered as she moved closer to me.

I took her face between my palms, threaded my fingers through her hair, and kissed her with every bit of passion I could muster. And she kissed me back with the same passion. Things really progressed from there. For all of her cool aloofness on the outside, she was a ball of fire in the bedroom. When I made love to her that night, and every night after that for the next few years, I felt it from the top of my head down to the tips of my toes. In bed, the movements of her lithe body turned me on like no other woman ever had. Neither one of us had to work very hard at pleasing the other. As we touched, explored and tasted each other we were easily mutually gratified just by the sensations it brought.

...

I knew I had to ask Loraine to marry me. We had been dating for two years by this time. I was almost thirty-three and she was only a couple of months behind me. I felt I could spend the rest of my life with her. It was time to join our forces and our assets.

I made the night special. I took her to a fine restaurant overlooking the city and I proposed, ring in hand. She said yes! Actually, she said, yes, yes, yes—with tears in her eyes. We had a small wedding in a chapel in her church. Her parents and sister attended the ceremony, along with a handful of people from her office. I had only my boss and his wife there. After the ceremony we had a dinner in a private dining room at a local high-end restaurant. Her father insisted on paying for everything. I believe he felt he was getting off easy since a larger affair would have been so much more expensive.

We left for our honeymoon right after the dinner. I had that all mapped out—two nights in Niagara Falls, two nights in the Pocono's, and then on to Atlantic City for fun in the sun and the casinos at night. We had a blast.

Chapter 24

Right after we returned from our honeymoon I began moving my things into Loraine's house. It was a beautiful gray stone ranch with three bedrooms, office and a den in addition to a large kitchen and dining room and living room. There were three bathrooms in the house—the main bathroom, which I called the public bathroom, one in the master bedroom, and one in the larger of the two other bedrooms. The house came with a big back yard and patio with a gas grill installed. Loraine said she bought the house about six months before she met me because it was a steal. I didn't mind moving into it since I really didn't want the hassle of house hunting and then moving furniture from one place to another. I would pull my weight with the household expenses and mortgage. I took all of my assets and put Loraine's name on them, but I kept two small savings accounts in my name only.

One of the first things we did after I was moved in was plan a back yard cookout for our friends and co-workers. I really thought about sending Richard an invitation. When it came to friends, I could only claim two—and one was dead. I did invite some of the other salesmen and their wives and of course, the secretaries, the office notary, and office manager. We had about thirty-four people in the back yard. Loraine had badminton, lawn darts, and volleyball in the basement and I was employed to erect all of it. Everybody seemed to have a great time and I felt I had done well in the entertainment department. I did the entire grill cooking while Loraine handled the sides.

Loraine was an excellent cook. She made nutritious, healthy meals which was probably a good thing since I had a love for junk food. I ate junk food almost every day for lunch so going home to a meal that was cholesterol-free and healthy was in my best interest.

Life was good. Loraine was neat and tidy like I was, and so we shared the household cleaning. We didn't have a lot of social life but we did go to dinner, special events, and attractions quite a bit. After convincing Loraine to go, I even revisited Kennywood, that amusement park, once. She had just as much fun as I had. We were great companions with a satisfying sex life. Marriage couldn't get any better than that. I was truly happy, and I think she was, too.

...

We celebrated our first anniversary with a trip to Hawaii. At age thirty-four, Loraine looked stunning in her bright green bikini. Her skin was flawless and her muscle tone was awesome. We walked the beaches like brand new lovers and ate in the finest restaurants the islands had to offer. Every time I looked at my wife I felt like I had really lucked out. She was the complete package. I tried not to think about my past but every once in awhile it would slip into my thoughts. Here I was in the best life situation that I could imagine after coming from a home life where I was hated and abused, and then sent away to live in a shelter—a modern word for orphanage. I was truly blessed. This was my reward for all of the misery, hurt, and pain inflicted on me as a child.

Our little world at home did not affect our careers. We both excelled in our positions and Loraine was promoted to vice president of operations by the time we celebrated our third anniversary. I was in the process of changing jobs at that time. I had been selling insurance all this time and really wanted to get into something a bit more interesting. Not that insurance hadn't been good to me—I just wanted something different and modern. I found what I was looking for. A major electronics corporation was looking for a new salesman. The position was meant for a person who could develop contacts in the corporate world, strike a rapport, and become the man the corporations came to for all their electronic needs. I felt that the job was meant for me, and apparently so did the human resources team who hired me. We were right—all of us. I fell into the job and immediately began excelling.

It's funny how when you're on top of the world, the world suddenly does a flip-flop. I had just landed a major contract and I planned on taking my lovely wife out for a celebration dinner. I walked into the house to find my wife in tears.

"Loraine? Honey, what's wrong?" I remember asking her.

"Oh, Nelson….I just found out that I can't conceive." Her voice quivered just before she let out another sob.

I went to her had wrapped my arms around her. It

never dawned on me but ever since the first time we made love, I had never used a condom. I figured Loraine must have been on the pill or something since she never turned up pregnant. My mind instantly went back to the little joke I made to Richard about my being sterile.

"Have you been tested? Should I maybe get tested?" I didn't even know she wanted kids. I never really thought about having them.

"No....there's no need for you to. I can't get pregnant. It's *me*." She started crying again. She explained it to me but I still didn't really understand it. It had something to do with the size of her uterus and the way it was positioned.

"Honey....it's okay."

"Is it? Is it, really? Nelson, I wanted a child. I thought maybe you would want one, too. You're the last of your family name. Don't you want to carry it on?"

"Gee, Honey....I never really thought about it. I've just been so happy with you I never even thought about us having kids. Do you want them?"

"Yes! Yes, Nelson....I want them. This is breaking my heart." She cried even harder and all I could do was hold her. There was nothing I could say. I held her and thought about a little kid calling me daddy. I just couldn't picture it, but the more I thought about it, the more I knew I wouldn't mind it.

"Do you want to maybe check out adoption, Honey? Maybe we could adopt one. It might not be the same, but we would love it as much."

I had hoped that was the right thing to say. Loraine got really quiet except for the sniffling. I just held her and waited.

"Yes.....Nelson, can we? I want to be a mom....I really do."

"Then of course.....let's look into it."

"Thank you, Nelson....thank you. I love you." She smiled as her eyes still glistened with tears.

"I love you, too....and I want you to be happy."

And I meant that.

...

It was not meant to be. We went to adoption agency after adoption agency. We were on waiting lists, but no child ever came our way. Our marriage began to change. Loraine became distant. We still got along, but the spark in our love life was just not there any more. We had functional sex and that was it. We had needs and sex took care of them, but there was no wild abandon like there had once been. Loraine felt guilty about not being able to carry on my name for me. Personally, I didn't care about carrying it on. I just wanted us to get back to being the way we were. I began to feel emotionally and sexually abandoned. We even stopped having fun, so I was surprised when she suggested we go to her Christmas party that year.

It was a loud, fun party with booze flowing everywhere. I was never really much of a drinker and neither was Loraine, but they kept the drinks coming and we kept drinking them. Loraine got up to mingle with people and I spied her across the room once head to head and laughing with a good-looking man who appeared to be much younger than we were. I was feeling left out as I sat there all alone at our table. She should have been laughing with me. I was feeling a little jealous when someone grabbed my hand.

"Come on, Nelson…get up and dance with me."

It was Loraine's secretary. She had recently been jilted by some guy she met through some dating service and she was getting really drunk in order to get over it. She told me all this on the dance floor as she teased me by running her tongue along my jaw. I tried to keep her at a distance but I was also getting drunk, making my reflexes slow. I looked across the room for Loraine and spotted her kissing the young guy on the cheek. Anger and jealousy flowed through me—both of which were new feelings. I quickly turned to the little sexpot in my arms and locked lips with her. She responded and I immediately pulled away.

"My God….I'm sorry. I've had too much to drink and so have you. I didn't…mean anything. Are you okay?"

"Yeah, Nelson….just fine. Don't worry about it. It's partially my fault." She admitted.

I helped her to her chair and sat her down just about the time Loraine was coming back to the table.

"I'm sorry. I got a little involved over there," she told me.

"Yeah…I know….I watched." I gave her a cold stare and then looked away.

"Nelson….please don't be mad. That meant nothing. I just kissed his cheek because he….well, he helped me get a project out on time the other day."

We didn't speak all the way home and when we got into bed I turned my back on her and slept way on the edge of the bed. Maybe I was being silly, but I felt hurt. I didn't really know anybody at that party and there I was sitting by myself, being taken for granted, while my wife was kissing another guy. My anger felt justified.

But it was short lived. I awoke to breakfast in bed the

next morning. There on the breakfast tray was a note of heartfelt apology. I couldn't stay angry.

Chapter 25

We had given up the idea of adoption. We were both past forty by now and the idea of a small baby or even a toddler was not something either of us was sure we wanted to deal with. I was positive I didn't—Loraine wasn't sure. But Loraine still had that nurturing side of her that needed fulfilled. That's why I shouldn't have been too surprised the day she threw me a curve. I didn't see it coming but I should have. As I walked through the door after a long drive from Columbus, Ohio I could smell good things coming from the kitchen and I heard my wife singing. It had to be a good night! I set my briefcase down and made my way to the kitchen where she immediately poured me a glass of wine. I remember thinking how nice it was and that maybe I had the old Loraine back.

"Well, you're in a good mood," I remember commenting.

"Uh-huh......I am," she answered me.

"What's the occasion?" My curious mind wanted to know.

"Well....let's sit down to eat....and then I'll tell you."

We sat down and I stared at my wife who for some reason unknown to me had suddenly lost about ten years off of her face. She looked young and radiant. I knew whatever it was she was going to talk about made her really happy.

"Well? Come on....the anticipation's killing me." I laughed.

"Nelson....I think we'll both agree that we're past the years of wanting or needing a baby....right?"

"Yes....I think so. Why? What are you talking about?"

"Well...I was thinking about a foster child. A foster teen."

"Are you serious? That can be a whole lot of problems, Honey."

"Well...remember when you were sent to the shelter? Didn't you feel scared and all alone?"

"Yeah...of course I did. I *was* all alone."

"Okay. I talked with an agency worker about this and she said they prefer to place these kids into good homes rather than shelters. It eliminates that initial fear and anxiety...not to mention they don't get the chance to feel like orphans being sent to an institution. Nelson, I want to try to get one here...a foster child, I mean."

"Honey, are you sure?"

"Yes....what do you say?"

"Do I get my old wife back? The loving, hot ball of fire one?"

"Have I been that bad?"

"Yes....you have. I've been feeling pretty unloved and uncomfortable lately."

"Oh, Nelson....I'm so sorry. I'll try to make it up to you. I promise."

"Then let's go for it."

The smile on her face told me we were doing the right thing for her and for our marriage. We made an appointment and went to see a worker at the agency. She told us we had a very good chance of getting a foster teen. We filled out the paperwork and began preparing for the many inspections we would have to go through. We knew our house would pass inspection since there was plenty of room, fire alarms in every room, and the house was in good repair. We both had good positions and were in good standing with our companies and the community. We didn't go to church, but the agency worker didn't see that as a problem unless a certain child's religion was important to his or her culture. Both Loraine and I were in good health, and had no bad habits, unless you want to include junk food and a healthy sex appetite as bad habits. Since our decision to go ahead with this foster parenting thing, our sex life was on fire again.

The call from the agency finally came. They told us there was a seventeen year old girl living in an unapproved unwholesome environment and there had been a court order issued to have her removed from the home. If everything went as planned we could have her in our home the Friday after Thanksgiving. We scrambled to get the room ready for a teenage girl. Loraine and I went shopping for bedding and curtains that would suit a girl that age. Loraine laughed at me when I walked up to the cashier holding a large shaggy stuffed dog.

"Girls like this kind of stuff....don't they?"

"Yeah, they do," she conceded.

We worked at cleaning and freshening up the room so there was a pleasant clean scent in it. Loraine put girlie things in the bathroom for her. Scented body washes and nylon net scrubbers, skin care products, hair dryer, shampoo and conditioner, and a curling iron now filled the bathroom we had never used.

"Loraine....what if she's really homely...and doesn't use stuff like that? What if she prefers Lava soap to that scented stuff?"

"Nelson....stop it," she snapped, but she was laughing at what I said.

We cleared our schedules so we would be available for her that whole weekend. We were invited to Loraine's sister's house for Thanksgiving and planned to be with our new foster child all weekend. We decided it was wise not to say anything at the Thanksgiving dinner, since we wanted to get acquainted with the teen first before everybody else knew about her.

Finally, it was the Friday after Thanksgiving. Loraine had jitters all morning. I volunteered to cook breakfast just to keep her from burning herself or something equally as disastrous. She must have gone into that bedroom and checked everything about a hundred times, in between looking out of the window to see if she arrived yet. After breakfast, she had baked cookies for the girl's arrival.

Finally, the brown sedan was in the driveway. Loraine's heart must have been racing a mile a minute. I could tell by the flashing in her gray eyes that she was full of anticipation like a child waiting for Santa Claus. Thank goodness she stopped and took a deep breath before she darted out the door. Otherwise, she may have come across as a manic, crazed lunatic. Actually, it was good to see her so excited.

After her deep breath she opened the door and walked out with dignity. Loraine was a class act. I followed her and immediately went to the back of the car when I saw the trunk automatically raised from inside. I took out the girl's one suitcase and book bag while Loraine was being introduced. Even before I reached the side of the car I could see the love in Loraine's eyes. I walked up to Loraine and focused on this newcomer who was to be part of our family, and my mind did a flip-flop. She was a gorgeous half-woman-half-teenager. Immediately, I was taken by her. Her blue eyes were red rimmed at the moment since she had been crying, but they drew me to her. She was sad and heartbroken; I could tell. There was something about her that made me want her and I was ashamed of myself. I recovered from my lustful thoughts and introduced myself. Her name was Belinda and she was sweet. Sweet and delicate. She said everybody called her Lindy and I told her that we would, too.

I took her to see her room and set down her suitcase before we joined the two ugly broads from Social Services in the kitchen. Man, those two were ugly!

Loraine immediately gained Lindy's trust, but I could tell she was a little put off by me. Maybe she felt the lust I had to push back down. God, I didn't want to hurt this girl. I wanted to help her. I remembered what it was like to be orphaned, but I was a boy. This small teenaged girl who looked like an angel was frightened—and sad.

When we joined everyone in the kitchen, the older of the two women made a threat to Lindy about going to a detention home and my hackles went up and I immediately came to her defense.

Loraine saw the two hags out and we sat down with Lindy. Loraine asked her about herself and the tears came. This poor sweet girl told us her whole life's story within two hours, crying the entire time. She and her boyfriend had lost a baby. This started Loraine's tears. Now this sweet girl had been through the wringer. First, her mother died and her father simply ignored her for three years. Then when he did pay attention to her, he severely beat her with a belt for being pregnant. Then he came looking for her and shot her! Actually, according to Lindy, it was her boyfriend, Ricky he wanted to shoot. She was in surgery for hours and they had to take the baby. The baby, a boy, died after about seven or eight days of fighting for his life.

Next the boyfriend gets arrested for killing the girl who told Lindy's father where to find her. He was released after they found the real killer. Then just when she thinks everything is going to be fine, these two hags show up and drag her out of the home where she was living with her boyfriend and his uncle. Apparently the boyfriend was who she lived and breathed for. She told us she felt safe and loved with him and that he cared for her and would never harm her.

I couldn't get over how sweet she was! Even after all she'd been through she was still sweet and fragile-looking just like one of those angels you buy from a Hallmark store. We spent the weekend trying to win her affection. On Friday evening, Loraine made dinner and Lindy offered to set the table. She was quiet throughout the meal, only speaking when spoken to, and only eating enough to be polite. She went to bed early and Loraine and I sat up talking.

"Isn't she beautiful?" Loraine asked me.

"Yeah, Honey....she is. She is so sad though. I feel almost like we're responsible for it. If we hadn't agreed to taking her in, she would still be in the place she loved."

"But that's not true. If we hadn't, somebody else would have. I'm glad she's with us. Oh, Nelson....I want to do so much for her! I want to make her smile and be happy."

"I know you do, Honey. And you will. I'm sure of it."

On Saturday, Loraine helped Lindy unpack her things. We took her to the mall and told her she could have anything she wanted, but that was a futile effort since all she wanted was to go back to Ricky. Loraine bought her a pair of jeans and a couple of tops anyway. We treated her to a movie and then to dinner before returning to the house. Since it was still early, we played gin for awhile before Lindy said she wanted to go to bed. I could tell she was warming up a little, but I knew deep down that she was in such emotional pain. I could see it in her beautiful blue eyes. Those eyes haunted me. It was like I had seen them somewhere before. After she went in to bed, Loraine and I watched a movie but mostly we talked through it.

"Do you think she was a little warmer towards us today?" Loraine asked me.

"Yeah, Honey, I do. Remember...she is really heartbroken. I'll bet she cries herself to sleep."

"It makes me wonder if the social services system is correct...I mean...how right can it be if Lindy is in this much emotional pain over it?" Loraine looked to me for my response.

"I don't know. Honey…aren't these people supposed to be trained to know what's best?"

"They're trained to follow guidelines. Human emotion is not involved. Look at you! Did they even consult you when they…whoever they are….decided you needed to go to a shelter? Your feelings or thoughts weren't even considered."

"Yeah, that's true…you're right there. Are you thinking of sending her back?"

"Oh, NO! She would only be put somewhere else. I'm just really considering letting her see her boyfriend. He could come here….while we are home, of course."

"Loraine, those two bitches said she couldn't see him at all."

"But why, Nelson? *He* didn't hurt her….*they* did. Anyway, I'm just considering it. I can't stand seeing her so unhappy. If she could see him once in awhile, she would be happy to be here."

"Just think it through thoroughly, Honey. I don't want to see you get in the middle of something."

"I will," she said to me, and she smiled and cuddled up next to me on the sofa.

We made love that night and Heaven help me, it was Lindy's face I was seeing as I made love to my wife.

Chapter 26

I THINK I need to stop here for a moment. I promised myself that I would be honest about everything when I wrote this. It's not that I haven't been honest—it's just that I left out a big part of my story. That is sort of dishonest, so I think I need to back up and tell the parts that are missing so far. I mentioned that Loraine was not the same person I married, and that part is true; but she had a good reason to change.

It was right around the time that Loraine got her big promotion. We had been married three years then. Suddenly Loraine got all high and mighty about her new big position and how she was a college graduate. Well, maybe she didn't—not really—but I felt like she did. She had made a couple of snooty remarks to me about not having a degree, and she even went so far as to say she achieved so much more than I did because she came from a good family with better values. At first I was hurt because my wife thought she was better than I was and she was looking down her nose at me. Then I got angry. I no longer rushed home to her. Instead, I began going to nice hotel lounges and began meeting women—women who didn't think they were better than me. I swear I just wanted to have someone to look up to me—to talk to. I never thought anything would go beyond that. I was a married man.

It was on a Thursday. Loraine always worked late on a Thursday. I had called her from my cell phone while I was on the road just to see if she wanted to catch a late dinner somewhere. She declined and added that she had more on her mind than just where to eat. She said it like I was a lowlife for even considering dinner. Well, I went to the nearest hotel and went into the lounge and ordered myself some dinner and a glass of wine. I ate in silence as I listened to the piano music. Out of nowhere I hear a female voice. I looked up and there she was.

"You look lonely," she said to me.

I just shrugged.

"Do you mind if I sit with you?"

"No....go ahead. Can I buy you a drink?" I was being polite.

I bought her a drink and she asked me my name and if I was married. I was honest with her.

"Nelson...and I'm married. I'm lonely at the moment, but I am married."

"Why are you lonely?"

"I don't know. I guess my wife and I are going through a rough patch right now. I called her a while ago and asked her if she wanted to meet me for dinner and she made me feel like shit," I told her. "I don't even feel like going home," I added.

"That's a shame. Some women don't appreciate it when they have a man who is considerate. I mean...if I was married and my husband called me on a whim and asked me to meet him for dinner, I'd be so grateful."

"Yeah, well....my wife is a big executive....I'm just a salesman. Not that I don't do well....just no title."

"Well, Nelson....tonight I'll crown you king...if you're interested."

I hesitated. Would Loraine even care?

"Come on," she insisted as she tugged at my arm. "I have a big room upstairs and I'm lonely, too. I need some company."

I became a little wary. "Why do you have a room upstairs? Are you from out of town?"

"Yes, of course. I flew in for a job interview. I'm leaving at noon tomorrow. Say you'll come up for one drink?"

Well, I went. One drink turned into two and two turned into sex. I'm only human. Loraine and I hadn't had an active sex life for awhile, and she was treating me like I didn't matter to her any more. I figured this wouldn't matter either. I didn't know that Loraine was having an emotional crisis about getting pregnant at the time.

I left Olivia's room about midnight, thinking I would never see her again. Boy was I wrong about that! The company she came into town to interview for was my company. She was hired into my department as an I-T Specialist so I got to see her almost everyday. It became awkward, especially after Loraine broke down about not getting pregnant. Olivia and I were having an affair, I'm ashamed to say. After I found out about Loraine's problem I ended it with Olivia. Loraine was my wife.

Well, Olivia called Loraine and told her about us. That vindictive bitch! Loraine didn't do anything to her. Why did she want to hurt her? I knew that Loraine knew about it the minute I walked into the house. The look on her face was a cross between hurt and anger. I stood there waiting for her to speak, throw me out, cry, something. When she finally spoke I was surprised by the control in her voice.

"So....this affair," she challenged me calmly. "Is it over?"

"Yes," I answered—because it was. "Loraine...I....."

She held her hand, palm up, towards me indicating that I was not to speak.

"What was the attraction, Nelson?"

"I don't know," I told her. "I was just becoming so lonely. You started treating me like you didn't care if I was even around. I don't know....maybe that's no excuse....but I was hurt. I called you to ask you out to dinner, and you snapped at me....making me feel like I was some sort of low life far beneath you. That's when it started. I thought it would only be that one night....until she showed up in my office a week later. She works there now."

"I see. You say it's over?"

"Yeah, Loraine....that's why she called you. For revenge...because I told her it was over. I'm sorry, Loraine. There isn't anything else I can say. I'm sorry."

"No....Nelson....*I'm* sorry." With tears in her eyes, she turned and walked into the bedroom and shut the door. I spent the night on the sofa.

...

I was glad it was Saturday when I awoke. I was stiff and sore from the sofa. I wandered out to the kitchen and saw that there was a pot of coffee awaiting me, but no Loraine. I stretched my neck to look down the hall toward our—the bedroom, and saw that the door was standing open. The house was quiet, indicating that I was home alone. I checked out the bedrooms and the bathrooms and sure enough, I was alone. Where would she have gone? Did I need to find a divorce attorney? Was she going to evict me from her house?

I took a cup of coffee into my office and started going over some contracts, just to keep my mind off of what my fate might be. She was gone for hours. Around four o'clock I heard her car pull into the garage. Loraine always parked in the two-car garage. I only did when it was raining or very cold outside. I heard her trunk open and I could hear her rummaging around in the back of her car. I put my pen down and just sat and listened. Finally she came in through the door that connected the garage with the kitchen. I didn't know what to do. Should I go out there or pretend like I didn't hear her come in? I didn't have to do either one. She knocked on the office door.

"It's open," I told her.

She opened the door and WOW! She was standing there looking gorgeous! She had her hair cut and styled, added some blonde highlights to it and her nails were done to perfection. She was wearing one killer outfit! I know I couldn't cover the shock on my face. It took a moment for me to say anything, but I had to.

"You look gorgeous," I told her. "Where have you been?"

"I was out spending some of my hard-earned money. Is this enough to keep you home?" She asked as she held her arms out for me to view her entire body.

I got up and walked around the desk and held out my arms.

"You didn't have to do all that. Just be nice to me," I

said. Then I added, "I'm sorry, Loraine. It won't happen again.....I promise."

She fell into my arms and I knew I was forgiven. I guess Loraine loved me more than I realized. Maybe if she hadn't forgiven me so readily and so quickly, it might not have happened again. But it did happen again, and again, and I have no excuse for doing it. I had a wonderful wife at home and I was cheating on her—cheating on her with women who couldn't even hold a candle to her. The thing was—these women fell over themselves to get to me. They made me feel like I was awesome.

Loraine found out about my other indiscretions and she always turned a blind eye on them. It made me feel guilty and the guiltier I felt, the more I did it. It was like I was cheating on her just to prove I didn't deserve her and that her superior attitude towards me was warranted.

Just about a week before Lindy came to live with us Loraine decided to put me on notice, so to speak. I was surprised by her fierce words on that Friday before Thanksgiving. I walked in from work around six o'clock. I had been on the road traveling back from Dayton, Ohio for the past four hours, and I was exhausted. When I walked in I saw her face and I knew I was in the doghouse for something—or someone. She started in on me right away.

"Sit down, Nelson."

I knew that tone so I sat down and stared at her, waiting.

"Nelson, we are getting a foster teen next Friday. Fortunately your little...indiscretions...haven't stopped that from happening. The cheating stops now, Nelson..... or you are out of here. I'm not going to have you mess this up for me. I want that child....and I'll not have you and your little whores take the privilege of having her here away from me. Do you understand, my darling husband?"

"Loraine, I....want the child, too. If it means being a model husband, I will be. I don't want to mess this up for you....for us. I swear....Loraine; I swear on my father's grave that I will never cheat on you again. Loraine....I love you."

There. I said it. And I meant it, too.

Now that all that is out in the open, I can continue with my story.

Chapter 27

It snowed that first Sunday after Lindy came to live with us. I talked her into going outside to build a snowman with me. Reluctantly, she went. Surprisingly, Loraine joined us. Lindy seemed to be a little more animated after Loraine came outside. I guess I was a little jealous since I wanted Lindy to like me and look up to me. The afternoon wasn't a complete bust, though. Loraine threw a snowball at me and hit me in the face and that made Lindy laugh. She and Loraine formed an alliance and attacked me with snowballs and I retaliated by taking them both on with my own snowballs. The afternoon ended with the three of us fleeing the outdoors and entering the house cold and wet. We all changed into dry clothes and Loraine made us hot chocolate. As we drank the chocolate and ate cookies, Lindy seemed to enjoy watching Loraine and me mock arguing about who won the battle. By evening, the three of us were like a happy family. Loraine had a roast in the oven all afternoon. Lindy set the table while I mashed the potatoes as Loraine put the finishing touches on the meal and then we sat down to eat. While we were eating,

Loraine asked Lindy about her brother. Lindy's face lit up as she told us all about him and where he was. I silently marveled at how beautiful her face was. She seemed so fragile—like fine China—and she once again reminded me of those Hallmark angel figurines they sold in card shops.

Lindy offered to clean up after dinner and I offered to help, telling Loraine she deserved a break after fixing such a fine meal. Lindy cleared and wiped the table while I rinsed the dishes and stacked them in the dishwasher. We chatted a little while we did it.

"Ricky and I always do this together whenever there is a family gathering," she informed me.

"Yeah? The family is lucky to have you two. Most people hate this job."

"Well, we work so well together that it doesn't take us any time at all to have everything done. It always seems like it should be our job even though Ricky always does most of the cooking."

"Your boyfriend cooks?"

"Yeah....he's great at it, too," she added, smiling.

Her whole face lit up again as she talked about the boyfriend. Once again, when she smiled I thought about how beautiful she was. I decided to keep her on the subject of the boyfriend since it gave me ample opportunity to win her over.

"So you get along with his family?"

"Uh-huh. Not with his mother when she found that I was pregnant though. She got downright ugly about it. Uncle Nick and Aunt Liz were on our side from the beginning. Ricky's mother...well, she came around eventually."

"He must have a terrific family."

"Yeah....he does. Like mine was when my mother was alive."

"You must miss her a lot."

"I do. So what about your family and Loraine's? Are they around here?"

"Loraine's is. We just had Thanksgiving dinner at her sister's house. My parents are dead and I was an only child. No other relatives as far as I know."

"How old were you when your parents died?" She asked me.

"Almost Seventeen," I revealed to her.

"Oh...wow...so you know how it hurts then."

I just nodded, knowing it wouldn't accomplish anything by telling her about my hateful mother and her cruelty. I guess I could have said something about how it hurt when my dad died. By the time the kitchen work was done, I believed Lindy and I had made progress toward a relationship. Armed with slices of an ice cream cake, we joined Loraine in the living room and put a movie into the VCR. It was a perfect ending to a perfect day, and I really felt as though we were a family.

In the morning I wished Lindy luck on her first day in a new school. Loraine was driving her there to get her registered and would pick her up after school. We had talked about it and decided between the two of us, Lindy would be driven to and from school rather than have her ride the school bus. I would pick her up on the two evenings that Loraine worked late, which was usually Monday and Thursday. Loraine wasn't going to work late on Lindy's first day of school, so she would be picking her up on that first day.

I watched Lindy as she put her coat on and my heart went out to her. I could see she was nervous but I also saw the sadness. I'm sure she was thinking about school without Ricky and it must have hurt her. I had to say something to her, and I gave it my best shot.

"It'll be okay, Kid. You'll see," I tried to reassure her.

She gave me a weak smile and a tiny nod before she walked out to the garage with Loraine.

I left for work shortly after they left. All day I thought about Lindy; I couldn't help it. I kept seeing her sad face and I imagined just putting my arms around her and holding her close—in a fatherly way, I believed I was thinking. Before I left the house, I checked to see if everything was turned off, and as I walked past Lindy's room I noticed that the bathroom light was on. I went in to turn it off and discovered the CD on the dresser. I picked it up and realized that the CD had been recorded by Lindy. I stuck it into my pocket and left the house with it there. As soon as I was in the car, I dropped it into the CD player. Man, was I shocked! What a fabulous voice she had! I couldn't believe my ears! I played the CD all the way to Wheeling where I had to meet a client. I played that CD over and over, every day after that. What a find!

I didn't say anything to Lindy about the CD and she didn't mention that it was missing to anybody, so I kept it.

Chapter 28

God help me....what did I do? I swear—I swear on my father's grave it wasn't my intention. It was Thursday. I was there at the school to pick Lindy up at three-fifteen. I watched her walking and talking with another girl as she came toward the car. I was glad she was making friends, and even gladder that it was a female friend. I knew her heart still belonged to Ricky, so I guess I didn't really have to worry about boys in her life. She was quiet when she got into the car with me and I sensed that she was nervous. I didn't think she was comfortable being alone with me and I tried to get her to warm up to me. I asked what kind of junk food she wanted and we agreed on deep dish pizza. All I did was touch her thigh and she stiffened and jerked away from my hand. It was only a friendly gesture on my part, and I remember saying something to that effect. Quietly, she apologized to me, I remember. She also asked me about my job. She said she had a paper to do on modern technology and I promised to bring her some literature on it. I brought it home the very next day.

When we got to the house she went to her room to

do her homework and I went to my office to go over the contracts I had written during the day. I finished them as I heard her come out of her room and I quickly joined her at the glass doors as she was standing and staring out of them. I ordered the pizza before I came out of the office and we waited for the delivery. I told her to go ahead and select a DVD for us to watch and I watched her from the corner of my eye as she busily leafed through them, reading the titles. I got out the soft drinks just as the doorbell rang, alerting us that the pizza had arrived. We ate and watched a comedy, laughing at the good parts. She went into her room and I went back to my office after the movie was over and the pizza was cold. She didn't eat very much, I must say. I had three pieces and there were four pieces left when she went into her room. It was an eight-slice pie. Anyway, I wanted to see if she wanted any more pizza before I put it into the refrigerator so I went down the hall and tapped on her door. I remember I opened the door and there she was, sitting on the bed brushing her hair. A wave of desire came over me right then, and I think for a moment I snapped. I don't remember it all, but I remember entering her and the soft feel of her. No woman had ever felt that good to me. I couldn't stop. I became a madman and I just wanted to stay there inside of her and feel her. My movements were frenzied and it was when I let myself release into her that I got hold of my sanity again. It was too late. The damage was done.

Lindy was sobbing and I felt like shit. But I was also scared. What had I done? I made up a story about the last girl who told. It wasn't true, of course. I had never hurt another girl, but I had to make Lindy believe I hurt one who told on me. I couldn't let her tell Loraine or the police so I tried that scare tactic.

I'm not proud of myself, but I became Lindy's tormenter after that. I wanted her so badly every time I looked at her. There was something about her—something that made me lust after her like I never had over any female before.

It happened again on the following Monday, right after we got home that day. I knew she probably had planned on locking herself in the bedroom to deny me, so I took her as soon as we got home. Never in my life had I ever wanted anyone like I wanted her. It turned me into an animal. When I made love to Loraine it was Lindy I was seeing, and I felt guilty as hell. Lindy became my new fantasy, and it was her I thought of when I was on the road driving to a client's location. God, I was sick!

Loraine announced that we were going to her Christmas party the following Thursday. I was annoyed because that was my night with Lindy. I suggested to Loraine that maybe we shouldn't go since Lindy would be home alone, but she told me she already spoke to Lindy. Lindy told her that she would be fine and that she would feel guilty if they didn't go because of her. I wanted to volunteer to stay home but I knew Loraine would have a fit. I made up my mind that I would have Lindy twice the following Monday to make up for my loss on Thursday night. I was obsessed with her.

...

The Christmas party sucked. I thought so, anyway. Loraine's bonus of ten thousand dollars made it a little easier to cope with the whole thing though. On the way home we discussed the bonus and also what to get Lindy for Christmas. Loraine wanted to get her something really special. Well, so did I—I cared about her, too.

Not wanting to wake her, we tip-toed into the house quietly. Loraine opened her bedroom door and peeked in. Lindy was sleeping peacefully so Loraine pulled the door shut. We went to bed and made love quietly in the dark. That night I made a promise to God and myself that I wouldn't touch Lindy again. Just wanting her was wrong, and I knew it. I asked God for the strength to stay away from her; for the sense to look at her as a child—my foster child. I was hurting her, and that made me no better than any of the others in her life who had hurt her.

But the next day, Lindy was gone.

Chapter 29

I REMEMBER WALKING into the house on Friday night and seeing the distress in Loraine's eyes. She questioned me right away.

"Do you have Lindy with you?"

"No....I thought you were picking her up."

"I waited at the school for her but she didn't come out. I waited until there were no other kids at the school. I was hoping she was with you for some reason...."

"No, Loraine...have you looked in her room?"

I went down the hall and into her room. Just on a hunch I opened the closet.

"Loraine? Her clothes are gone. She's gone."

"What? Why? We treated her like our own daughter! Why would she go? I have to call those social workers," she said as she ran her fingers through her hair.

Loraine was beside herself. Already there were lines of emotional agony showing in her face. She was worried, upset, and distraught all at once, and she didn't know in which direction to go. She sat down and began to cry a heartbreaking cry. I went to her and held her.

"Want to bet she's with the boyfriend?" I asked her.

She didn't answer me. She just cried. I felt like shit because I knew why Lindy left. Not only had I hurt sweet Lindy but I also hurt my kind, loving wife.

...

I was nervous the first few days after Lindy left, but when I hadn't heard anything about what I had done to her I figured she just bolted and decided to not pursue any type of legal action against me. I began to relax. Loraine was adapting to the fact that Lindy was gone and wasn't coming back but I could see the pain in her eyes. I knew she wondered what we had done to make her go. All I could do was shower Loraine with love and affection and be very attentive to her in order to help her get through the emotional pain. I was guilty—guilty as hell. I didn't deserve this good woman; I knew.

It was two days before Christmas Eve. I decorated a small tree for the house and put up some outside lights, but I really didn't feel like doing it. Loraine had such high hopes of a wonderful holiday with Lindy and those hopes had been shattered. I caught her in front of the tree just crying. The tears were streaming down her face as she wrapped her arms around her chest, shielding her broken heart. I went into my office to work. I just couldn't watch any more. When she tapped on the door to call me to dinner, I was relieved that she had stopped crying. In fact, she actually smiled a little when she spoke.

"You know, Nelson....I hope she *is* with Ricky. I know she's happy if she is. I just hope that she will be okay. I love her, Nelson."

"I do, too, Loraine. To know her is to love her. She's just that easy to love."

"Yeah....she is...isn't she?" Loraine had a genuine smile on her face. It was bittersweet.

After we ate, I went back into the office to finish up a contract and Loraine cleaned up the kitchen. I didn't hear the doorbell when it rang, so I was surprised to hear Loraine call for me. I was even more surprised—no, shocked—to see the police standing there telling me I was under arrest. That little bitch turned me in after all!

...

I was handcuffed and taken to the police station. The ride to the station wasn't exactly pleasant. The two uniformed officers were stiff and silent and the detective who sat in the back with me wasn't all that congenial either. I tried to question him.

"How can you arrest someone on the word of a teenaged girl? Especially one who has already been put into the system?"

"Evidence....there's evidence. You'll hear it all when we get there."

He ended the conversation abruptly and I knew not to press it. I wondered what kind of evidence he was talking about though.

I was led to a room at the station—I guess it was an interrogation room—and I waited for Loraine, hoping that she was able to get in touch with our lawyer. The detective came in, sat down, and began leafing through papers in a folder he had carried in with him. He began to question me.

"Mister Sutter....tell me about Belinda Riley."

"She...she's a troubled teen. We took her in as a foster child. We tried to...help her....but she....well, some kids are well beyond help, I think."

I know. I was being unfair by trying to make Lindy look bad, but I was scared for my life now. Prison was a scary thought. The detective—Bruno I think his name was—didn't seem all that receptive to my words though. I was glad for the interruption when Loraine came in. She began asking questions and I thought at first that she was on my side. Boy, that changed in a hurry! She spoke to the detective.

"Detective, what is this about?"

"Do you know Belinda Riley?"

"Yes, of course. She was our foster child. Something hasn't happened to her, has it? She ran away."

"She has accused your husband of rape...and she left evidence to back up her story."

"What kind of evidence?"

"Well, she wrote a letter and turned it in to the school telling the whole story and she said she left underwear with your husband's semen on it in her locker. We found the underwear—two pair of panties in her locker."

"And was my husband's semen on them?"

"Yes, Ma'am.....I'm sorry."

The detective offered to let Loraine read the letter Lindy wrote and I tried to stop her.

"Loraine, you can't believe what a troubled teenaged girl says. She probably wants money from us," I pleaded.

"Shut up, Nelson," Loraine said flatly, as she read the letter.

Loraine handed the letter back to the detective, stood

up and put her coat on. I felt the panic well up inside of me. She couldn't just leave me here!

"Loraine, where are you going?"

She turned on me and slapped me—hard. I felt my teeth cut the inside of my mouth and I felt the sharp sting of the slap on my cheek. But the hate and anger in Loraine's eyes stung more than anything. Loraine's anger was overwhelming.

"You did it, didn't you? You *raped* her! *Raped* her! You *pig*!"

"Loraine, it's all lies," I countered.

"No! It isn't. Lindy isn't a liar! How could you? That sweet child!" Tears were sliding down her face as she screeched at me. Then she turned to the detective and said, "You might as well keep him here. He no longer has a home to go to."

And she walked out. Forever.

...

My attorney, Dave Watson finally showed up, but after I was placed in a cell. He wasn't all that happy about the charges, but then again, neither was I. He glared at me.

"Just tell me why, Nelson. You have a beautiful wife. Why would you do that? And to a child!"

"She's seventeen," I defended.

"And you're forty-two! What the hell's wrong with you? My God, Nelson...what were you thinking?"

"Dave, I...I don't know. I'm disgusted with myself. I... just....I don't know...I wanted her from the moment I saw her...I don't know what it was about her. It was like I was possessed or something."

Dave sighed and shook his head. "Well...I'll defend

you, but I can tell you that the evidence is pretty strong. All I can hope for is to get you as little time as possible. You really screwed up here."

"I know, Dave. I wish I could go back and fix it."

"You'll be arraigned in the morning. I'll see about bail..."

"I'm not even worried about that. Loraine threw me out. I have nowhere to go."

...

Bail was denied. After the arraignment, I was taken to the local county jail and processed in, and then placed in a cell with another guy. Before they took me away, Dave advised me not to tell anybody what I was arrested for so I didn't. The other guy in the cell with me was in for multiple drunken driving offenses. I let him believe I was in for the same thing.

The attorney said that there was one thing in my favor. No Lindy. She had vanished. Dave said he would push for and insist on going ahead with a speedy trial. After all, she was the one and only witness. And her presence in the courtroom wouldn't exactly be a plus, Dave said. He had seen her picture and said what everybody else always said: "She looks like an angel."

Chapter 30

Jail was no fun. I never liked a lot of people around me and in jail either it was in the small cell with the cellmate or out in the yard with a bunch of guys who all had big attitudes and muscles to match. Now I was no puny guy, but I really wasn't much of a fighter either. I had that one confrontation back in the shelter when I was seventeen, but since then I'd become soft on the defenses. These guys would have liked nothing better than to mess up my pretty face, so I steered clear of them.

I didn't like taking showers with guys either. I think that is the most degrading thing about jail. I don't want to see other guys' privates and I don't particularly want them seeing mine. I tried to take showers when there were the fewest guys there. Maybe that was my mistake the day I was beaten up. There was nobody around when I walked back from the shower. I had just finished my shift in the prison laundry and was given permission to shower before I went back. I had a pass from the guard in charge of the prison laundry. I knew when I heard that strange noise that there was trouble, and I shouldn't have stopped, but it was a natural instinct.

I don't remember much of the beating because I was rendered unconscious for some of it but for most of it the first blow caused me to be numb. I remember the rape. Four guys raped me. *That* I remember, and *that* I felt. I figured it out right away. In the prison yard the day before, I heard someone call the name, Riley. I wondered if it was Lindy's father, and then when he started staring me down, I knew it was. He was talking to some black guy and pointing to me while he talked. I knew it was best to stay away from Riley and his black buddy. What I didn't know is that the buddy had buddies. It was they who worked me over. I remember thinking then that I would make Lindy pay for it somehow.

I awoke in the hospital in more pain than I had ever imagined possible. It hurt to breathe, move, talk, anything. I was one injured puppy. Then I find out that the hospital has listed my condition as the result of an accident. Accident? Yeah, right. My rear hurt so badly from those guys. I remember one asking me how I liked it. Well, I didn't *exactly* do the same thing to Lindy, now did I?

After nine days in the hospital, I was released and sent back to the prison infirmary for another two weeks. At least I could see out the windows in the infirmary. The weather was starting to get nice. It was late March and except for the stay in the hospital; I had been in this prison since two days before Christmas. I was anxious to know if there was even going to be a trial or were they just going to forget about me for the next twenty years? It came as quite a surprise when I was told that I was getting out. No Lindy. They couldn't find her so I was free to go. If she turned up I would be arrested again and then tried for the rape of a minor.

I walked out of that prison a determined man. I was going to find her and stop her for good! I wasn't going back to that place or any place like it. The authorities couldn't find Lindy? Well, I sure as hell would. At this point I had nothing to lose. No home, no job, nothing. I had my two bank accounts that I kept in my name only. I would use the money in there to find her and shut her mouth for her. That was another one of my mistakes.

My first step was to find a motel room. I needed to wash the prison stink off of me and I needed a good night's sleep. I looked in my wallet they had confiscated and found that I still had over three hundred dollars in it. First I bought myself some clean clothes and then I got a room at a Red Roof Inn and just stood in the shower until the water began to cool down. I wasn't sure I would ever be completely clean again.

After the shower I felt a lot better, and I was hungry. Pizza. It would be the first time in almost four months that I tasted pizza. I ordered an eight-slice with everything on it and planned on eating the whole thing. While I waited for the pizza I began to map out a strategy on the motel stationary. I was sure Lindy didn't go alone. The boyfriend had to have gone with her. Now...if I were a young girl and guy wanting to run away, how would I go? Plane? Too expensive and you need identification. Train? Maybe. Greyhound? Perfect. They would find that sort of romantic. That would be where I would try first. I needed to find a picture of Lindy somewhere.

The knock on the door signaled to me that the pizza had arrived. I savored every bite of that pizza! I sat in the one chair in the room with my feet up, eating pizza and watching TV. Just like old times—almost. I thought about Loraine. I wondered if she would speak to me if I called her. Damn Lindy! I had a nice life with Loraine!

As I munched on the last of the pizza I pondered the problem of getting a picture of Lindy. The school yearbook! I could go to the library where they kept copies of each year's yearbook from Lindy's school before she came to live with me and Loraine! I was sure there would be a picture of her in there since she was so pretty. Any photographer would want to capture her face on film! With that much decided, I turned in for the night and slept fitfully for the first time since—well, since before Lindy came to live with us, actually.

Chapter 31

I WAS UP bright and early, eager to start looking for leads to where Lindy might have gone. I sauntered into the diner that sat next to the motel and ordered myself a breakfast fit for a king. That food tasted almost as good as the pizza! After eating that prison slop for over three months, I had forgotten how delicious food could be. After my second cup of coffee, I reached into my wallet to get some bills to pay for my meal and I discovered a credit card that I hadn't activated. It had my name on it and I wondered if I would be able to activate it and use it, if necessary. There was a number to call in order to activate it, so I went back to the motel and dialed it. What luck! The credit card was still usable and it had a five thousand dollar limit on it. I went ahead and activated it. Then I walked to the closest branch of my bank and checked on my accounts. I had forgotten that I made a deposit into the one just before Lindy took off, so I was surprised to find that I had over ninety-five hundred dollars in just that one account. I could buy a car! After all, if I were going to find her I would need transportation. I knew where there was a used car lot not too far down the highway. If I started walking I could be in a new set of wheels before noon.

Luck was in my corner for once. Not only did I know cars, but the car salesman knew me! We recognized each other instantly and I knew he was going to question me about my legal problem. He was very direct.

"Nelson....good to see you. I heard you had some kind of trouble."

"Yeah, Roy....you know how teenaged girls can be."

"Story was that you raped her..." Roy looked at me expectantly, waiting for my reply.

I began my acting career that day as I let out a huge sigh before I answered him.

"Roy, you know me. Have I ever had to chase a skirt?"

"No....as I recall they all chased you."

"Yeah, and this one was no exception. I pushed her away from me....I mean, hell, Roy, she was only seventeen! Anyway, because I turned her down she decided to get even with me.....and make up a story about how I raped her. The police bought it, Loraine bought it, and that's all it took to ruin my life."

"So you're out of jail?"

"Yeah, the kid took off. Nobody knows where she went so they let me out. No crime, no trial."

"So you're looking for a car? I have a nice one for you."

"Sure....let's see it. Oh, and remember....I know cars."

"Yeah...I know you do. I always had the utmost respect for your car knowledge. I certainly wouldn't try to screw you."

He began walking and I followed him around to the other side of the building. He pointed to a white Honda Accord.

"There it is. Low mileage, great condition. Here....let me open it up for you. Great interior...not a mark on it. Body is in perfect condition. And.....this one didn't come from an auction. I bought it outright from a guy. His wife was pretty sick and she couldn't drive it any more. They needed money for medical bills. True story. I can show you the paperwork."

"How much?"

"For you...fifty-five hundred. It's only three years old. Take it for a test drive."

I drove the car for a couple of miles and knew that I was going to get a good deal. I returned to the lot and laid five thousand dollars down in front of him.

"Okay.....I guess you're bargaining with me. Fine..... this will do it. Now....you need insurance and a registered plate....there will be tax at six percent....let me work it all up for you."

I drove off the lot at three minutes to noon, my pockets about sixty-three hundred dollars lighter than they were when I went in. But at least I had good, reliable transportation.

As I drove up the highway, I saw the golden arches to my right and I did a ninety degree turn into the drive. I hadn't had a Big Mac in months and my mouth was watering just anticipating it. I ordered the Big Mac and a Quarter Pounder and large fries, a chocolate shake, and the all time famous apple pie. It was an artery-clogging feast! I took the food back to the motel and stuffed myself with it.

I had paid for my room for three nights. If Lindy was somewhere in the state of Pennsylvania, I had three days to find her. If she wasn't, I would be on the road to wherever she was just as soon as I could be. After I ate, I drove to the local library and searched for the yearbooks. They were in a special Alumni section of the library. It was in a separate room. I stopped dead at the plaque with the dedication on it at the entrance of the room. William Stockwell was the dedicatee! Stacey's father! Stacey. This had to be an omen—a good one.

I found the yearbook from the previous year with no trouble, and I dropped down into a chair to search through it. She would have been a junior in this book. And what do you know—here she was at the prom. She and Ricky were together in this one. I earmarked the page and continued to look. I found her again, only this time it was a better image. There were two more pictures of her, both great photos. I took out the razor blade I remembered to bring and cut out all of the pictures and stuffed them inside my shirt. Next stop—the Greyhound Bus terminal. It was slow moving since I was coming up on rush hour traffic. I got to the terminal around four in the afternoon. I had to take the time to make the pictures look like they hadn't been cut out of a yearbook so I had to stop and buy a small photo album and arrange the pictures in it. I think I did a pretty good job. I found a parking space and dropped several coins in the meter before I headed toward the ticket windows. I had my story down pat before I approached the windows. A woman about my age was the ticket seller so I figured that was the best window to start with. I pulled up my most adorable smile as I approached her.

"Hi.....how long have you worked here?" It was a start.

"Seven years....why?"

"Well, my daughter ran away last December and she has not been found. I just discovered that the police hadn't even bothered to search for her so I'm doing my own search. Let me show you her picture....maybe you'll recognize her."

I produced my small family album, and forced myself to tear up as I opened it. I set it down for the clerk to see, visibly wiping my eyes for her benefit.

"Oh....she's so pretty! I think if I saw her I would remember. You and your wife must be frantic."

"Well, that's the problem. My wife left me last September and my daughter was very distraught over it. I believe she may have gone to try to find her. I tried to tell her that her mother didn't want anything to do with us. She left me for a thirty-year-old guy! Can you imagine? Of course, my wife looked that young herself, but....well, anyway, my daughter is sick. She needs medical attention but she doesn't know it. The day after she left the family doctor called to tell us...my daughter could die without medical attention."

"Then you must be frantic...you poor guy! Check with some of the other windows, and then stop back here."

Well, I knew what she had in mind. No ring on her finger meant that she wanted to console me. What the hell—why not?

Nobody recognized Lindy from the photos but they all told me to come back early in the morning when the first shift was on. They worked seven to three-thirty. I stopped back at the first window and was disappointed to find it empty. I turned to leave and she was standing behind me.

"Hi....no luck?"

"No....they all said to come back in the morning, so I guess I will." I turned to walk away and just as I knew she would, she called to me.

"I'm sorry....my name is Peggy—Peggy Simpson. Have you had a home cooked meal lately?"

"No....I haven't. And my name is...Jonathan Riley."

"Well, Jonathan Riley...how about I take you home and cook you a nice hot meal?"

"Oh, I don't want to put you to any trouble, Miss Simpson."

"It's no trouble at all. I'd love the company, and the name is Peggy."

"Okay....Peggy...where is your car?"

"Oh.....I take a bus to work."

"Well, then we'll go in my car," I said as I smiled agreeably.

Peggy was not a bad cook. Nothing like Loraine's cooking, but the food wasn't bad. When we got to her place, she quickly changed into a pair of jeans and a tee-shirt and I could see she didn't have too bad of a body either. Her face was cute—forty-year-old cute. She told me she was divorced. Like me, she lost her spouse to another man, she said. After being married for fourteen years, he decided that women weren't his cup of tea. He took up with his personal trainer at the local gym and they moved to California. Cute.

As I sipped the wine she had poured for me, I listened to her woeful tale of catching her husband in the act. I was not impressed. Obviously, she had never been to prison where it wasn't all that uncommon.

"So Jonathan, tell me about you."

"There's not much to tell, Peggy. My wife left with a younger man and all I had was my daughter. When my daughter left I just felt like dying. She was all I had. I think she may have taken off with her boyfriend…because I haven't seen him around lately either. But I'm more concerned about her health."

"Maybe you'll have better luck when you talk to the morning shift."

"I hope so. You know, I would have thought the police would have combed the bus station looking for clues that she had been there."

"They rarely do. If she didn't commit a crime, they wouldn't be looking too hard for her."

"No….I guess not. Now, would you like some help with the dishes?"

"I'm just going to stack them in the dishwasher."

"Well, let me help."

We rinsed the dishes, stacked them in the dishwasher, and wiped the counters and table before we took our coffee to the living room. I was beginning to think that this dinner was just an act of kindness on Peggy's part and quite frankly, I was a little disappointed. I was horny, to say the least, but I never made the first move, remember. (I know….I heard you….except with Lindy. Yes, except with Lindy, okay?")

"What is you daughter's name? You never told me."

"Didn't I? Brittany. That's her name."

"Pretty name…for a very pretty girl," Peggy whispered as she cupped my shoulder. "Oh, my…you are tense. Let me work out some of those kinks in your muscles for you."

Before I could answer she was massaging my back and shoulders, and I have to admit, it was a better massage than Renee gave me. Experience is the key, I guess.

"Wow, Peggy....that feels so good. I haven't had a woman's hands on me in...well, it's been awhile. I'd almost forgotten how good it can feel." I told her as I turned to face her.

Her lips were right there, waiting. They were soft lips. The first kiss was soft, and then all of her need was unleashed on me. She was like a wanton she-devil as she practically tore my clothes off. It was almost scary. We didn't make it to her bedroom—hell, we didn't even make it lying down. She straddled me as I sat on her sofa and she sank down onto me. It was wild, it was exciting, and it was gratifying. I almost screamed when I came. She screamed when she did. Wow!

"How long has it been for you?" I had to ask.

"Two years."

"Two years! My God, woman....why?"

"Because I don't know many men who are single and available."

I spent the night there, having sex in the bed this time, and gave her a ride to work the next morning. I had to go see the morning shift people anyway. I kissed her in the car and promised to call her, even though I knew that wasn't going to happen. I made a note to send her flowers—soon.

I showed Lindy's picture around to the morning shift with no luck. One guy had a suggestion.

"Listen...two of the guys who work here are on vacation

right now. They would have been on the windows back in December. One of them will be back on Monday and the other will be back on Wednesday."

I thanked them and walked past Peggy's window and winked at her. Her smile brightened up her window.

I decided I needed to get more clothes, so I went to a local Wal-Mart. I bought several items of clothing and another pair of shoes for half of what I would have paid at a men's store or a department store. The clothes didn't look too bad either. Okay, so I was used to expensive clothing and shoes. Those days were gone, but I wondered what Loraine did with my things. I was tempted to call her and ask her. But I didn't.

Chapter 32

It looked like I was going to have to stick around for awhile since the only possible leads were on vacation at the time. I decided it wouldn't hurt to check out the train station and the airport while I was waiting around. Both came up empty. The train station was a definite negative and the airport was no help. Unless I was a law enforcement officer, they refused to cooperate with me. I didn't think Lindy traveled by plane anyway.

I paid for my motel for another week, using my new credit card. I assumed the bill would go to Loraine. I didn't care. She owed me. After all, I had put her name on all my assets when we got married and she threw me out with nothing. If worse came to worse, I figured I would ask her to give back my half of my own assets. That was only fair. I had another idea. I sat down and wrote her a letter telling her to pay the bill on the credit card with my half of my assets. Since it wouldn't be all that extensive, I figured she might not mind. I only planned on using the card as little as I had to. I would send the letter about a week before the credit card statement was due to be mailed—probably in about three weeks.

Since I had time on my hands, I decided to get some exercise in at the local YMCA. I paid the small amount needed to use the pool and the exercise equipment and started going there on a daily basis. With all the junk food I was woofing down I figured I needed the exercise.

I decided to change my mind about seeing Peggy, too. I called her one evening and asked her to go out to see a movie and have dinner. She sounded like a little kid about it. I thought it was kind of cute. I spent quite a few more evenings at her house. I'm not sure if she was stupid or just trusting, but she never questioned me on what I did for a living, or where I lived, or anything. She just accepted me as I was, no questions asked. She was kind of sweet and not a bad cook and she went out of her way to please me. The perfect woman—not to mention that the sex was incredible.

On the following Monday I went back to the bus station. The guy who had been on vacation didn't recognize Lindy. He said check with Ben who would be back on Wednesday. On Wednesday I made my way down to the bus station again, but this time I had Peggy with me since I had spent the night at her place. I noticed a few raised eyebrows when we walked inside the bus terminal together. Oh well, it's too bad some of the guys she worked with didn't pick up on her needs. Ben studied Lindy's picture for quite awhile.

"She is certainly a pretty girl," he told me. "I think I would remember her if I had seen her. No…I haven't seen her," he added as he handed the album back to me.

I thanked him for his time and stopped by Peggy's window to tell her I'd call her later. That didn't happen.

On my way out of the city via the main street—Liberty Avenue—I saw a sign from the corner of my eye: TRAILWAYS BUS COMPANY. Another bus company! I went around the block and found a parking space behind the building and went inside. There were only two ticket windows open and I approached the first one. An elderly man was writing on a tablet of some sort and I had to clear my throat to get his attention. Just my luck—he was hard of hearing. I had to repeat myself more than once. He said he hadn't seen her and was fairly useless to me. I approached the next window which was covered by a younger fellow, about twenty-five. I set the pictures down in front of him.

"Listen, Pal....this is my daughter. She left home in December, and I need to find her. Would you have seen her here maybe buying a ticket?"

He took the picture album and studied it. I noted that his name was Matt as I stared at him while he drooled over Lindy's picture.

"Yeah....she was here. She was with a dark-haired guy...tall. Another guy bought their tickets. I remember her because....well, it's obvious why I would remember her," he said as he smiled at me. "She and the kid stood in the background and this big dude, fair, light hair, about six-two bought the tickets for them. I remember thinking how lucky the guy was—the one she got on the bus with."

"Do you remember where they went?" I was getting impatient hearing this guy mooning over her.

"Let me think....yeah, they went to South Carolina." He wrote down the name of the town where they went.

"It's the last stop for this bus route. They took it all the way to the end of the line. They would have had to get off in this town," he reaffirmed to me as he tapped his pen in front of the resort town.

"You're sure of that? How do you know that?"

"Hold on....I'll pull up the driver's log."

I waited while he searched.

"Yeah....two people got off in that town. The last two on the bus."

"Thanks....I appreciate it," I told him with a big smile.

"You say she's your daughter?"

"Yeah," I assured him.

"Mister, you have a beautiful daughter. I hope you find her."

"Me, too. Thanks," I said again, and then I walked out and got back into the car.

Bingo! All I had to do was get myself checked out of the motel and get ready to travel to South Carolina. I started packing up as soon as I got back to my room, but I decided that I would get a fresh start in the morning, since I had one more night paid for anyway. I ordered another pizza and sat back and relaxed while I waited for it to be delivered. Yep! I was going to find that little bitch, but first I had to find myself a little handgun. Being in prison made it easy for me to know where to get my hands on one, and I went there right after I ate the pizza. Within five minutes I was hooked up with a small revolver, fully loaded. I hated to part with that kind of cash—three hundred—but it was necessary. I left at daybreak.

Chapter 33

I HAD NO idea how to find this little resort town that the guy in the bus ticket window told me about. He said that the bus driver would know but he was driving a bus somewhere in Virginia. I had the name of the town and the name of the state—I would find it.

Even though I always enjoyed driving, I tired quickly since I hadn't done it in awhile. I stopped for lunch somewhere in Maryland—I have no idea where. I saw the sign for Burger King and steered toward it. I ordered my usual burgers and fries and a large coffee. I ate slowly, savoring the taste of the fattening high cholesterol food. I was a junk food junkie—I knew that. I think it was because I was deprived of things like McDonald's and Burger King when I was little. The only time I ever got anything like that was when my father rewarded me by taking me out, away from my mother. Fast food reminded me of those times. I *think* that's why. I don't know for sure.

I got a coffee to go and got back on the highway.

Virginia is one big state! I seemed to be traveling in Virginia forever! When I entered Richmond, Virginia

I was exhausted, so I looked for a motel for the night. I could wait one more day since I had waited this long for my confrontation with that little tattle-tale bitch.

There was a small restaurant next to the motel and I decided that I would go there for dinner, after a shower and a change of clothes. Feeling refreshed I walked over to the little place and found a booth to sit in. An attractive auburn-haired waitress hurried over with a coffee pot in her hand and I turned my cup over for her to fill it. She gave me a menu and a smile and I couldn't help but notice her prominent green eyes and the sway in her hips as she walked away from me. I opened the menu for about thirty seconds and then shut it. The special was country fried steak and I wasn't sure what that was, but I was going to try it, served with mashed potatoes and gravy and corn on the cob. Maybe I would have dessert after I ate, thinking that the dessert might just be the auburn haired waitress. I noted her name on her name tag—Lois. I loved how she purred out her southern accented words when she took my order. She made it a point to let me know that I was her last customer for the evening and she was off until the day after tomorrow. Was that an invitation? I would find out.

Country fried steak is pretty tasty, I discovered. After I finished the meal, Lois hurried over to see if I wanted dessert. Here came the game.

"Oh, no....I'm sure you want to get home. It's still early. You might be able to go do something with your husband or boyfriend. I'll just grab a candy bar out of the vending machines back at my motel."

"Nonsense! Let me get you something special. I don't have a husband or a boyfriend." She sprinted away and came back with something that looked like a waffle with a scoop of vanilla ice cream, cherries, chocolate sauce, and whipped cream. "Here you go! Black Forest Supreme.... you'll love it....it's delicious."

She was right. It was delicious, and I loved it. I finished my dessert and paid the bill at the register and walked out full, but a little disappointed. I was full but not sated.

But there she was! It looked like she was cleaning out her car and throwing things into the dumpster, but I played it like she was having car trouble. I'm not stupid.

"Hey...Lois....problem?"

"Oh....no....I'm just throwing out some trash out of my car. I have a tendency to leave things in the car rather than carry them in to the trash, so they start accumulating."

"Oh.....yeah....I'm bad for that, too," I told her.

"So it's not just me," she laughed.

"No. By the way, my name is Jonathan Riley, and I'm from Pennsylvania. Just traveling on a little business trip. Do you have to be right home? Maybe you could show me some sights while I'm here. It's still early."

"Sure.....come on. Hop in. There's a carnival in town. Does that interest you?"

I remembered my two trips to Kennywood in Pittsburgh and remembered how much fun I had, so that sounded good. We rode the wild rides and played some games and then went into a picture booth. We sat together and had our pictures taken and then decided we wanted to do it again. This time, inside the booth, I pulled her into my arms and we got four pictures of us in the middle of a passionate kiss. She was happy with those. We left the carnival at closing and she drove me to my motel.

"Jonathan, I had so much fun with you tonight! I wish you weren't leaving in the morning," she purred.

"Well, give me your address and phone number and I'll keep in touch. Maybe we can see each other again some time."

She smiled. "I'd like that. I need something to write on."

"There's pen and paper in the room. Want to go in?"

She nodded and got out of the car. I gave her the motel stationary and a pen and she wrote down her address and phone number.

"Here. Let me give you *my* address."

The devil had a part in this, I'm sure. I wrote down Loraine's address, in care of Loraine Carter, and gave it to her.

"Loraine is my mother. I'm staying there until my condo is completed. We have different names because she went back to her maiden name after she divorced my father." I was silently chuckling to myself, just knowing how disrespectful I was being to Loraine.

She nodded, and stuck the paper into her purse. We stood there staring at each other for a few moments before she reached for me and draped her arms around my shoulders. My lips found hers and it was lights out. I ran my fingers through her silky auburn hair and then down the length of her body, and she melted against me. We quickly undressed each other and fell onto the bed. The sex wasn't bad. Peggy was better. Lois, for all her worldly looks and talk, was not all that experienced. She wasn't a virgin, but she wasn't a sex goddess either. She was adequate. I worked at pleasing her and she let out a loud moan when it happened. This excited me more than

I thought possible and when my release came it felt like an internal explosion. We slept wrapped in each other's arms that night, parting reluctantly in the morning with a promise to keep in touch. After one last kiss, I jumped into my car and drove away as she stood there, tearfully watching. I was reminded of Jennifer way back when I was sixteen.

Chapter 34

I STOPPED FOR lunch somewhere just east of Raleigh, North Carolina. With any luck I would be in South Carolina by dinner time. I spotted an Arby's and decided that a couple of roast beef sandwiches would be great. I pulled into a parking space and took my map inside with me, planning on studying it while I ate.

As I was eating and looking at the map, a woman was sweeping the floor near my table. She just had to speak to me.

"Looking for something in particular?"

I looked up at her and inwardly cringed. There ought to be a law to determine a cut-off on how ugly a person could be in public. They could put ugliness on a metered scale and if a person goes over the ugly limit he or she must not go out in public. The ugly law. If there was such a law, this woman just broke it.

"No....just checking to make sure I'm on track."

"Can I help? I know all the roads in North and South Carolina," she boasted.

I'll bet she did—probably from being run out of the towns.

"No....I know where I'm going."

"Can I get you anything?"

"No....thank you...I'm fine." 'Go away,' I added silently.

She stood there and glared at me, making me wonder if I had spoken that out loud. Annoyed, I looked up at her.

"Is there something you want to say to me?" I asked her, showing my displeasure.

"No....just studying you. You need some help. You've got something going on inside of your head that ain't right." She turned to walk away, and then turned back to me. "You're not going to win. And...yeah, I *know*....I'm ugly."

I got the hell out of there. All the way through the rest of North Carolina I kept hearing her words. They were damn spooky, if you ask *me*. I kept hearing her and I kept seeing that ugly face looming around me. I shivered.

I crossed over into South Carolina at six in the evening. Besides lunch, I had made a couple of stops for gas, something to drink, and a bathroom. I kept the speed at fifty-five to sixty, not wanting to get stopped for anything. I think I made pretty good time.

I pulled off to check the map again. I had no idea where this resort town was. I figured I would just drive along the coast and run into it. I passed Myrtle Beach and kept going south. Since it was dinner time and close to dusk, I decided to find a place to stay for the night. I didn't want to be floundering around in the dark, looking for Lindy, so I pulled into a small motel that had its lights on showing a vacancy. There was probably more than one vacancy since the tourist season wasn't started yet. I figured the next move would be to find a small restaurant and strike up a conversation with the wait-staff. They would know where the resort areas were.

...

"It's about forty-five minutes from here. Nobody there, though. The town closes up for the winter. One or two people stick around but mostly everybody goes somewhere," the chatty waiter told me.

"Thanks....how is the view of the ocean then? I guess there wouldn't be a lot of people obstructing it about this time of year."

"No...there won't be anybody around. Too cold for sunbathing, too. If you go out on the beach you'll probably be alone."

"That's the way I like it. Thanks," I said, as I stood up, dropping an adequate tip onto the table.

I went back to the room, showered, and then turned in for the night. I didn't realize how tired I was until my head hit the pillow. Sunlight was streaming through the window when I opened my eyes again.

I was almost giddy as I showered and dressed. I was going to find her today—I just knew it. I had breakfast at the same restaurant I was in the night before and quickly got back onto the highway in search of my destination and Lindy's fate.

The waiter was right about the time. Exactly forty-five minutes later I saw the name of the town as I entered it. It looked like a ghost town. The waiter was certainly right about everybody going somewhere else. I pulled into a convenience store parking lot to collect my thoughts and get something to drink. I was about to get out of the car when the door opened and two women walked out. I felt my mouth go dry and my heart jump. One of them was Lindy! Wasn't it? Yes! It was her! I watched her as she spoke to the older woman, smiling. They got into a tan colored late model Chrysler and pulled out. I sat there gripping the steering wheel and then snapped to life. I had to follow them! I pulled out and started looking for the car, but it was nowhere to be seen. Shit. Where had it gone? I went back to the convenience store and bought a can of Pepsi, and then set out to search for that car. The town was not that big. That car had to be somewhere. I drove up and down every street but that car was not on any of them. I went back and drove them all again. Nothing. I was beginning to get frustrated—and hungry again. I left the small town and found a lonely restaurant just outside of the next town and went in to have lunch. I noted the time on the wall clock. It was already two in the afternoon. The calendar next to the clock said it was April eighteenth. Lindy had turned eighteen just four days before. She was no longer considered a minor.

After I ate and paid the bill, I began to search again. I turned down a road that led to the beach and sat there for awhile. Motion at the closest motel attracted my attention. A blonde girl was coming down the steps from the second floor and heading toward the office. It was Lindy! I surveyed the rest of the motel property. There was a Toyota parked beside the steps and there it was! That tan Chrysler! This was where she was staying! I wondered where the boyfriend was. Maybe he didn't come with her after all. Who was that woman Lindy was with? A relative? I began thinking about a plan to get to her. I was so engrossed in my thinking that I almost missed the boyfriend coming out of the door on the second floor. He was with an older man. Another relative? I watched as the two of them walked toward the office, both wearing suits. 'They're probably going out to dinner. Not a care in the world,' I remember thinking.

I watched until both men were out of sight. Now I had to decide how to get to them. I got out of my car and moved furtively along the high grass that grew on the beach. I stopped at the side of the motel building and looked up. I was about to head toward the stairs when I heard another car pulling into the parking lot. I stepped back as the car found a parking space. There were two people inside the car. Another car was coming in. I ran back to my car and jumped in. As I watched, still another car came into the parking lot. I saw the boyfriend emerge from the office door and run back up to the motel room. He went in and was back out in a moment, and I watched as he locked the door before he went back down to the office. I remember sighing as I sat there. Nobody else came in or out of the office door the entire time I sat there. What the hell were they doing in there? Some sort of religious service? I doubted it.

I decided to leave. I had no idea where to spend the night but I certainly wasn't going to spend it sleeping in the car on the beach. I drove inland and found an open Holiday Inn. I got a room, paying with my credit card, and checked in for the night. I would get a good night's sleep and then get there early for my surprise reunion with the lovely little Lindy. I knew I would have to kill the boyfriend first. He would never let me hurt his precious girlfriend without inflicting some bodily harm on me. I began to pace my hotel room, and I began to have second thoughts. Was this stupid? Yes. NO! She ruined my life! Maybe I should just go home and forget about it. Get a job—start over. And let her get away with it? Oh, hell no! She could have kept her mouth shut, but oh no—she had to tell!

I did not sleep well that night. I tossed and turned and had dreams all night. In one of my dreams I was with Richard again out on the highway. In the dream I said I was sterile. That woke me up. I sat up and began to wonder about that. Was I sterile? I had never, to my knowledge, ever gotten a girl pregnant—even when I didn't use condoms. Of course, it would have been too soon to tell with Peggy or Lois, I guessed. Anyway, the night was a rough one for me. Common sense told me to go home and forget about it. My stubborn ego told me to stay. I arose at six in the morning, took a long shower and dressed carefully for my planned confrontation, just after breakfast.

I parked the car where I had been the day before and made my way to the end of the building. The sun was high in the sky already. Checking my watch, I saw that it was already eight-fifty-five. The temperature was a pleasant sixty-five degrees. I stared at the ocean for a moment, noting the sparkle of the sun on the waves. I had planned on climbing the steps and just knocking on the door. When they opened it, I would just burst inside, gun in hand. I was just under the steps when I heard their motel room door open. What luck! Lindy was coming down the steps—coming right to me! I held my breath and waited. When she hit the bottom step I reached out from behind the steps and grabbed her by the throat. I felt her stiffen and then I felt her shiver.

"You didn't think I'd let you ruin my life and get away with it, did you, Sweet Cheeks? I was in jail for three months because of you; I lost my job, my wife, my home, all of my assets because of you. You have to pay for all that. Not to mention that your daddy had me worked over while I was in jail. You have to pay for that, too. Now... where's the boyfriend? Upstairs? Let's go visit him." I thought I sounded really tough. Tough enough to scare *her*, anyway.

I half-carried and half-dragged her up the steps, holding her close to me. I set her down in front of the door and told her to open it.

"NO!" She challenged.

"Yes, or I'll kill you right here and then go in and kill him. You won't even get to say goodbye to the love of your life."

She opened the door. The boyfriend was standing there wearing nothing but a pair of sweat pants. I could tell he was shocked to see me there holding a gun on Lindy.

"What the hell? Who are you? No....never mind...I *know* who you are. Let go of my wife."

It all happened fast. I remember he said something about me raping Lindy and I remember telling him that she loved every minute of it, and then saying that after I killed him, me and Lindy were going to get it on for awhile before I killed her. That's when the shit hit the fan. Lindy went crazy.

I felt the slice in my arm and saw the blood just before I felt the pain in my groin and saw the stars. I remember going to the floor and hearing the explosion of the gun. I was wounded. I started to black out but then the door flew open and there were cops everywhere. Lindy was holding the gun and pointing it at me. She had blood all over the front of her. I saw the boyfriend take the gun out of her hand and she was saying something to the two paramedics who were leaning over me, and then she collapsed into her boyfriend's arms. No—he was her *husband* now? They got married? Was that yesterday when I saw him dressed in a suit?

I was wheeled out on a stretcher and a police officer put me in handcuffs. Not again—shit. I don't remember much about the ride to the hospital but I do remember hearing that I would be taken into custody and transported back to Pennsylvania when I was released from the hospital. What about my car? What the hell! Was I going to lose my car now? Again? I lost the Benz when Loraine filed for divorce. She sold that one. This just wasn't fair! I vowed as I was transported to a prison cell after the overnight stay in the hospital that I would eventually get even with Lindy for all the grief she caused me. Didn't I tell Loraine that taking in a foster teen could be a lot of problems? I was right about it, wasn't I?

Chapter 35

"NELSON, YOU'RE AN ass! What the hell did you go there for?" My attorney was scowling at me as he spoke. "You might as well just plead guilty....you don't have a prayer of getting off on this."

"Dave, I can't go to prison! My God, Dave! I'm not cut out for it!"

"Look, Nelson....going after her was a major mistake... can't you see that?"

"What am I going to do?"

I was scared. I realized that I had made an awful error by finding her. She may have just gotten on with her life. She was married now! Maybe she would have started a family and forgotten the whole thing. I should have listened to my head when I was down there having second thoughts.

"Nelson, I'm going to suggest that you waive your right to a trial and just sign a confession," Dave told me.

I looked at him like he was crazy. "Confess to it? Then I'll go to prison!"

"Nelson....you're going anyway. By making it easier

on the system, you can get the minimum sentence. With time off for good behavior, you could be out in...say... fifteen years."

"Fifteen years! Fifteen years! I can't do fifteen years!"

"Well, then we go to trial and you are found guilty and get the maximum...possibly life....since you went after her."

Suddenly fifteen years didn't sound so bad. I agreed to it, signed a confession and wrote a letter of apology to Loraine and Lindy. That was Dave's idea. He said it would help my cause. I also sent the letter to Loraine asking her to pay my credit card bill with my half of my assets. Hopefully she would do that much for me. After all, they were my assets to begin with. I was whisked away to a prison in the middle of Pennsylvania. Funny...here I was back in the central part of Pennsylvania where my life began. It made me start thinking about my father. I knew he would be so disappointed in me if he were still around. I felt very sad about that. I remember I had made him a promise to keep on the straight and narrow path once, and I kept that promise until....Lindy.

One thing about prison, you get plenty of time to think. I thought about everything and everyone I knew. I began counting all the girls I had had sex with. I remembered all their names and what I liked about them. I thought about Renee, wishing she was still in my life. I felt so comfortable with her and I believe I truly loved her—in my own way.

One thing I learned about myself is that I don't have a big reservoir of love. I guess I loved Renee and Loraine—as much as I was capable of love, that is. Outside of my dad, I don't really think I truly loved anybody the way I was supposed to. I loved Renee because she was comfortable and good company. I loved Loraine because with her I had a nice life. By the end of the first three months of my sentence served, I realized that I was one sorry-assed individual.

My thoughts turned to Stacey. I wondered where she was and who she married. I knew I was never good enough for her and didn't I just prove it by landing my ass in prison? I wondered if things would have been different if she had given me a chance. I knew I would have given everything I had to make her happy. At least I thought I would have. Maybe I would have been just as bad a husband to her as I had been to Loraine.

One other thing that worried me about myself was that I did not feel guilty about anything. I believed I should feel guilt and remorse but I didn't—not for all the women I was with when I cheated on Loraine or for the forced sex with Lindy. I actually felt guilty for not feeling guilty!

Another thing I kept thinking about was *why*. Why did I force myself on Lindy? I never forced the issue of sex on any girl ever in my life. Why Lindy? I remember that I wanted her to look up to me—like me, even. I wanted her to respect me and lean on me when she needed something. I wanted to be the one she ran to. I sure as hell blew that one!

Chapter 36

I WAS ASSIGNED to the laundry duty again. That didn't bring back any fond memories. Not only was it torrid in the laundry room, but it stunk as well. Did some of these guys shit the bed, or what? I hated it. One of the guys who worked along side of me struck up a conversation with me on his last day in the laundry. Mitchell was an okay black dude who was in prison for shoplifting. He got fifteen years for shoplifting! It was what he shoplifted that got him the fifteen years.

"I learned the hard way that you can't steal a new car right out of the showroom," he chuckled. "You should have seen the faces on those people!"

"I'll bet. Did you drive it through the window?"

"Oh, hell no. The same way they got the car in there I drove it out. When they opened the big doors to bring in another car, I started up that brand new Thunderbird and drove it like a bat out of hell....right out through that door."

I started laughing, because of course I knew how those cars were brought into the showroom.

"Anyway....I'm moving on up," Mitchell continued. "This is my last day in laundry....and you might want to think about this, too."

"Think about what?" I asked. My interest was already piqued.

"Well, tomorrow I start college classes...from in here."

"How do you do that?"

"Well, first you apply....and then if you get accepted.... you do mostly online courses...or some correspondence courses. You seem pretty smart. Maybe you should think about it"

"Hell yeah.....I will."

We worked the rest of our shift just making conversation, but my mind was turning. No more laundry and an education to boot. Right before our shift was over I asked him how to get the ball rolling for that.

"Ask to see a counselor. They can't refuse that. When you see a counselor, tell him you always wanted to get a degree but life got in the way of your plans. If he suggests a trade, tell him you're no good with your hands. You have no particular skills or talent. What were your grades in school like? High school, I mean?"

"I was an honor student."

"Well....shit....you shouldn't have any trouble. You were an honor student? Really? And you ended up in here? Well, damn, dude....you're a victim of white man justice.... and you're not even black! I like you, Nelson. Hope to see you in class!"

We left the laundry room together and went into the showers. I learned from experience to always go into the showers with someone you can trust. We talked a little more about college classes and I was more revved up than ever to get to see a counselor.

...

I was on the list to see a counselor. That list must have been quite long because I didn't see a counselor for another month. When my turn came, the guard in charge of the laundry pulled me off the line and handed me a slip of paper.

"You have counseling today, so you're excused from the laundry for the rest of the day. Take this pass and go down toward the infirmary. The guard down there will get another guard to take you the rest of the way. Your appointment is in ten minutes, so leave now."

I thanked him and quickly made tracks out of there, feeling like it was a holiday. Any time I could escape laundry duty felt like Christmas. I mentally rehearsed what I would say to the counselor as I made my way down toward the infirmary. I spent an hour with the counselor and the interview went well. His name was Bob, he told me, and he began by asking me questions.

"So Nelson....where did you grow up?"

"Not far from here. Down closer to Bedford. I was raised on a farm."

"Yes....it says here that you were orphaned at seventeen. Want to tell me about that?"

I shrugged. "It was a long time ago. My dad was killed while he was working on an old car, and my mother died of a massive coronary about a month later. I was sent to live in a shelter."

He nodded, because he already knew that. "How did that make you feel?"

"Well...sad...scared...unsure of what was going to happen to me. See, I loved my father....but I loathed my mother. She was.....cruel...to say the least. She told me she never wanted me and that she would have had an abortion except my father found out she was pregnant and wouldn't stand for an abortion."

"That must have been....upsetting to hear that."

"Well....by the time she told me that....I already hated her. See, I caught her in the barn with another one of the farm hands. I learned that day that my father was not my biological father. I hated my mother long before that, but that sealed it. I also loathed the man she cheated on my dad with. I mean....my dad didn't deserve that. He was a good guy. He knew about it. He told me that he wanted me and that was all that mattered."

Bob stared at me and I could see compassion in his eyes. I knew it was the right time to hit him with my rehearsed plan.

"See....I was a really good athlete, and an honor student in school. My mother never acknowledged any of that. But I was determined to do well. After I got out of the shelter I went to work and took night classes at the college. But I only got one year in. I ran out of money. After awhile I just gave up on the idea. My wife always acted superior to me because she had a degree and I didn't."

"Let's talk about your wife for a moment. Were you happy in the marriage?"

"Yes....I was. Loraine is a wonderful woman. We had a good life together. It was just the college thing that bothered me. I always wanted that degree but life just kept interfering."

"Nelson....it sounds like a college degree is really important to you. Is it?"

"Yes.....I wish I had gotten a degree. Maybe I wouldn't have felt like a second class citizen in my wife's eyes. Other people's eyes, too. I always wanted somebody to look up to me...like I was awesome to them."

"When you went to college....what were your grades like?"

"Honor. A three point two. I worked full time while I attended school."

"That's not too shabby then. Listen.....if you're interested.....we have a college program in here. You can take classes and earn your degree. Your sentence is long enough that you could actually earn your Bachelor's degree. What do you think? Would you be interested?"

"Well.....yeah....of course I would be. What do I have to do?"

"Well.....I'll set up the testing for you. It will be about three days of testing...all types. We test for IQ, achievements, psychological....just a lot of tests. One stipulation of course."

"What's that?" I knew there had to be a catch somewhere.

"That you agree to continue on with counseling. There are areas we need to get into....focus on. You must agree to see me at least twice a week. If you are chosen for the college program you will be exempt from all work detail.... so there will be plenty of time for counseling sessions."

"Of course I'll agree to that. Why wouldn't I?"

"You'd be surprised by how many guys turn counseling down." He smiled just a little. "Everybody needs counseling of some sort. Everybody. A lot of guys don't think they're everybody. So you agree to it?"

"Yes," I assured him.

"Okay…." He turned around a retrieved a couple of sheets of paper from his file cabinet. "Read these over and sign them….if you agree."

I read them. One was a release form, and another was an agreement to counseling. Breaking the agreement would mean giving up the college program. I signed them both.

"Now….the school will send for your transcripts….so fill this out. They need to know where to send for them."

"How does this get paid for?" I asked while I filled in the information required.

"It's federally funded and state aided."

"You mean that all the while I was struggling to pay for college all I had to do was commit a crime and it would have been paid for?"

Bob laughed—sort of. "It's not *exactly* like that… but being in the prison system qualifies you for certain…. programs. It's part of a rehabilitation program. Not everybody qualifies….and you may not either…..but let's give it a shot."

The following Monday I was scheduled for three days of testing, and I waited for the results. I had the answer back in four weeks. I qualified! I was scheduled to start classes the following January—only five weeks away!

Chapter 37

My counseling sessions began almost immediately, so by the first week of January I had already had about eight sessions. I didn't mind them, but that was because so far we had not talked about the reason I was in prison. We started at the beginning of my life and in eight sessions we were only up to the part where I had to start the eighth grade looking like a refugee.

My first class began right after the New Year. It was a computer class and I knew I would ace it. The class was held in a prison classroom and was twelve weeks long. After the twelve weeks, I received my first A grade. All the classes lasted twelve weeks. Along with the computer class, I had a correspondence English class and algebra class. I earned A's in both of those. At the end of the first semester I was carrying a four-point-oh. My counselor, Bob was proud of me. In counseling, we were now at the stage of my first girlfriend, Jennifer. So far—so good. Prison life was actually tolerable. My second semester began with one classroom class, one online class, and one correspondence class. It was a nice variety. We had run across a snag in the counseling area, though. I made the mistake of mentioning Stacey. I didn't want to talk about Stacey but Bob kept bringing her name up.

"Look.....Stacey was a fantasy. I was never good enough for her except in my dreams and fantasies."

"What did Stacey look like?"

"She was a goddess. Long silky blond hair, big blue eyes, the face of an angel. You know...just an average girl." I joked.

"And you were in love with her?"

"Who wasn't? She was gorgeous."

"What were the fantasies like?"

"They were private. Mine. I don't want to talk about them."

"I think you should. Something about Stacey has kept her a clear vision in your mind. That's worth talking about."

I shrugged.

"Nelson, you need to open up about her. There is something there that you're not seeing...I'm not seeing. I sense it, though. Tell me about her. What kind of interaction did you have with her?"

"I danced with her once....at homecoming. All the football players did. It was a tradition. I talked to her in the diner once. She was preoccupied though....because she was looking for her boyfriend," I told him.

"That's all?"

"Yeah...that's all. The rest is in my head."

"Are they....sexual fantasies?"

"N-no....not really....well, some of them are. I mean.... we're never having sex....just working up to it...or lying together after it. Most of the fantasies are where I rescue her and she regards me as her hero," I admitted to him. After all this time, those fantasies sounded pretty lame.

"Do you still have them?" I knew he was going to ask that.

"No....but I still think about her."

"Any idea where she is?" He asked me.

"No....no idea at all." I responded. "Is it time to change the subject?"

Bob smiled. "Yeah....I guess it is. Tell me about Renee."

"Renee's name always brings a smile to my face," I confided to him. "She was more than a girlfriend and a lover. She was my best friend, my pal. She shared her family with me. I never had that...family life, I mean. I *loved* being with Renee."

"So what happened?" He had to ask.

"I don't know. She just stopped coming around. She was a student at Edinboro University...I guess she found someone who was educated. I know I missed her for a long time."

"What happened after she stopped coming around?"

"Well, nothing. I worked for Big Jim selling cars until...."

"Until what, Nelson?" He asked, watching me expectantly.

I surprised myself by getting choked up. "Jim sold out. He was....terminal."

Bob was quiet for a few minutes. I guess he knew that talking about Jim bothered me and he let me get myself together before we continued.

"So....you lost Renee and Big Jim in the same year?"

"Yeah....and the little old lady across the hall. That was a bad year for me."

"Tell me how you felt."

"Sad, angry, lonely. I wondered why everyone I cared about went away."

"And what did you come up with?"

"That I didn't deserve anybody. I wasn't good enough to have good people in my life." I actually admitted that to him. Bob was good at forcing things out of me.

These counseling sessions left me drained emotionally. After every one of them I had to go into my cell and sleep for a couple of hours. Somehow, the sessions were making me feel better, too. I felt sort of cleansed after each session.

At the end of my first college year Bob and I were at a stalemate in the counseling sessions. Over the past year, many of the sessions had been about being married to Loraine. I didn't mind talking about *her*. Loraine was a fine woman. It was the extramarital affairs I didn't want to focus on. Bob *did*.

"Do you get off on hearing how many damn women I screwed?" I asked him.

"You must have gotten off on screwing so many women. Otherwise you wouldn't have cheated on your wife so often."

"I told you....Loraine made me feel like I was beneath her."

"And all the women? They made you feel....." He left his question dangling.

"Like shit...because I was cheating on my good wife."

"Nelson, nobody can make you feel like you are beneath them or like shit unless you already feel that way." Bob, the brilliant one challenged.

"Yeah…well maybe that's how I felt."

"Were you trying to make yourself feel better by being with other women?"

"Yeah….no…I….just…I just wanted to be awesome to somebody. I wanted to feel like somebody really, *really* thought I was the best guy they had ever met."

"Did you ever get that feeling?"

"No."

"Why is that?"

"I don't know."

"Yes, you do," he countered.

I sat there and stared at him for the rest of the hour. What did he want me to say? I went back to my cell and wrapped up in a blanket and slept the rest of the afternoon. I knew the sessions had to continue. My other option was giving up the college classes and going back to the laundry detail. I couldn't let that happen. I knew I was going to have to come to terms with what he was saying and trying to make me say. My self- esteem was in the toilet.

Chapter 38

My Associate's degree was in the bag. After two years of college I had finally earned a degree of some kind. Two years of college and two years of counseling were under my belt. In those two years' time, Bob had not asked me anything about why I was in prison. I guess he knew, but he didn't bring it up. After the last final was taken and graded the guards actually threw us a little graduation party. It was kind of cool. Lame—but cool. Mitchell was in the graduating class with me and we hung out together at the party—if you could actually call it that. The guards had a cake and sandwiches and sodas brought in and we gathered in one of the class rooms. Some of the guards were kind of friendly that day, but there was no mistaking the ones that hung back with the weapons close at hand. All in all, it was a generous effort—I have to admit. We had three months off before we started on our classes toward a higher degree, and the best news we got was that instead of laundry or kitchen duty, Mitchell and I were assigned to library duty. The prison had a fairly good sized room for the library and they had just received a giant shipment of used books from somewhere. All of them had to be catalogued and assigned to shelves. Since Mitchell and I both had a 4.0 GPA we were assigned to this project. It was a well-appreciated lucky break.

Our new assignment started the next day. Mitchell and I walked down the hall to the library and were met by the library guard.

"Now…I'm going to be nearby….but you two are going to be on your own for the most part. We're trusting you. Don't make us regret it."

"No problem." I replied. "We can't climb into one of these books and fly out of here….so I guess you can trust us. Just show us what to do."

"Okay, funny man….let's get started." He growled.

We began by putting all the books into categories, and then in alphabetical order, by author's last name, and when we were done, he showed us how to catalogue and assign library numbers to them.

It took us all summer to do this task, since more books, magazines and newspapers kept coming in. It was a pleasant assignment, though. It got even better. The guard in charge came in right before school started.

"You two….come here," he bellowed.

We thought we were in trouble for a moment. We stared at each other and made our way to where he was standing.

"Okay….listen up. This is going to be your assigned duty. I know you both take classes, but not at the same time. When one of you is in class during the open hours, the other will have to be here. Here are the library hours." He handed us each a schedule. "You two work it out. Your classes start day after tomorrow. Make damn sure this library remains open at the times it is scheduled to be open. If you have correspondence classes, you can do the work while you are here. The same with online classes. That computer at the front desk can be used for that. Finish up in here and take the next two days to work out a schedule between yourselves."

"If we both are free, can we both be here?" I had to ask that, didn't I?

"Yeah....I don't see why not. This place will be your responsibility....the two of you. Don't screw up."

He walked back out into never-never-land, or wherever the hell he went to hide. Mitchell and I stared at each other and then just smiled. The smile turned into a grin—a big grin. We finished up and got out our school schedules. It was determined that while I had two classroom classes on Tuesday and then again on Thursday, Mitchell had two classes on Monday and on Wednesday. My correspondence class could be done in the evenings, and his online class could be done at the library or in the computer classroom. I had no online classes that first junior semester.

Classes started and Mitchell and I managed the classes and the library like clock work. For the next two years we handled the library tasks and our studies and there were no complaints from the guards or the other inmates. It was one of the better times spent behind bars.

It was on a Sunday when I saw Lindy's picture in the paper. The prison library received three city newspapers a day—three of each. One was the State College newspaper, another was the Harrisburg paper, and the third was the Pittsburgh Post Gazette. The library wasn't busy that day so I sat down with the Pittsburgh paper and started leafing through it. When I got to the featured articles, I stopped and stared, feeling my insides crumbling. There she was on the front page of the features page, smiling into the camera, looking like an angel. She was in a musical, at the university she attended. She played the lead role in "The Wizard of Oz" produced at the university by the music and drama departments. The write-up included her musical accomplishments, her personal data, and her address—well, at least half of it. The article mentioned the street she lived on as being the same one she grew up on. She was married to Ricky, her high school sweetheart. Touching. I filed this information away in the back of my brain, and for the life of me, I don't know why. I never intended on ever using it. After I read the entire article, I sat and stared at the photo. She looked just as I remembered her—fragile and angelic. Why did I hate her so much then? I didn't know. I hated her and.......I wanted her. I was sick.

I didn't hear the library door open as my eyes burned that picture into my brain. I jumped when I heard the voice behind me.

"Man....that chick is *hot*!" I heard the inmate exclaim. "I need to get hooked up with that!"

I wasn't real familiar with this guy, but at that moment I wanted to punch him square in his face. What the hell was wrong with me that I had such messed up feelings and emotions where Lindy was concerned? It shouldn't matter to me what any guy said about her, but for some weird reason, it did. I cut the picture out and saved it.

From that day on, I scanned through every Pittsburgh paper every day, just wanting to see her name or her picture again. That day came as I finished my last year in college. Lindy and Ricky both achieved their Bachelor's degrees the same time I did. How about that? We had something in common. They were both going on for Master's degrees. *'Must be nice,'* I thought. *'At least they will have the chance to use their degrees. When I get out of here nobody is going to hire me. Thank you, Lindy.'*

If I were sane where Lindy was concerned, I would have realized that my being in prison was not her fault. I had just completed my first six years in the penitentiary and had a Bachelor's degree to show for it. What could I accomplish in the nine years I had to go? Nothing. Nothing, unless they allowed me to further my education by obtaining a Master's degree.

I decided to run it by Bob to see what he said. I had been an excellent counselee for the last four years. Maybe he would go to bat for me.

Bob was on vacation and I had to postpone my quest for a whole month. In the meantime, Mitchell and I had another major task at the library. Some books were being taken off the shelves because they were worn out, but there was another shipment of books to be categorized, catalogued and stacked onto the shelves. We had a job in the library all summer. After that, we both wondered what was next. We kept hoping that our education would keep us out of the kitchen and the laundry. Sometimes it pays to hope....especially when you get your wish.

Chapter 39

When Bob returned, I was actually glad to see him. I almost missed our sessions, but not quite. I liked Bob but I didn't like having my personal life delved into, nor did I like having my head examined, so to speak. But at least I knew that Bob was in my corner, for the most part. I decided to approach the idea of working on a Master's degree as a sort of joke. I took my best shot.

"So, Bob…now what. Master's degree?"

"Do you want a Master's, Nelson?"

"Well, of course….hell yeah. Who wouldn't?"

"Let me do some checking for you. Just remember…. you have to stay in counseling."

"Yeah….I know. How else would you get your jollies? Bob, did I ever tell you about the time my mother sent me into the chicken coop, knowing that there was a rattle snake in there?"

"No….tell me about it."

I told him the story and watched his face. He was truly a compassionate person.

"So when can you let me know about additional

education? I really got the bug now. I just want to go on and on."

"I'll start checking into things today. That's a promise."

The rest of our session was spent just talking about my marriage. I got up to leave at the end of the session and he promised to have something for me when I returned in two days.

...

"Nelson, I found a school in England that will let you do correspondence courses to earn your Master's. You will be funded, of course. But if you want to do it, I'll send for the application." Bob started out our session this way.

"Oh hell yeah! Thanks, Bob," I answered enthusiastically.

This was the news I had waited and hoped for since our last session. Loraine didn't have a Master's degree. I would be more educated that she was! I was so enthralled with that notion that I almost missed what Bob was saying.

"Nelson...did you hear me?"

"No....sorry....what?"

"I think it's time we get into your counseling more in depth. I've waited all this time just making sure you were comfortable with me....and I think you are. Am I right?"

"Well, yeah....sure. I mean...you're *okay*." I responded.

"I hope you think so in a year from now...or longer. Hey, listen...people pay big bucks for me to get into their heads. You're getting the service free. Take advantage of it. Learn why you did what you did. Apply that knowledge when you get out of here. So you don't make a mistake again."

"Mistake, you say?"

"Yeah....mistake. You screwed up. It happens. Learn why and move on. Grow and become a better person by what you discover about yourself."

Bob labeled my crime as a mistake. I liked that. We finished our session that day by talking about the job I had before I got arrested. I knew that by the next week we would be touching down on hallowed ground—Lindy. And I dreaded it. I didn't want to talk about it. I didn't want to talk about *her*. I didn't know why I did what I did, or why I felt the way I felt about her, and maybe I just didn't want to know. But I knew Bob was not going to let it slide. Also, I knew way down deep inside of me that what I did was wrong. It was the *why* that frightened me. I had asked myself why I did it at least a million times over those past six years. Now I was going to have Bob asking me the same question, only he would do it in such a probing way that I would feel naked and exposed before him. I shuddered when I thought about it like that.

One thing that still really bothered me was that I still felt no remorse for what I did to Lindy. Sorry that I ended up in jail over it—yeah—but sorry that I did it? No. And that bothered me. Would I do it again? Maybe—maybe not. Not if it meant going to prison over it. But even after six years in prison, I still wanted her badly—and I hated her for it.

Chapter 40

"Tell me about Lindy, Nelson." Bob began our very next session that way.

"What about her?" I tried avoiding the subject.

"Well, let's start with the day she came to live with you. Tell me about her that day....from the first moment you saw her."

"She was really sad, I remember. She was crying...a lot. Those big blue eyes....they haunted you....you know what I mean?"

"No....I'm not haunted by them. What do you mean by haunted?"

"I don't know....they drew me in. Her eyes were very expressive...and so sad. I wanted to...just hold her. I remember she was so sweet and....fragile. She looked like an angel....delicate and just so pretty. Beautiful, really. She was beautiful." I smiled a little just remembering that day.

"Were you attracted to her?"

"Yes.....no, not really."

"Which was it...yes or no?"

"Well, the moment I saw her I was....but after listening to her story I just wanted to protect her and make life nice for her. I swear I never wanted to....have sex with her. I mean I didn't think about it. If you could have seen her that first day...she was just crying...she was heartbroken. I just wanted to make all her pain go away."

"Why was she crying?"

"She had been through it...I can tell you. That poor kid had been through hell....and then they take her away from her boyfriend. They had a baby together and the baby died...because her father shot her. There was much more to the story. All she wanted was to be with the boyfriend. It broke Loraine's heart. Loraine was going to arrange for her to see the boyfriend."

"So tell me about Lindy living there before you...."

"Raped her?"

"Up to that point....yes. Tell me what the three of you did together."

I told him about the snow and the snowman and snowball battle, the trip to the mall, and how Lindy and I cleaned up the kitchen together.

"So it was a parent-child interaction at first?"

"Yes. I wanted her to look up to me, come to me when she needed something...I swear that's how I felt."

"So what changed?"

"I don't know."

"You don't know?"

"NO....I *don't know.* It kind of happened fast. I knocked on her bedroom door and then opened it. She was sitting on the bed in some kind of nightshirt or something. It wasn't even sexy-looking. I don't know what came over me. I saw her and it was like I went berserk. I just had to have her. I was like a madman. It was like I was suddenly possessed."

"But it happened more than once...."

"I know. I don't know why. I really had a hard time with it afterward...but I knew it wasn't going to stop. When she took off I was sort of relieved...because I knew it was the end of it."

"Describe Lindy to me. What did she look like?"

"Long blonde hair, big blue eyes, the face of an angel, and a gorgeous figure."

"Can you still see her today? I mean exactly what she looked like?"

"Well, that's not too hard considering I just saw her picture in the paper a month or so ago. She has the voice of an angel, too. She sings. Her picture was in the paper because she had the lead role in the Wizard of Oz at her college."

"What happened when you saw the picture? What was your reaction?"

"I was kind of startled, I guess. I mean her face just jumped right out at me. She *is* stunning."

"How did you feel when you saw the picture?"

"Well, surprised, then angry, then sad, then I just wanted her again. Oh, when one of the guys made a comment about her...he was looking over my shoulder....I wanted to punch him."

"Nelson, our time for today is just about up. Listen.... we have a lot of work to do, I can see. These feelings you have...for Lindy.....I'm missing something there. I have to think about it, but....there is something about the whole... situation. There is some significance there....I need to think about it."

I was in deep thought when I walked back to my cell. What was it that he thought he was missing? I hoped he figured it out because I sure didn't have a clue what it was.

Unfortunately, I never saw Bob again. There was a major pile-up on the interstate and Bob was right in the middle of it. He didn't actually die, but from what I read in the newspaper, he was in a vegetative state and the odds of recovery were not in his favor. At some point down the road, I believe his wife consented to pulling the plug on him. I was saddened by it, of course. That was just one more person I allowed close to me that I lost.

I also lost the chance for a Master's degree. Bob had all the information somewhere and the new counselor assigned to me had no idea what I was talking about. The only good thing that came out of it was that as long as I agreed to counseling, I would have the job in the library. Of course, the new counselor had to start at square one with me, and I made damn sure I didn't mention Stacey to him.

Chapter 41

PRISON LIFE BECAME fairly routine for me. I worked in the library, keeping it neat and clean, and keeping all the books properly catalogued and in their right spots on the shelves. Mitchell was still my partner and we worked well together. We talked a lot, along with a couple of the other more educated inmates. They enlightened me on a lot of things, including how to get fake ID's.

"Nelson, we got our degrees but believe me, we won't be able to use them. People don't hire ex-cons," Mitchell informed me. "Not in this country, anyway. Now you take your degree to South America or somewhere and nobody has to know you're an ex-con—a felon. Here, if you don't put that down on an application and they find out you lose the job. You put it down and they don't hire you."

"I guess I never looked at that part of it. So what do we do with the degree?"

"Say we have it. People ask you if you have a college degree, you nod your head, because you have one. That's about it."

"So we wasted the tax payers' money by putting in the four years of education paid for by the government?"

"Yeah....pretty much...." He hesitated a little. "But at least we spent four years doing that instead of laundry."

I nodded in agreement, but I was disappointed. I guess I never thought about the consequences of doing the time for a felony. I really regretted what I had done now, but it made me even angrier at Lindy. I kept thinking, 'yeah... okay...maybe I shouldn't have done what I did, but she didn't have to tell either. She could have just left and kept silent. It didn't ruin *her* life. She still married Ricky and they live happily ever after. It ruined *my* life though!'

...

Working in the library was a way to connect with other inmates who had ways and means of obtaining things. Mostly all of the inmates came to the library at one time or another. Many of them spent hours looking up statutes and things like that, just looking for a loophole to relieve them of their sentence. Library time was something that couldn't be denied an inmate unless he acted out or ended up in solitary for something. Every inmate was permitted two hours a day of library time. Most of them took advantage of it, too. Since I was the librarian I met them all. Some were okay, and some were just plain assholes. It was in the library where I met Juan Juarez. He was an asshole with a skill. He could forge documents. He bragged that the documents he forged were flawless, and would never be questioned. Somehow I knew that in the future, he would come in handy for me. Juan was originally from Mexico but he had a girlfriend in the Pittsburgh area. When his time was up he was going to be staying with her until he could eventually talk her into moving to Mexico with him. The girlfriend came to visit every visiting day.

Most of the inmates had visitors. I did not. I served my entire sentence without having even one visitor. Sad, isn't it?

I began thinking about that. Why didn't I have anybody? From the time I was sixteen, women were drawn to me. I could have had almost any woman I wanted, except for Stacey. Now, in my time of need they're all gone. None of them would give me the time of day. What was it about me? Why wasn't there anybody there, weeping because she missed me so much? I brought it up in my next counseling session.

"Well, Nelson....apparently this is something you've been thinking about a lot. What do *you* think it is?"

I shrugged.

"Tell me how your relationships usually ended."

"The girls just went away. Well, Renee did. I think I loved Renee....but she just disappeared."

"Nelson, did you ever let any of these girls and women know that you cared about them? Did you ever indicate that you appreciated them being there?"

"Well, no....I mean...they were there and I was, too. I just assumed that they knew I wanted them there....or I would have left them."

"That's not quite how it works. Women like to be told they are cared for. Women like to know that a guy wants them there. You just seem....cold. You're very noncommittal. I can imagine that women do not feel secure in a relationship with you. It's like you're not totally there with them. Does that make any sense to you?"

"Sorta...I guess," I answered. I never knew I was

supposed to tell women I cared about them and that I was glad they were there. I had to ask him. "Do you think Renee might have stayed if she knew how I felt about her?"

"Maybe. I don't know that for sure. Nelson, from all you have told me, it sounds like you went along with the program but never initiated anything. You put no effort into any relationship."

"No....I guess I didn't."

I thought about it for a moment and I began to wonder if it would have been different if I had made a pass at Stacey. Would she have gone for me? I guess I'll never know the answer to that one.

"Nelson...did you feel bad when these women left?"

"Some of them, yeah."

"Like who, for example?"

"Renee. Just Renee, I guess. But I also feel real bad about Loraine....my wife."

"Tell me about that."

We spent the next four counseling sessions talking about Loraine and what I did to her. I figured it was all leading up to Lindy, and I was right. Before we started talking about Lindy I admitted that I felt bad about the one night stand I had in Virginia. And I did, too. She was a nice woman. If I hadn't gotten arrested again, I may have gone back to her. I didn't mention it to him, but I also felt bad about Peggy. Now there was a good woman! I should have just stayed with her and never left Pittsburgh. That was a stupid move—I admit it. I often wondered if she would answer my letters if I wrote to her. Maybe if I was honest with her and told her the truth, she would. She might even visit me. I never wrote to her because to be honest, it wouldn't have been fair to her. Is that a sign that I'd grown, I wonder?

...

Since furthering my education was now a thing of the past, I almost looked forward to my counseling sessions. I was learning a little bit about myself, as much as I didn't like to admit that. My counselor made me realize that because of the cold, unloving relationship I had with my mother, I was cold and unloving in my relationships with women. He said I didn't like women, as a rule. I was both surprised and sad about that, because I always thought women were wonderful, and it was just my mother who was rotten. He said something about the subconscious, and that I really wasn't aware of my feelings about women. I had to believe he was right. After all, I was the one who was all alone with nobody to love me.

Chapter 42

I WAS DOWN to the last third of my prison stay. I now had five years to go. It seemed as though I'd been in a lifetime already. I'd all but forgotten what it was like on the outside. For all ten of the fifteen I was to serve, I had been a model prisoner, by prison standards. I didn't cause any trouble, I didn't get into fights, and I didn't break any rules. I don't know whether the other prisoners liked me, but at least they didn't have a desire to hurt me. I knew that, and that's the best you can hope for in prison.

There was lots of time to think. I did a lot of that. I did a lot of reading as well. I read everything from the newspapers to the encyclopedias, and every novel in between. I read in my cell at night and in the library while I worked. I would never get that Master's degree but I would have knowledge way beyond it when I was a free man.

It was right around my tenth anniversary as an inmate when I saw the announcement in the newspaper. I read the Pittsburgh newspaper every day. That's where I saw it. My eyes honed in on it like some kind of built-in magnet or radar. 'Lindy and Ricky DeCelli…proud parents of a beautiful baby girl. Samantha Renee, born March eleventh at seven-thirty-four in the morning, weighing seven pounds, two ounces.' Now I *never* read the birth announcements. I didn't know anybody, let alone anybody who was pregnant. But somehow that grabbed my eye.

'Well, well…' I thought to myself. *'Life goes on now, doesn't it?'*

I don't know what I felt, but it was something out of the ordinary. Jealousy? Sadness? Whatever it was, it put me in a dark mood for the rest of the day. In fact, I brooded for a week. My counselor noticed it immediately.

"What's going on, Nelson? I sense there is something bothering you."

"It's…..nothing," I answered.

"Nothing doesn't put you in this kind of mood. Nothing is *something.*"

"It's really something I can't really explain. You don't want to hear it."

"On the contrary, Nelson….I certainly do want to hear it."

I stared at him for a moment and then decided that I had better just spit it out or he would badger me the whole hour.

"Lindy had a baby."

"Where did you hear this?"

"It was in the newspaper under birth announcements."

"Why does this bother you?"

"If I knew the answer to that I wouldn't need you, now would I?"

"It *does* bother you, though…..doesn't it?"

"I guess," I responded.

"Let's talk about Lindy for a few moments. Nelson, we need to figure out why you have this.....obsession with her. We also need to explore the fact that you blame *her* for everything. You know....there are many beautiful girls in this world. It's not a crime or a sin to be beautiful. Why do you subconsciously punish Lindy for it?"

"I don't do that!" I was becoming angry.

"Yes....you do."

"Look," I sighed. "I made a mistake. I shouldn't have done what I did....but she didn't have to tell. She could have just gone on with her life and let me go on with mine. It's not like she was some virgin that I deflowered."

"But you took her against her will...."

"Yeah....okay....I did." This conversation was getting tedious.

"Nelson...would you have any idea what it's like for a girl who has been raped?"

"No..." I answered. I guess I really didn't.

"As long as you were free she would always be looking over her shoulder. There would be nightmares and the feeling of never being completely safe. Depression and anxiety disorders could possibly develop."

"But she has Ricky to lean on. He keeps her safe."

"But he can't be with her twenty-four hours a day. And I'd like to point out to you, Nelson...rape is a felonious crime. The girl may be a woman now, but she was seventeen years old....a scared kid."

"But she and the boyfriend were sleeping together. They had a kid together."

The counselor sighed. "Look....Little Red Riding Hood may have been sleeping with the woodsman but she was still afraid of the Big Bad Wolf. What you did wasn't bad, Nelson. It was horrendous. Violating any woman is a horrendous act. And that is what you did. No, you didn't deflower her…you didn't necessarily take away her innocence….but you violated her. Now we need to work on remorse. You should be remorseful for what you did. I guess we need to start with making you cognizant of your crime first."

We spent many hours just going over the same stuff. I admitted that I shouldn't have done what I did, but I could not understand why it was so terrible. The counselor said it had something to do with catching my mother in the barn that time. That is why I don't see any form of sex as being against a woman's will. Maybe I'm sicker than I thought I was. Maybe my childhood really did warp me and I never knew it. (Thanks, Mom….you ruined a perfectly normal, sane kid. I hope it's hot enough for you down there.)

I tried to see it the way the counselor said I should. Lindy wasn't at fault. I did something wrong and now I'm being punished for it. I hurt Lindy. I deserve to be in jail for it. Fine. But I couldn't see it that way. What I did took ten minutes, if that. Okay, so it was ten minutes, twice. How does that equal fifteen years of my life? Oh yeah, I could have gotten twenty years or better, so I should be grateful. I forgot about that.

Chapter 43

I CUT OUT the birth announcement and put it in my cell alongside the clipping of Lindy in the musical that I had already cut out years before. That one was getting faded. I don't know when I got the idea that I was going to make Lindy pay me for all my years in prison. I just know that one day I woke up and started planning it. The idea just came to me. I was going to take her child and keep her until Lindy and her husband paid me to get her back. The plan began to formulate and the more I thought about it, the better it sounded. Mitchell said I could use the degree I earned in South America. Well, that sounded like a good place to relocate. I would need money—lots of it. Lindy could help me obtain it. I settled on five million dollars. That would be plenty. I knew I had to find out where she was living and then how to get into the house and get the kid. Since I had never even been near kids, other than Renee's niece, I had to find out what I would need to care for one during the time I had her. I had no desire to hurt the child—just use her as a tool to gain my wealth. I wondered where Lindy was gong to get that kind of money, but put that thought aside. It wasn't my problem. It was hers.

My new cellmate had a five year old daughter on the outside. He was in for breaking and entering and he told me he did it to get money to feed his wife and daughter. He talked about his wife and daughter a lot and I just let him talk. Because of that, we became good cellmates. I encouraged him to talk about his daughter and I eventually brought up the subject of the expense of raising a child. I asked him what all a kid needed and he obliged me by telling me. I soaked it all up like a sponge. I was particularly interested in what kids liked to play with that would keep them occupied. I had to find that out since I didn't know anything about keeping one occupied.

"Jim, what does a five year old play with, anyway?" I started out.

"Mine plays with dolls, and other girl things. She wanted an easy-bake oven for Christmas last year. I couldn't afford it," he obliged me. "She's real smart too, and she likes to color and draw a lot."

"In coloring books, you mean?"

"Yeah….she does real good at it, too. Stays in the lines pretty well."

"So what else do they like?"

"Oh, I don't know…..there are lots of things that intrigue her. Cameras, sunglasses, purses, things like that. She likes grown-up things geared for a child."

I filed all of this information in my brain. I would make sure that Lindy's little girl would have enough to occupy her while she was in my company. I wanted her to be as comfortable as possible because the alternative may have been having a crying, screaming brat on my hands.

It was obvious he loved and missed his daughter, so I had to ask the next question.

"Jim, what would you do if your daughter was ever kidnapped…or something?"

"Kidnapped? You mean somebody taking her?"

"Yeah. What if somebody just took her and demanded a lot of money for her return? You don't have that kind of money, so what would you do?"

"I'd get it….somehow. I don't know how, but I would get it…..and just pay it. My daughter is worth more to me than any amount of money."

"How would you feel? Emotionally, how badly would you hurt?"

"Nelson, you cannot imagine the pain that would cause. As a parent, there is nothing worse than losing a child. The pain would be unbearable. I miss my daughter so much now and I know where she is. If I didn't know where she was, I wouldn't be able to stand it."

He fed right into my hand, and it was just what I wanted to hear.

…

I had three years left on my sentence. My days were still the routine of the library and the counseling sessions. I was reading the paper in the library one Sunday when the birth announcements reached out and grabbed me again. Lindy and Ricky had a second child—a boy this time.

'Michael Raymond, born March sixteenth at five-sixteen in the morning, weighing seven pounds, fifteen ounces…'

"Life still goes on," I mumbled to myself. "What's it like in Camelot, Lindy?"

I saw an anniversary announcement for Peggy in that same paper. She and her husband were celebrating their tenth anniversary. Well, good for her. Some guy was reaping the benefits of being with that good woman. Good for him. I was really glad for Peggy. She deserved to have a good someone in her life. I stared at her picture for a little while. She looked radiant. At least I could quit feeling guilty about disappearing on her. She faired far better with me out of the picture.

I went back to the birth announcement. I had the choice of two now. I was still leaning toward the first one since I knew more about little girls, thanks to my cellmate. Besides, there would be less maintenance for the older one. By the time I got out she would be five. I knew they could carry on a conversation by then. At least Haley could, from what I remembered.

I worked at perfecting my plan every chance I got. I changed and rearranged it many times in the next three years, but the end result was still the same—Lindy's daughter for my financial freedom in another country. Brazil came to mind many times, and I believed that was where I was going to go. I began counting the days until my release.

Finally the day came. Juan had been released two weeks before me and he left an address and phone number with me so I could get in touch with him when I was released.

I'll never forget that first moment of freedom when I stepped outside those prison walls. I carried my belongings in a paper bag as I walked along the road toward—I had no idea what. I was alone, friendless, and had no resources, but I was free. Once again, as I had done the last time I walked out of a jail, I checked my wallet. I had quite a bit of money in it. I had forgotten all about the money I had taken out of my bank account to buy a car and then travel to South Carolina. I still had bank accounts but I knew that was going to be a hassle since they would have to be searched for after fifteen years. Briefly, I wondered how much interest had accrued in fifteen years.

As I slowly walked along the road, it dawned on me that I had nowhere to go, let alone no way to get there. I spotted a clearing, walked over to it, and dropped down on the grass, clutching my bag holding all my worldly possessions in my lap. I was now fifty-seven years old, with no prospects, no chances of legal income, no pension, and probably no social security available to me. Whatever happened to that kid with all the potential? Lindy. Lindy happened.

I sat for awhile and just enjoyed the scenery. Cars passed me, but nobody paid attention to me. I watched a car fly by in the direction I had come from and wondered what his hurry was. I saw him turning around and coming back toward me. *"Uh-oh….what is this? Trouble?'* I remember thinking. The black Chevy slowed down and pulled over, and his passenger side window went down.

"Hey….are you Nelson?" The driver yelled.

"Yeah…." I answered as I stood up, brushing the grass off of me. "Who are you?"

He got out of the car and extended his hand to me. "My name is Jack—Jack Everett. I'm your parole officer."

"I don't think I was paroled. I served my time."

"Well, yeah….but you should have gotten twenty years. The five they took off for your confession is going to be served as parole. That should have been explained to you.

Hey, I'm easy to work with. Just stay out of trouble and you'll be fine. Anyway....sorry I'm late. I agreed to come get you when you were released but there was an accident on eighty....a bad one. Traffic was backed up. Let's get you in the car and head toward Pittsburgh. That's where you want to go, right?"

"Yeah....do I have much choice?" I answered as I got into his car.

"No....not really. It's a long drive so we'll know each other pretty well by the time we get there. Where are you going to stay?"

"No idea. I guess a motel until I can find a place."

"Yeah, okay...but remember...you're classified as a sex offender, so you have to be mindful of where you stay."

That sent a sharp stabbing pain right through me. Sex offender! Why didn't he just say pervert? It was the same thing, wasn't it? He must have caught my reaction.

"Hey...I'm not going to judge you. You were already judged. My job is to see that you follow the rules. I don't know what happened....I wasn't there.....so it doesn't concern me."

I was glad to hear him say that. If I thought prison was bad, this had to be worse. Going through life having people back away from me, hide their kids from me, protest me living in their neighborhood—I was a marked man. If I ever even thought about changing my plans to get the hell out of the country and go to South America, this convinced me otherwise. I had to go where this stigma wouldn't be on my head.

Chapter 44

We stopped to eat somewhere off of Interstate Seventy-Nine South. Jack chose the place. I would have been in hog heaven had it been a McDonald's or a Burger King, but he chose a small home-style restaurant. The food was good, I have to admit. But after fifteen years of prison swill, flour and water would have tasted good.

When we arrived in Pittsburgh, Jack pulled into a small motel.

"Older people stay here, so you won't have to worry about kids."

"Is it an old-folks motel or something?"

"No," he laughed. "It's just that older people seem to prefer it. No pool, I guess. There is a small coffee shop and the price is reasonable. Do you have money?"

"Yes, I do. I guess it's safe to say that prison officials aren't thieves. The money I left in my wallet was still in there."

Jack laughed again. "You're lucky."

I checked in at the motel office and the desk clerk handed me a room key. The room was all the way at the other end of the motel, but that was okay because I wanted some privacy after just spending fifteen years having somebody always there. Jack came into the room with me and sat down in the chair that he pulled out from under the small round table that was positioned in front of the window.

"This isn't too bad," he said, as he lifted the blind a little. "You have privacy and you can open this blind if you want. Not too bad of a view out there. It looks like there is a creek running behind this place. It's pretty green back there. You must have missed that...didn't you? Green grass, trees, and bushes...."

"Yeah, I guess I did. But you don't think of that stuff. On the outside we take it all for granted. You don't know you miss it until you get out and see it again. I'll appreciate that scenery out there. I hope it will be okay to just walk out there."

"Yeah, I think it should be all right. Now....what section of Pittsburgh do you want to live in? My area of Allegheny County is mainly in the south or southwest."

"That's good for me. I like that part of Pittsburgh."

"Now you'll need to get a job....and then a car. I can help with all that. It's mandatory that you work."

"How do you get a job after you've been in prison?"

"It's not that easy....but it can be done. What kind of work have you done in the past?"

"Sales. Cars, Insurance, electronics."

"Try a used car lot then. There are plenty of them around. Hell, most of the owners have been in jail themselves. As a matter of fact...." He stopped and pulled out a pen and a card. "Here....I'll write this down for you.

Go see this guy…hand him my card….and you'll have a job….guaranteed."

"Thanks. If I get a job there then I can find a place to live right around there."

"Yeah…there are a lot of old houses turned into apartments. You shouldn't have too bad a time finding a place. I'll get out of your way for awhile, but remember, I'm a phone call away. I'll stop back in two days to see how you're doing. Follow up on that lead. It's easy to get there on a bus. Maybe a trip downtown to the Port Authority might be a good idea. Get yourself some bus schedules."

Jack left. At this point I could have sat down and cried. I didn't know anybody, I had no place to live, and no job, no car, and now he wanted me to ride a public bus. I used to drive a Mercedes! I brought home two thousand a week! I lived in a beautiful home! I had finally been somebody! Then Lindy came into my life. Now I'm nobody…again!

I stretched out on the bed and just felt sorry for myself for a couple of hours and then I got up and ordered a pizza. Pizza! How long had it been? Fifteen years! That's how long it had been! While I waited for the delivery, I showered the prison dirt off of me and wrapped a towel around my waist. I really hesitated putting those same clothes back on, but then I thought about the delivery person. What if it was a girl? I'd end up right back behind bars. It's a good thing I thought about that because the pizza got delivered by a cute brunette around seventeen. Oh boy! That could have been a big problem.

I felt better after I ate my pizza. In the morning I would head out to find this car lot and then look for a place to live, but for the evening I was going to sit and watch television—alone—and just luxuriate on the bed in my underwear. I had ice in the ice bucket and a two liter bottle of Pepsi that came with the pizza. I was free.

Chapter 45

In the morning, after I showered and dressed I went to the coffee shop for breakfast. After eating the ordered special, I found a bus stop and took my first public bus ride since working for Big Jim. I had no trouble finding the Port Authority and I went in. At the information window I told the clerk what area I needed to get to and he told me what bus schedule to find. He also told me about purchasing bus tickets to save myself a couple of dollars. I purchased ten for the price of nine and then took a couple of schedules for different areas. I found the stop to get on for the address I had and stood and waited for a bus. One came along before too long and I hopped on and then got off at the appropriate stop.

The used car lot was right there. I stared at the lot and at the shack with the office sign above the door. I had seen better places, but beggars couldn't be choosers, I guessed. I sighed and resignedly walked to the door. The first thing I saw was a help wanted sign so I pulled the door open.

"Can I help you?" A voice floated in the air.

Because I had come from the bright sunlight into this

darkened room, I couldn't see anybody at first. When my eyes adjusted they rested on a very large, balding man of about fifty-fifty-five, sixty maybe.

"My name is Nelson Sutter and I was told you may be looking for some help."

I handed him Jack's card as I spoke. He stared at the card for a moment and looked up at me.

"When did you get out?" He asked.

"Yesterday."

"Ever sell cars?"

"For many years. I started selling used cars when I was eighteen and left to sell new cars in my twenties. Selling is how I made my living before...." I left the end of the sentence hanging in the air.

"Were you in jail for a white collar crime?"

"No."

"Stealing?"

"No."

"Can you start on Monday? Today is Friday. Enjoy the weekend and be here Monday at nine. Lot opens at ten. There will be some paperwork to fill out and I'll show you around after that....okay?"

I nodded and thanked him. When I left, I surveyed the area. I spotted two 'for rent' signs and decided to check them out. The first place was exceptionally nice for the area, but the man stood firm on my providing references for the past ten years. I only had one reference and I didn't think he would have been too happy with it. The second place was not as nice, but still not bad. It was clean and furnished, just like my first apartment when I was eighteen. The landlady showed me the small apartment and told me how much it was, and I breathed a sigh of relief that it was affordable. She studied me for a moment.

"You just get out of jail?"

I was startled that she asked that and I immediately turned to leave. I thought about lying but decided that wouldn't be wise, so I answered her.

"Yes. How did you know?"

"My husband spent ten years in jail, and my son is in prison right now. You have the same look in your eye. Hopelessness. All you can do is keep plugging away. Don't give up though. When do you want to move in?"

"You're going to let me have the place?"

"Yeah. I appreciate honesty. You were honest with me. Hey....everybody makes mistakes. You paid for yours. You shouldn't have to keep paying."

"How soon can I move in?"

"You have money for the first month's rent? It's three hundred, plus a security deposit....that's ninety-nine dollars."

I opened my wallet and took out four hundred dollars. When I handed it to her she handed me a key.

"No loud parties, no pets, no profanity. That's the rules. There are laundry facilities in the basement. They take change only. Rent is due monthly, the due day being the day you sign the lease. It's the tenth for you—every month. Sign the lease and the place is all yours."

There was going to be enough money for a couple of new pairs of pants and shirts. I would need them to work in, so I took a bus to a local shopping center and found a K-Mart. After I made my purchases, which also included new underwear and shoes, I headed back to the motel on a bus. I got off a stop early when I spotted a McDonald's.

I walked the rest of the way, carrying my bags of burgers and fries and the K-Mart purchases. I had accomplished a lot in one day—a job, an apartment, and new clothes.

After I ate my McDonald's feast, I decided to walk along the creek and just leisurely enjoy my time and freedom. As I strolled along the creek, I began to wonder what Loraine was doing. Would she see me? Speak to me? No, probably not. I knew I would eventually have to see her and get what few things I may have left there. But then again, she may have thrown everything out. Maybe there was nothing of mine there any more. It wouldn't hurt to check.

...

Jack Everett showed up early the next morning. He seemed impressed that I had not only landed a job but a place to move into as well.

"Okay....you have tonight paid for in the motel, so tomorrow I'll come by and take you to your new place. You'll probably have to go shopping for some food, too. You can't afford to be eating out every day. I'll take you shopping. Are there any cooking utensils in the apartment?"

"I don't know," I responded. "I didn't check. Oh, and the landlady knows I was in prison, by the way."

"Very good, Nelson. Just remember to be up front with everybody about that. It closes some doors, but in the long run it frees you up from lying all the time."

...

When Jack arrived the next morning, I checked out of the hotel and we rode to my new apartment.

"It's small, but not too bad," I informed him.

Once inside, he checked the cupboards and discovered that there were a couple pots and a frying pan, and a small set of dishes.

"Do you drink coffee?" He asked me.

"Yes....but there is no coffee pot here."

"Place up the street has a sale on coffee makers. Twelve dollars for them. Got that much?"

"Yeah, I guess. That's a necessity, isn't it?"

"Yeah....for me it would be," he admitted, chuckling.

"Nelson, do you drink as a rule? You know that's not allowed, right?"

"I don't drink....never did. Maybe some wine once in awhile, but that was it. That won't be a problem."

"Good."

Jack took me shopping and helped me carry the bags inside. I set up the coffee pot immediately and started a pot of coffee. I had bought a couple of mugs where I got the coffee pot since there were no coffee cups in the apartment. I began washing them out with the new dish detergent I had bought. All in all, I had spent another seventy dollars. I was getting down there in the money department. At least I could walk to work.

When the coffee was done, Jack stayed and had a cup with me. We talked a little, going over the rules some more, and then he asked me about my crime.

"Jack, I have been over it and over it many times....with counselors and in my own mind. I don't know why I did what I did. I don't know what came over me. Lindy...she just....I don't know what it was. When it happened...I was shocked myself. I...I don't know. I can't explain it. I know I have never done anything even close to that before.

Hell, I never even came on to women. They always made the first move."

"You know to stay away from her, I hope."

"Oh hell, yeah. I won't go near her again."

"Good. So you'll be okay? I'll be stopping by every now and again over the next couple of weeks. I go on vacation for two weeks toward the end of March. There is a festival in Canada I go to every year."

"But what will happen to me while daddy is gone?" I joked.

"Usually a sub is assigned to you. The guys split up the case load...usually." He got up to leave. "I'll stop by the lot in a couple of days to see how you're doing there. Remember to keep your nose clean, Nelson.....and you'll be fine."

Chapter 46

I SETTLED INTO my apartment and started my job the very next day. I was happy to see that I hadn't lost my touch. I sold two cars that first day. Jay was impressed and very pleased with me, I could tell. That first week whipped by and I ended it with a total of seven cars sold. I immediately put three hundred dollars away for my next month's rent and began thinking about a car for myself. Jay let me have a gray Ford Taurus for four hundred dollars. It was an older model, but in good shape with low mileage. I registered it and bought the required insurance and once again, I had wheels. I pulled the car off the lot and drove straight to Loraine's house. It was harder than I thought it would be. She opened the door and I saw her face twist up with hate.

"What do *you* want?" She snarled.

"I was just wondering if....you still had any of my things here. I don't have any clothes."

"I'll open up the garage door. There are a couple of garbage bags with your things in them. Take them and go. Don't come back here again."

"Loraine....I'm so sorry. I never meant to hurt you."

"Just get your things and go, Nelson. We have nothing to say to each other."

"For what it's worth....I loved you, Loraine."

"It's worth nothing, Nelson. Don't ever come here again."

She shut the door and I heard the garage door begin to open so I stood there and waited. She met me in the garage and pointed to the garbage bags. I grabbed them and started back out through the garage door.

"I won't bother you any more, Loraine."

"See to it that you don't. If you do I'll get a court order to keep you away. Do you understand me?"

"Yeah....thanks, Loraine. Have a great life."

She didn't answer me but just walked back in through the door that led to the kitchen. As soon as I cleared the garage door, it started to close. I remembered the credit card bill and I thought I should ask her if she paid it. I wanted to know if we were divorced and what about my half of the assets? I went back and knocked on the door.

"I'm warning you, Nelson," she growled when she jerked open the front door.

"I just had a couple of questions to ask you. First, are we divorced?"

"Absolutely, we are."

"Well, did you pay that credit card bill I had sent here?"

"Yes, actually...I *did* pay it. Anything else?"

"What about my assets? Shouldn't I receive half of what I brought to the marriage if not the entire amount?"

"Your lawyer took most of it. I'll have my attorney

draw up financial papers for you. If there is anything you're entitled to, you'll get it."

"Do you want to know where to send it, if there is anything?"

"It will be sent to Dave. He was your attorney, wasn't he? Good-bye, Nelson."

And she shut the door a second time. There was nothing else I could do except get in my car drive away. It hurt. It hurt a lot. I remembered how much Loraine loved me. Now? She hated me. I drove back to my apartment and toted the garbage bags up to the second floor into my apartment.

I made myself some bacon and eggs for dinner and after I ate, I began to go through the bags. The first things I pulled out were a couple of letters—letters from Lois in Virginia. Damn! She actually wrote to me. I'll bet Loraine had a fit over that! I read the letters and smiled. She was a truly good person. Hopefully, by now she was married to a really great guy who appreciated her.

The rest of the stuff was unremarkable. There were some shirts and pants that I could probably still wear. There were also some ties and shoes and socks and underwear. At least she didn't destroy everything. The last thing in the bag surprised me when I pulled it out. I don't know how Loraine missed it but it was the CD of Lindy singing. She had to have taken it out of the Mercedes and just threw it in the bag without looking at it. If she had, she certainly would have taken it. There was a cigar box with some things in it. That was something I left in the garage when I lived there. It had a picture of Stacey and a letter I wrote to her once. In the letter I told her I loved her and some day I would make it big and come back for her. Obviously

I never mailed the letter. Loraine must not have looked in the box since the rubber band I put on it all those years ago was still there. It snapped and broke at my touch.

I decided to wash the clothes that I could wash. There were two suits in the bag that needed to go to the dry cleaners. At least I'd have them if I needed one. When the bags were empty I was satisfied that at least I would have clothes to wear. The clothes were still like new since they were originally all very expensive.

I found the laundry room and threw in the clothes. I had no detergent but I found some on the shelf, silently promising to replace it when I bought some. I had just enough change for two washer loads and two dryer loads. It was enough to do the entire contents of the two garbage bags. There were hangers in the closet, left by the last tenant, so I ran up to get them so I could hang my shirts and pants on them. I didn't have an iron so I couldn't let the stuff get wrinkled. After all these years, I was finally learning how the other half lived.

I finished everything up by nine o'clock and just dropped down on the sofa and turned the television on. A movie was just starting so I grabbed a glass of Pepsi and the bag of Oreos and settled down onto the sofa. I wasn't paying attention to the movie. It was more like I was staring into space. The strangest thing happened. I began to cry.

Chapter 47

It was rather early when I awoke on Sunday morning. I don't remember much else after I started bawling the night before. I guess I must have fallen asleep on the sofa because that's where I was when I woke up. The television was still on and there was some kind of church services going on. I got up off the sofa and put the coffee on, then went in to take a shower. I felt like shit and when I looked in the mirror, I could see that I looked like I felt. My life couldn't go on like this. I thought maybe I should just throw in the towel—quit. I was lonely, dejected, sad, and lost. All I ever wanted was for someone to love me and look up to me—treat me like I was their hero. That's all I ever wanted to be—somebody's hero—like my dad.

The shower made me feel a little better. I wandered out to the small kitchen and poured my coffee. I knew I had to go shopping today, but after counting my money, I realized that I would have to budget what I had, until next week. I was out of eggs and bread. I would allow myself thirty dollars to spend and no more. I wanted to get some detergent to replace what I borrowed in the laundry room. I say borrowed because I'm not a thief.

I got dressed and I have to admit that it felt good wearing some of my old clothes. The jeans fit just as they did fifteen years ago. I pulled a sweatshirt on over my head and put on my socks and sneakers and then left for the grocery store. Grocery shopping was becoming my big event of the week.

I managed to keep my bill under thirty dollars after all. As I was lugging my plastic bags up the stairs I saw Jack pulling in. Leaving the apartment door open, I set the bags down on the counter and immediately put on a pot of coffee. It was brewing when he walked in.

"I smell coffee. Did you put that on for me?"

"Well, yeah, kinda. I drink it, too but I thought I would offer you a cup."

"Thanks. I appreciate that," he said as he helped himself. "So how's it going?"

"Good, I guess. I'm getting used to being alone and doing everything for myself. I guess I should get a couple of books to read."

"Not a bad idea. Actually, I wasn't scheduled to stop here today, but I thought since I was so close that I would just run in to see how everything was going. Did you sell any cars this week?"

"Seven."

"Seven? I'm impressed."

"Thanks. The commission isn't all that great, but I'm managing."

"Good. That's good, Nelson. That's what we expect. By the way, you know that you have to avoid any contact with anybody under eighteen, don't you?"

"I figured. I don't know anybody at all, let alone someone under eighteen."

"Well…just wanted to remind you of that."

"What happens if I'm on the lot and somebody comes by with their kid?"

"Ignore the kid….that's the best thing to do. Look….. maybe what happened was a fluke. Maybe you're not a threat to anybody….but you have to follow that rule."

"I got it, Jack."

"Good. I'd better get going. I have to go make an arrest. Some of the parolees aren't as smart as you are."

Jack left and I was once again alone. I decided to go up to the drugstore and find a good book and maybe a deck of cards. It's too bad I had never taken up a hobby now that I would have the time to do it. On my way to the drugstore I changed my plans and went on to Wal-Mart. I found a couple of good mysteries I hadn't read and a deck of cards. I went into the toy and hobby section and found a ship building kit. That appealed to me so I bought it.

I realized that I couldn't spend much more money until I sold more cars. I had the rent money for the month and I didn't want to chance not having it when it was due. I took a mental inventory of my refrigerator and cupboards and mentally made out a small list of things to get. I had been to the store that morning, but when I left Wal-Mart, I went back to pick up the items on my list. I was going to make a big pot of spaghetti sauce and have that for lunches at work. There was a microwave in the office, so I would be able to heat it up every day at lunch. I could alternate between spaghetti noodles and shells. I was really getting the hang of being poor! Poor and alone. I thought about Renee again. It would have been great just to invite her over for spaghetti and a movie. I wondered where she was. Married, probably, with about six kids.

I made a note to get a VCR-slash-DVD player and then I could rent movies to keep myself occupied. After the initial purchase, that would have been cheap entertainment for me.

After I put the ingredients for the sauce into a pot, I assembled my ship building kit and began working on my ship. It was actually a large sailing ship that looked a lot like a pirate ship. There were many intricate parts so it kept my attention all afternoon. It still wasn't completed when I turned in for the night. At least having a project gave me something to come home to. I had almost forgotten my plot to take Lindy's child for ransom. I probably should have given up the idea and just made my way selling cars again. Maybe I would have if I hadn't seen her again.

Chapter 48

It was after work on Monday when I decided to just take a drive and explore the area. I discovered that I was not living too far from the shelter where I spent my seventeenth year. I remember passing the high school I went to back then. It was the same high school where I used to deliver the porn videos to the janitor. He had shown me the tunnel and how to come in and out of it.

I guess I should mention why I was giving porn to the janitor. I swear I never watched porn flicks myself. I remember helping the old guy lift a couple of cases of floor cleaner and I saw the porn videos on the top shelf of the janitor's closet. I pulled them off the shelf and saw that they were teen porn. During the time I was selling insurance I came across a whole box of teen porn videos so I took a couple to the janitor and sold them to him. Every other week or more I would show up with more videos for him. He paid well for them, the sick bastard. Anyway, that's all there is to say about that. I sold them all to him eventually.

Anyway, when I passed the school I realized after all

this time that Lindy had gone to the same school until she came to live with us. As I drove a little further I began wondering where she lived. I glanced up at a street sign and discovered that I was on Carlisle Street. That was her street! I remembered it from the article in the newspaper! I followed the street until I came to a small shopping area. There was a newly constructed McDonald's right next to the Blockbuster Video Store. I knew it had to be new because there were signs announcing that it was the grand opening. I pulled in when I saw the sign that said that Big Macs were being sold for eighty-nine cents and for two dollars you could get two Big Macs and fries. I just pulled right in and parked the car. The drive-thru was not opened yet so I knew I would have to go inside. As I was about to step out of my car, I saw her. She and Ricky and the children were coming out of the door. Ricky was carrying the little boy and Lindy held onto the little girl's hand. The kids were holding balloons and their faces had pictures drawn on them. Ricky said something to Lindy and it must have been funny because she laughed. I watched as they climbed into a silver SUV which looked almost brand new. *Must be nice,* I thought to myself. I watched as they strapped the kids into their seatbelts and then got into the front seat, Ricky driving. Before he started the car, he leaned over and kissed Lindy. After the kiss she turned to the back seat and was talking to the kids. They were smiling and laughing. It hurt me. It made me sad and it made me want for someone to be with me. They were one happy family. How I wanted that at that moment! Oh, to be part of someone's life again! As I watched them pull away I wanted Loraine so much right then. I started my car and put it in drive and followed them up the hill. I slowed as Ricky signaled for a left turn into a driveway of an attractive ranch home. The house was blue and the one thing that caught my eye was the very large solid paned windows. *'Must get a lot of sunlight in there,'* I remembered thinking. I drove up the street and turned around, so I could pass the house again. I drove past and then went down a little further until I found an intersection. I wanted to see if there was a way to get to the house from the back. There was an alley behind the house. As I drove down the alley I spotted the back of the ranch home. The yard was fenced in and I could see that there had been a large addition added to the back of the house. Probably a game room or something similar. I briefly wondered if Lindy and Ricky had built it or had her parents done it. My eyes took in the back yard. There was a swing set and what I believed may have been a sandbox. A basketball hoop stood tall on one side of the yard. The area around it had been cemented, for bouncing the ball, I guessed.

I never did get my Big Macs. I drove home with a heart heavy with loneliness and just heated up a plate of spaghetti and went to bed. I had dreams all night and most of them had Lindy in them. By the time I awoke on Tuesday morning I was angry with her, and full of anxiety. I wanted what she had. Hell, I wanted *her*! Not sexually, necessarily. I wanted to be a part of her life. I wanted to be sitting at her dinner table, playing basketball in her back yard, and yes, sleeping in her bed! I knew I couldn't stay in the country. If I did, I would violate the rules and go knock on her door. God, I was so sick when it came to her! Why? But WHY? I wish I knew.

Chapter 48

THE VERY NEXT morning I went to my bank and had them start searching for my accounts. Since it was going to take awhile I just went on to work and told them I would call the branch later. I checked back at noon and was told that they were successful in locating my accounts.

"Great. I'll be there in about thirty minutes," I told them and then hung up.

I added a couple of bucks to each account to make them active accounts. When the interest was calculated, I was surprised that the account had grown that much, but after all, it had been fifteen years.

I returned to the lot and sold two cars within an hour. As the day wore on I could feel my mood darkening. Lindy and her family were in the back of my mind all day. At the close of the day, Jay told me that he was going to a car auction in the morning and that I was on my own.

"Nelson, I believe I can trust you. That's why I decided to go to this auction. I'll bring back some good cars at a good price. You know how to run this place, so you're in charge tomorrow."

He handed me a set of keys and lightly punched my arm as I walked out. I should have felt good about myself because he trusted me, but at that moment I couldn't care less.

As soon as I got home I dug out the pictures of Lindy that I had saved. I sat and stared at them for a long time. She was supposed to be the victim and yet *she* had everything. I had nothing. *She* was surrounded by family and people who loved her. I had nobody. *She* was happy. I was sad. I was one sick puppy.

It was that night that I thought about just forgetting my plan and to just work my way up. I was already working at accumulating a bank account. It was only Tuesday and I had sold three cars already for the week. Tomorrow I would sell more since I would be by myself on the lot all day. I could work my way back up to where I was before, I was sure of it. I put Lindy's pictures away and went to bed believing that I could succeed once again. It's too bad that fate hadn't planned it that way.

...

I sold my first car not long after I opened up on Wednesday. By noon I was writing up my second deal. This week would yield a good paycheck. By three o'clock in the afternoon I had three cars sold for the day. I silently hoped that Jay would bring back some good cars because I was clearing out his lot. Around four o'clock, as I was writing up my sales report for the day, two big men walked in flashing badges. I felt my blood curdle when I saw them, but it wasn't me they were after.

"Where is Jay Booker?" The bigger one asked.

"He's at an auction....a car auction," I answered. "Is

there something I can help you with?" I was trying to appear calm but my heart was going wild.

"How late do you work at night?"

"I get off at five every day."

"Then this doesn't concern you."

I breathed a sigh of relief and silently thanked God.

"Is this him pulling in right now?"

I looked up and saw the car hauler pulling in with four cars on it.

"No.....that would be the truck driver who hauls the cars. Jay should be showing up right behind him."

I noted the four cars and was pleased with what I saw. Two of them were high-end sellers. It's too bad that I never got a chance to sell them. That could have been the deciding factor on whether I left the country or not.

I saw Jay's car pulling in and I indicated with a nod of my head that he was coming. The two big guys with badges were joined by four others. All six of them were quiet as they waited for Jay to enter the office.

"What is your name?" The biggest guy asked me.

"Nelson....Nelson Sutter. Am I in trouble?"

"No....I don't believe so. You have to stay here until we clear you. You'll have to start job hunting after today though."

"Oh....no.....what about what he owes me for this week? I've already sold five cars. I can't just forfeit the pay."

"Figure out how much he owes you and we'll see to it that he pays you before you go. Sit tight."

I sat. When Jay entered the office I saw the big guy approach him.

"Jay Booker? You're under arrest for the sale and

trafficking of an illegal substance. We have a search warrant to exercise a search of the premises. But before we begin I want you to settle up with this guy here."

Jay didn't resist, nor did he say anything. He sat down and asked for my sales report and wrote out the check. The big undercover cop reached for the check and looked at it before he handed it to me.

"You say you sold five cars and this is all he's paying you? He's been robbing you."

I took the check and looked at it. It was for eight hundred and six dollars. That was about right for the price of the cars I sold, but I didn't say anything as I put the check into my wallet.

"Cash that check first thing in the morning because all of his assets will be frozen tomorrow afternoon," the big guy informed me as he handcuffed Jay. "Write down your name, address, and phone number and then you're free to go. Donnie, get a picture of this guy's driver's license before he goes," the big guy told his colleague.

I pulled out my driver's license and was thankful that I had remembered to renew it when I bought the car. The guy called Donnie made a copy of it and handed it back. I wrote down my name, address and phone number, again being thankful because I decided to get a phone. I began to gather the few things I had there as they began their search. I heard the big guy tell Jay that they had him under surveillance for the past week. As I was walking out the door, I heard another officer yell to the big guy, "Storm, we found the mother load!" I got the hell out of there. I had no idea Jay had been dealing right out of the office.

First thing in the morning, after a restless sleep and many arguments with myself, I went to the bank and cashed the check and withdrew all my money from both accounts. I went home and paid another month's rent and told the landlady that I may be going out of town to work for a couple of weeks but that I would be back. I called Jack, my parole officer and told him what happened. He was sympathetic and told me to just start looking for work and don't give up. He said he would see me in two weeks because he was just getting ready to go on his vacation.

I filled the car with gas and began driving so I could think. I ended up driving out into the country and as luck would have it I came across a row of cottages in the country. A guy was standing in one of the yards when I decided to stop. He stared at me as I got out of the car.

"Hi, can I help you?"

"Yeah....my name is.....John Nelson. I was wondering if any of these cottages were for rent right now."

"No...not really. How long were you looking to rent a place? My name is Jim Heiser, by the way. I own this place."

"Well, I just wanted somewhere quiet to go for a couple of weeks. I'm just coming out of a bad marriage and a rough divorce. I'm still rocking in my shoes. My ex-wife had a hell of a divorce attorney. She got everything....and she's the one who cheated!"

"Kids?"

"No...that's the hell of the situation. No kids but they still awarded her everything."

"That's a tough break. So why do you want to rent somewhere quiet?"

"To lick my wounds and just regroup. I have to decide where I want to live and what I want to do. I just need to think, take a walk in the woods, relax," I told him.

"Well....I'll tell you what. We aren't allowed to rent this but if you can pay for two weeks up front, I can let you have this place for two weeks, three tops."

"That would be great....if you would do that."

"Yeah....well....nobody can know about it...so don't even tell the neighbors."

He wouldn't have to worry about that. I had no intention of socializing, and I made that clear to him. We settled on a price and I paid for three weeks.

"This is just between us. Hell, I can use a little beer and pretzel money. Don't break anything....leave the place like you found it," he told me as he handed me the key. "It's yours as of right now."

He smiled and left in his Lincoln Navigator. I checked the place out. It was perfect. Now all I needed to do was find a way to snag Lindy's daughter.

Chapter 49

I NEEDED A way out of the country. I called Juan Juarez. He was surprised to hear from me but was very accommodating where my needs were concerned. Our conversation was a lot longer than I had hoped for. I knew I needed him but from the moment he answered the phone, I despised that fact.

"So Nelson....I would have believed you to go the straight and narrow path and never need my services."

"Yeah....well....shit happens, I guess. I need a passport and matching identification to go with it. Use the name John Nelson."

"I can handle it. Give me about four days and you'll have it all."

"Now...Juan....what would be the best way to get out of the country?"

"Well....let me see. Plane....jet plane."

"Yeah....great. What should I do? Hijack one?"

"No....you can charter one. It'll cost you, though."

"How do I go about doing that?"

"I got a number for you. Call and ask for Ramon. He'll fly you wherever you want to go....for a healthy price."

I wrote down the number he gave me and thanked him.

"Listen....Nelson....." he continued. "I'll call the guy and pave the way for you....okay?"

"Yeah....thanks, Juan. I'll call him later today. I'll give you a call in about four days. Is that all right?"

"Yeah....talk to ya," he said just before he hung up.

I remember thinking that I put myself in the same league as he was in and that disturbed me. I was about to embark on a felonious act that far surpassed anything he had ever done, and for the life of me, I couldn't understand why. Why didn't I just give up this crazy idea? I don't know. I just knew that I couldn't.

...

I estimated Lindy's house to be about thirty-five miles away from the cottage, and I was not far off. I drove out past her house and saw that it was exactly thirty-four and a half miles away from the cottage. I drove past the house twice. The SUV wasn't in the driveway, but there was a light blue Toyota parked there. Lindy's car—it had to be.

I went back to my apartment and packed a suitcase, careful to leave some stuff behind so that the landlady wouldn't get suspicious. I had finished my ship and that was sitting on the kitchen table. She could keep it when she discovered I was gone. I left some clothes and a few other personal items. As I was leaving she walked into the entrance hall from the front door.

"So where are you going? I thought you were a car salesman," she asked me.

"I am. I have a chance to work a big auction in Ohio for a couple of weeks. My lot is closed for awhile so this is a way to make big money real fast."

"Oh....well good for you. How long will you be gone?"

"Probably about two weeks. See you when I get back." I force a smile.

She nodded, and held the door for me.

I was becoming a first-rate liar. The lies were just rolling off of my tongue at rapid speed and just as smooth as silk. I felt bad about lying to her. She was a good person and she had treated me fairly.

I drove straight to the cottage and dropped my suitcase on the bed in the larger of the two bedrooms. The smaller room had two single beds in it. The place was sparsely furnished, I could see. In the kitchen, however, there was a coffee pot and a toaster, dishes, pots and pans, and silverware. I turned on the refrigerator and filled the ice cube trays. I needed to go shopping.

...

The clerk rang up my grocery items as I stood there watching the total increase and increase even more. I had to get things that a child would eat and some things I would want, too. Funny how many of those things were the same. The whole thing totaled a hundred and twelve dollars!

By the time I got back to the cottage the refrigerator was cold, and clean, I noted. I put my purchases away in the refrigerator and into the cupboards and decided to check out the television set. There was a VCR there with it and both worked. I sat down and made myself a list of things I would have to get for when Lindy's daughter became my house guest. I would need some clothes for her, and some toys. Some kids' movies would be ideal. I began my shopping expeditions immediately, by going to K-Mart first. I bought five Disney movies there. They were on sale so I got a good price. I saw a woman holding onto a little girl's hand and the girl was about the same size as Lindy's daughter. I smiled at the child and then at the woman.

"How old is she?"

"She's five, tomorrow."

Yeah? Well, happy birthday!"

"Thank you, sir. I'm going to have a party."

"Well great! Hope you get lots of presents."

"I have a granddaughter her age. In fact, her birthday is this coming Saturday. What size does your daughter wear? My granddaughter is about the same size."

"She wears a five."

"What about shoe size? I know my wife will insist we buy shoes to match any outfit we buy her. My wife is back there looking at shoes right now."

The woman picked up a shoebox out of her cart and showed me the size on the side of it. I thanked her and headed back toward the shoes under the pretense of finding my wife. I picked up a pair of tennis shoes in the same size as the woman was buying. They were white with pink trim. I found a pink and white tee-shirt with a small bow and some lace around the neckline. I added that to my cart along with a pair of jeans. That was enough for one day. I would hit the Wal-Mart in the next couple of days. I didn't want to draw attention to myself by buying a lot of kids' things all at one time. People, especially women cashiers, had a tendency to be nosey.

It was time to take a ride past Lindy's house again. It was just getting dark as I rounded the bend right before her house. The family was just getting into the SUV when I passed. They were going somewhere! I could check out the house a little more closely. Since I didn't know where they were going, I would have to be quick. I drove into the alley I had found the first time I went past the house. When I was sure they were gone, I got out and climbed over the chain link fence.

There were privacy fences along both sides of the yard so I was certain I wouldn't be seen in the yard. I peered into a couple of windows in the back of the house. The master bedroom. Nice. I looked through the windows to the far right of the bedroom, into the added on room, and discovered a large family-slash-game room. I could see a pool table and a large screen television. Nice. I moved to the left of the house, passing another window. I quickly took a peek in there and saw a crib. It had to have been the little boy's room. I walked around the corner and found two more large windows. When I looked inside I realized that I was looking into the very room I wanted to find. It had to be the little girl's room—all pink and feminine-looking. I examined the windows and discovered that I could get them opened with just a screwdriver. This was going to be a cake walk! Didn't Lindy and her husband know any better than to let their daughter sleep in a room that was this accessible?

I decided that I would watch the house for the next couple of days. I had more shopping to do and I had to check out the drop-off point. My plan was coming together, especially after the jet pilot agreed to let me charter his plane to Brazil. It was going to cost me twenty grand but it was worth it. That much money would be a drop in a bucket when I had five million.

I had no intention of hurting Lindy's little girl. I wouldn't do that. I just needed her to get five million dollars. I continued my shopping for her, buying clothes and toys. It was in Wal-Mart that I found the most gorgeous lavender dress for her. I decided to buy it and save it for her to wear when she was returned to her mother. Funny how I thought of her as being only Lindy's daughter—never Ricky's. I'm sure a psychiatrist would have a field day with that one.

Finally everything was ready. Now all I had to do was go get little Samantha Renee. I remembered her name from the newspaper clipping. I needed something to keep her from screaming out when I took her out of her bed. Once again I called Juan. He had something that could help me, but told me it was dangerous. When he delivered my passport and ID he brought it to me.

"Don't use too much, Nelson. It can put someone out permanently."

"I don't want to do that, Juan....just enough to put someone out for about an hour."

"Is it a large person or a smaller one?"

"She's on the small side."

"Then only a couple of drops. Man, Nelson...you surprise me. I thought you would just go straight...go to work...earn a lot of money. Damn!"

"Yeah...well....like I said....shit happens."

"You said she...it is a woman then?"

"Yeah....all I want is what's mine...that is all. The bitch took everything. I'm entitled to something."

"I agree. Good luck, Nelson. Hope it works out for you."

After Juan left I took one last look on my list. I had everything I needed and I was ready to pick up my house guest. I made one last trip before it was time to go to Lindy's house, and that was to get gas in the car and to pick up a couple of prepay cell phones. I would need them for making contact and they were inexpensive. While I was in the store, I saw a voice changing device. It only took a second to make up my mind on that one. There was a possibility that Lindy would recognize my voice. I made my purchases and then sat in the car thinking about everything. Was I forgetting anything or overlooking anything? I couldn't think of a thing.

Once I was back at the cottage, I ordered a pizza and when it was delivered, I settled into the recliner chair eating and watching the television. Surprisingly, I wasn't nervous. I was even able to take a little nap. I awoke at twelve-thirty and made some coffee. I took a quick shower and donned black clothing so I wouldn't be seen as easily. On one of my trips I had noticed a clearing next to the road almost right across from Lindy's house. I planned on parking my car there and hoped that nobody else had the same idea. I would go in through the front yard. The neighbor's privacy fence afforded me the cover I needed. After a couple of cups of coffee, I was ready to go.

Chapter 50

It went off without a hitch. I was driving home with Lindy's beautiful little girl passed out on the front seat. I kept a blanket over her so she would not be detected. As I carried her into the house I silently congratulated myself on a job well done. I put her down on the loveseat and covered her. She was out cold. I stared at her features and realized that I was looking at a tiny Lindy with dark hair. I was also looking at five million dollars. I smiled and then reclined in the chair and fell asleep.

At eight o'clock I awoke and looked over at little Samantha. She was still sound asleep. Quietly, not wanting to wake her, I got up and made coffee. I drank the coffee at the kitchen table and had a bowl of cereal with it. I had no idea what to expect when she woke up. Would she begin crying and screaming? I hoped not. That would put me in a bad mood. I was not all that fond of kids, and I really couldn't stand crying kids.

I returned to the recliner and put the television on, making sure that the volume was turned low. Well—well—there was Lindy and Ricky on the screen. Lindy was a wreck, and Ricky wasn't looking too good either. I listened to them pleading with the kidnappers to give their little girl back.

"You will have her back, safe and unharmed, in exchange for five million dollars," I responded to the picture on the television.

I tried to imagine what they were feeling at that moment. Remembering what my cellmate said, I knew they were in a great deal of emotional pain. Good. *'Spend fifteen years in prison and see how that feels, little miss bitch!'* I remembered thinking.

...

Samantha didn't awaken until after four in the afternoon. I was getting quite concerned that I put too many of those drops on the gauze pad. I should have checked on her, I guess, but it was nice not having to deal with a crying kid for awhile.

During that time until she awakened, I had plenty of time to think about things. This whole thing was a mistake, I knew. But ever since I met Lindy, I had made nothing but mistakes. Now it was too late to back out.

I thought about my whole life during that time that Samantha slept. I tried to remember something—anything good about my mother. I couldn't come up with a thing. I thought about my dad. He would be so disappointed in me. That made me feel bad. I thought about all the girls I dated before I got married. Jennifer, and then Gwen. Jennifer was my first—my first girlfriend, my first sexual encounter, my first experience with female affection. Gwen was a blast. I wish I could have had more time with her. There was Kathy and then there was Renee—my favorite.

I wondered if she ever knew how much I cared for her. I thought about Ann. What a woman that was!

Loraine. Although I regret losing Renee, the biggest regret I have is the way I hurt Loraine—not just the thing with Lindy, but all the times I cheated on her. She didn't deserve any of that. She was a good woman and a good wife. I always believed that I cheated on her because she looked down her nose at me. That is not true. I just *thought* she looked down her nose at me. She treated me like an equal. I wanted to be put on a higher level. Counselor Bob was right. I thought Loraine was superior to me—*Loraine* never thought that. She would not have married me if she thought that.

Briefly, I thought about Peggy. I really liked Peggy. She would have been a best friend with benefits. Then there was Lois in Richmond. I still couldn't believe that she actually wrote to me. I wondered if Loraine had read those letters and then sealed them back up.

I had just reached the end of the list when Samantha stirred. She wanted to go home. I told her that she couldn't go home unless her mommy paid me a lot of money and she began to cry. I nipped that right from the get-go.

"Just stop crying. I can't stand brats that cry." I think I told her.

She put up a brave front and stifled her cries, but I could see her bottom lip quivering and I could hear her sniffles. I sort of felt bad about that. She seemed like a nice little girl. I softened a little.

"Are you hungry?" I asked her.

"My mommy will make me dinner," she responded.

"Your mommy isn't here. You're going to have dinner

here with me." I answered. "How about a grilled cheese? Do you like that?"

"Yes."

I made grilled cheese and added some potato chips to the plate after I started the Disney movie for her. She wanted Cinderella, so that's what she got. When I took her the plate with the grilled cheese on it, I decided to try to make friends with her. The next few days would be easier that way.

"So which one is Cinderella?" I asked.

"The pretty one," she told me.

"Then....that would be *you*....you're prettier than all of them."

She smiled at me and said, "My mom is the prettiest of all."

"Yeah? You don't say. Well, you look like your mom, so that makes you just as pretty."

She really smiled at me this time. It was the response I was hoping for. This was going to be easy. We watched the rest of the movie in peace and then I asked her what she wanted to watch next.

"My mommy only lets me watch one movie a day."

"But your mommy's not here. You're on vacation so you can watch as many as you want. Let's watch this one."

I dropped in the movie called 'Babe' and it seemed to really hold her interest. In fact, I liked it, too. Talking farm animals—what an idea. I spent the day just talking to Samantha and watching movies. I discovered that she was a polite child with good manners. Silently, I commended the DeCelli's for their teachings. Samantha was not going to be a problem.

Since the knock-out drops were still not out of her

system, she fell asleep early. I covered her with a blanket and switched to the news channel. Nothing was new on the DeCelli kidnapping and they re-ran the clip with Lindy and Ricky appealing to the public. I dozed off and awoke just before six in the morning. I made myself a pot of coffee to wake up and then placed my first call to the DeCelli residence. It was a brief call, with the promise to call back. I had to remember to keep my calls short, impersonal, and above all, noncommittal. Calls had to be short and to the point, and hard as it was going to be, no taunting. I knew they were going to want to speak to Samantha at some point so I had to pave the way to make sure Samantha didn't give any information that would be a dead giveaway.

Telling her she was on vacation was a smart move. When she spoke to Lindy she told her she was on vacation when Lindy asked where she was. I told Samantha to call me John—a nice common name that couldn't be linked to me. The feds would have a heyday looking up all known kidnappers named John. I knew they would, too.

Chapter 51

I DON'T KNOW when the dreams started, but Lindy was in every one of them. Long blonde hair, big blues eyes—sometimes naked, sometimes not—screaming at me—or we're making love—or she's crying—trying to kill me—Ricky coming at me—all of them caused me to awaken with a jerk.

Anyway, I believe they started right after I called Lindy and told her I had seen her daughter naked. Lindy freaked! I think I did that because I had been so scared when Samantha didn't respond to me and I found her lying in the bottom of the tub. Hell, I didn't know little kids could hold their breath under water. She was washing her hair! It scared me though. I couldn't help but laugh when I saw her holding her hands up in front of her chest. That was priceless, and I just had to share it with Lindy. Afterwards, I took Samantha for a walk in the woods. We saw a nest of baby birds, some squirrels and a rabbit. Samantha was thrilled and that pleased me. We went to McDonald's after that. She sat in the back with the seatbelt on and didn't fuss at all. She was definitely a good child.

Something was happening to me. The little angel was getting to me and finding a soft spot in me. I think it was because she was so sweet and caring. She actually worried about me! Nobody ever worried about me before! And she was so adorable! I guess I could say she was a lot like Lindy.

We took another walk up through the woods again. The baby birds were gone. Samantha was upset about that until I explained that baby birds grow up and fly away to make homes of their own. That appeased her. On top of the hillside we could see sheep grazing in a nearby pasture. Samantha asked intelligent questions and I was happy that I could give her intelligent answers. After all, I grew up on a farm. She was an excellent pupil. She listened with interest as I explained about the sheep being shorn for wool in the spring, and then she listened to stories about my life on a farm. I was becoming very close to her, and I think she was beginning to feel that way about me. I'm not sure when I decided she should go with me to Brazil, but the more I thought about it, the better I liked the idea. I know it was before she got scratched on the red bushes. It happened when we were coming back from seeing the sheep.

"Ow!" She made a yipping noise.

"What's wrong?"

"I got scratched."

I pulled the leg of her jeans up and saw the scratch. It was only about an inch to an inch and a half long, and there were a couple of blood droplets coming from it. I took her inside and looked for something to put on it. I found some kind of antiseptic cream and figured that would be good enough. I covered the scratch with a band-aid. I thought that was going to be all there was to it.

I had found a swing in the garage and I thought she might like to swing on it, so I hung it in the big tree in the front yard. The day after our walk I was pushing her on the swing when she said she wanted to go lie down. At first I didn't think anything of it. She seemed warm and I thought she was getting a cold. Kids do.

Later, when I checked on her I felt how hot she was and I discovered the red line going up her leg. Damn, I was scared! I didn't know what to do. I chanced a trip to the drug store and got all the remedies I could find but Samantha kept getting hotter and more and more listless. She was calling for her mommy, and that was tearing me apart. I wanted to call Lindy but I knew that would bring the feds down on me. But I was worried about Samantha. She was really sick and I was afraid that she could die. I remembered the antibiotics I had in my shaving kit and I figured they might help. After all, they were to fight infection. I broke them in half since she was so small. They did seem to be helping but I only had five of them.

That's when I came up with the idea that Lindy should put a prescription of antibiotics in with the money. It unnerved me that Lindy had asked me point-blank if her daughter was sick. How the hell did she know that? It was that night that I had the tell-tale dream. Counselor Bob was right about something being significant.

In the dream I saw Stacey coming toward me. I reached for her and Lindy materialized beside her. It was then I knew what Bob was trying to figure out. Stacey and Lindy looked alike. I then realized that when I first saw Lindy,

Stacey was in my sub-conscious. It was uncanny that they looked that much alike. I wondered why I hadn't seen it before, or maybe I had and didn't know it.

It explained a lot to me. Now I knew why I was so obsessed with Lindy and why I reacted to her the way I did. She looked like Stacey did at seventeen and I wanted her as much as I did when I was seventeen. And I admit it, I was jealous. I couldn't have Stacey because she was with Tommy, and I became jealous over Lindy's love for her boyfriend, Ricky. I'm an asshole.

Anyway, getting back to Samantha, I was still at a loss as to what to do. Finally, I did the only thing that made sense. I told Lindy her daughter was very sick and about the scratch on her leg. I also told her to make sure she gets a prescription of antibiotics and puts it in the bag with the money. Lindy pleaded with me to just give her back and she would take care of her. There wasn't a doubt in my mind that she would, too. But life doesn't always work the way you plan it. Samantha was going to Brazil with me. I had already had Juan make up her passport and birth certificate. She was going to be Samantha Nelson, my daughter.

Chapter 52

Everything went as planned without a hitch. Those smoke bombs were a brilliant idea. I think if I hadn't have used them the feds may have nabbed me. But they couldn't get through the pungent smoke the bombs let off.

I remember watching Lindy as she went through the gymnasium doors with the heavy duffle bag. I guess she must have had a flashlight with her because it sure was dark inside with the lights off. She followed the instructions to the letter, like a good girl. I was proud of her.

My timing was perfect. I knew I had to be fast and everything had to be timed just right. It worked! It worked! I was the proud holder of five million dollars. I hurried home, hoping that Samantha was okay. I didn't want to leave her alone but she was sound asleep and I thought it would be okay. I had only planned on being gone for less than an hour. I didn't administer any of those drops. I didn't think it was safe since she was so sick.

I checked for the antibiotics as soon as I got into the cottage. They were there, as I knew they would be. Lindy would never do anything to jeopardize her child's life; I was sure of that. There were two bottles of pills. I read the directions and woke Samantha up and gave her one from each bottle, just like the directions read. She went right back to sleep.

To kill time, I cleaned up the kitchen. I couldn't get the pilot to budge on the time so we had a few hours to just lay low. I made sandwiches and put them in plastic containers in the refrigerator, hoping that Samantha would be hungry when I got her up at noon to take more medication.

She believed that her parents and her little brother Michael would be on that plane with us. She would never have been so agreeable to going if I hadn't told her that. I really didn't enjoy lying to her since that was a bad way to start out a relationship. I figured that I would tell her that her parents decided they didn't want to go and that she could live with me. Yes, that was cruel but I would make it up to her with lots of love and affection. I planned on getting her a pony and a dog when we got to Brazil. We were going to have a garden and a nice little house. Our life was going to be nice. Samantha could have whatever she wanted. I could afford it.

I checked her forehead when I got her up at noon. She felt a little cooler. She said she was hungry so I brought out the sandwiches and we ate them together. She liked it that I put potato chips on the sandwich. Years ago, Richard had shown me that. It makes a sandwich so much better, I think. I turned the television on before I ran to the bathroom. She was watching the scene from the school when I came back into the living room.

"Look, John…the school is on fire," she told me.

"Yeah….that's really something," I answered. "Want to watch Cinderella?"

She smiled and nodded. I was relieved that she seemed to be feeling better. Her forehead didn't seem so hot, but that read line was still going up her leg. It looked like it had traveled a little since the last time I checked. I was concerned about it but there wouldn't be anything I could do until we got to Brazil.

...

It was time to get ready to go. I got out the lavender dress for Samantha. I was smart enough to remember to buy dress shoes and lacey socks for her. She looked adorable in that dress. My heart melted when she came out of the bathroom dressed and ready to go. She asked once again about her parents and Michael.

"I just called them. They are on their way to the airport now, so we'll see them on the plane." I lied to her.

Her face lit up in a smile. I grabbed our suitcases and put them into the back seat and took one last look around. Everything in the cottage looked satisfactory, but I wouldn't have cared anyway. We were leaving the country. Let that Heiser guy worry about it. I did call him to tell him the key would be under the mat, but then I couldn't find the key. I left the door unlocked and as I pulled out of the driveway, I had a nagging feeling that I had left something behind. I figured it was just my imagination and the jitters all combined into one. I drove to the county airport.

I parked the car in the far corner of the lot and Samantha and I walked into the terminal. I checked us in and paid for the flight, met and talked with the pilot for a few minutes and then Samantha and I stopped to load up on vending machine goodies. I told her she could have anything she wanted and all she seemed to be worried about was finding something that her brother Michael would like. I told her to pick out whatever she wanted for both of them and to get a lot of things since the plane ride was long.

"What do *you* want, John?" She had asked.

"Well....let's see. Let's get some chips and some candy and some cans of soda. I like those cupcakes right there," I said as I pointed.

"Then we should get those for you," she responded.

God, I loved this child! In another hour she would be mine—my little girl. I felt so happy and warm about it, too. I couldn't wait to begin being her father. I would be a lot like my father was, and never anything like my mother. I held her hand as we started down the hall toward the tunnel that would come out on the field where the plane sat.

Everything from that point on happened so fast. First, Samantha collapsed and as I was about to pick her up, a blonde guy grabbed her. I started toward him when I felt someone grabbing my shoulder. I gasped in surprise when I turned around and looked into the furious eyes of Ricky DeCelli. Man, his eyes showed no mercy! Instantly, I knew I was in trouble. I really didn't remember him being that big!

I felt the first punch and after that I was bargaining for my life. He was relentless. I couldn't believe it when he snatched the gun out of my hand and threw it. The guy was crazed. I was almost relieved when the feds showed up. At least I wasn't going to be beaten to death.

It was over. My dreams, my life, and all my plans were finished. I was never going to see Samantha again. That hurt more than anything. I had truly fallen in love with that little girl, and I really had hoped to do everything I could to make her happy, to protect her, and to take care of her. After fifty-seven years of life, I had finally known what it was to love unconditionally and without motive other than to just care for another. Now it was over.

As the feds were leading me up the ramp, in handcuffs, I stopped short when I saw Lindy. I couldn't believe she slapped me, but what left an impact on me forever was what she said.

Chapter 53

"Stacey Stockwell was my mother, you son-of-a-bitch."

Those words will forever haunt me. Stacey, the love of my life was Lindy's mother—and she was dead. I was in love with Stacey for forty years. And I raped her daughter. If things had worked out like I wanted, she would have been my daughter, too. That thought made me want to cut my dick off.

And I kidnapped Stacey's grandchild. I didn't deserve to live.

God, what have I done? I hurt the child of the woman I had been in love with for forty years.

I still had to come to terms with the fact that Stacey had been dead for almost twenty years. Twenty years. I remember that pained look in Lindy's eyes when she talked about her mother. How she had missed her! Samantha would have had that same look when she talked about her mother when we were in Brazil. I would have been responsible for that pain.

NO! I would never have hurt Samantha! At least,

not intentionally—but taking her away from her mother would have hurt her!

I cry. Not for myself, but I cry because I hurt Stacey's daughter.

I'm sorry, Stacey. I'm sorry, Lindy.

I know sorry isn't enough but it's all I can do. I only hope that someday you can forgive me for what I did.

I didn't hurt Samantha. She was taken away from me before I could hurt her. No, I wouldn't have ever done anything to hurt Samantha. I only want Lindy and Samantha both to know that I truly loved that little girl and that I would have been good to her. I would have given her everything. Please know this, Lindy—and Samantha.

Please know this, too. I finally realize how wrong I was. I know what I did to Lindy, was wrong and I fully accept my punishment. If I could see Lindy again I would tell her this. I also would want Lindy to know that I didn't think I deserved the first fifteen years in prison until now. I deserved all of those years and more.

I would want Samantha to know that she changed me. I don't think I fully understood right from wrong until now. It is wrong to take another person's child, but is it wrong to love another person's child? That's something I don't have an answer for. All I know is that I fell in love with that little angel. It was through Samantha that I learned of what I had been missing all my life.

I sit and think about all of those who have passed through my life and I realize that there was always one important element missing with every relationship. Yes, I felt love and fondness for those in my past, but the element that was never there was the ability to love and be loved unconditionally and unselfishly. I never fully gave myself to anyone. I always held something back, like I was afraid of losing my entire self. The women in my life wanted me—my all. I had always settled for those who wanted me, instead of going after the one I wanted. I believe that I couldn't—or wouldn't—give all of myself to a woman because I was always hoping and waiting for Stacey. When I saw Lindy I saw my chance to have Stacey. So I took her. I finally had Stacey—or actually, Stacey's look-alike. The resemblance was uncanny. But then there was Samantha. Little Samantha taught me how to give of myself. I wanted to share everything I had with her. I had been searching for this love all my life. And now...

It's over

Epilogue

Nelson Sutter will remain in prison without parole until he is eighty years old, if he lives that long. His counselor, Mary Jo got the book into print just as she promised. Any and all proceeds from the book are to be put into the hands of Belinda DeCelli and she is to donate them to the charity of her choice.

At first Lindy refused the proposition until it was made clear that there were no strings and that it was Nelson's way of righting a wrong. Lindy chose to donate the proceeds to the research of ovarian cancer, a project that Dr. Nick Bazario has been working on.

As for Nelson, he has been assigned to the prison library again. He gets no visitors, writes to nobody, and makes no phone calls. He has made the prison inmates his only family and he gets along well with them. Because of his attitude adjustment, he is well liked by the inmates and the guards, and that is to his benefit, since prison will be his home for a long time.

About the Author

ALTHOUGH CURRENTLY RESIDING in Florida, Carole McKee is a native of Pittsburgh. Her love of the city comes out in the stories she writes. She began writing in 1996 when she wrote a tribute to her Labrador retriever after he passed away. Her first novel "Perfect" (AuthorHouse, 2007) was packed full of emotions, bringing laughter and tears to readers. "Choices" (AuthorHouse, 2008), a heart-rending story about young love began this series, followed by "The Bushes are Red" (AuthorHouse, 2009), a gripping tale full of emotion as Ricky and Lindy face a parent's worse nightmare. "The Full Nelson" completes the trilogy.

Breinigsville, PA USA
21 August 2009
222727BV00001B/1/P